Praise fo
L

"Although the suspense elements in this book are handled excellently, what makes this story truly great is the love Will has for Laura. The lengths he goes to to help her overcome her hangups and to unearth the truth of her past are outstanding." ~*RT BookClub* 4 1/2 stars.

"This insightful, though provoking novel will give readers much to ponder. Victims of abuse can take comfort." ~Huntress Reviews

"...emotional...poignant...refreshing...the author's style is so rich with emotion...a romance that shows the power of love and friendship." ~Fallen Angel Reviews 5 Angels

DISCOVERING VERONICA

"....well written and engaging." ~The Daphne du Maurier

"A romantic mystery that will build your tension to a fevered pitch." ~The Best Reviews

"I could not put it down until it was finished." ~Escape To Romance

"....an exciting contemporary romantic suspense...." ~Reader To Reader

"4 Stars....escalates with every turn of the page." ~Scribes World

"....filled with great characters and a thoroughly disturbing subplot...." ~Road to Romance

"Greenland manages a neat twist that catches the reader off guard in this strong debut novel." ~*RT BookClub*

Dear Reader,

When I met author Shannon Greenland, I was immediately enchanted by her personality. She has a zest for life and one of the most positive attitudes I have seen. She has a way of bringing you into her joy. Soon after, I picked up her first novel, ***Discovering Veronica***, and was so moved by her eloquent writing style that I could not put the book down until I had read the entire thing.

I could not be more pleased to invite you into Laura Genny's story [***Laura's Secrets***]. The realities of Shannon Greenland's stories and characters are mesmerizing and readers will be hard-pressed to find fault with even one word of these emotionally gripping tales.

Every day women are faced with a multitude of obstacles and hardships. Shannon writes stories that give women the courage and strength to be the best that they can be.

I hope you enjoy ***Laura's Secrets*** as much as I have.

Would you like to read more stories about women of strength? Don't miss ***That Devil Moon*** by Dana Taylor, available now from Echelon Press.

Happy Reading!

Karen L. Syed

To Mary -
Celebrate Life!

LAURA'S SECRETS

SHANNON GREENLAND

Shannon Greenland

Echelon Press

This is a work of fiction. Names, characters, places, and incidents are products of the author's imagination or are used fictitiously and are not to be construed as real. Any resemblance to actual events, locales, organizations, or persons, living or dead, is entirely coincidental.

Echelon Press Publishing
56 Sawyer Circle #354
Memphis, TN 38103

ISBN: 1-59080-415-5
www.echelonpress.com

First Echelon Press paperback printing: June 2005

Cover Artist: ©Nathalie Moore 2004 Arianna Award Winner
Editor: Kat Thompson

Printed in LaVergne, TN, USA

Dedication

Not many people can say they've been best friends with someone since toddler hood. Well, I can. This book is dedicated to my longtime, best friend, Jill Hockman. My childhood memories are unique and enriched because of you, Jill.

Acknowledgements

I'd like to acknowledge my critique partners, Tara Greenbaum and Terri Ridgell. Thanks for your candid input, available ear, and wine tastings.

One

Gripping the towel wrapped around her lanky, naked body, Laura stared at her closed bedroom door. She tiptoed to it, then placed her ear along the wooden surface.

Silence.

She glanced over her shoulder at the pink dress lying on her bed. Aunt Jane had given it to her earlier that day for her tenth birthday. Like everything else in Laura's closet, lace and ruffles adorned it.

Shuffling back across the room, she took one last look at the door and dropped her towel. Quickly, she reached for the white panties and jammed her feet into the leg holes. The door to her bedroom flew open. Laura gasped and jerked her underwear up.

Aunt Jane marched toward her, a scowl planted across her face. She grabbed the sides of Laura's underwear and yanked them back down her legs.

With a red tipped finger, Jane jabbed at Laura's flat chest. "Don't you ever try to hide from me young lady. There's nothing special about you, and you've got nothing I haven't seen."

Laura didn't flinch when the spittle from her aunt's mouth landed on her face.

Aunt Jane straightened, walked to the bay window, and then stretched out on top of the chaise lounge. She fluffed her dress and made a show of smoothing wrinkles, shook her brown hair back and took a deep breath. With a pleasant smile on her face, she lifted her index finger and twirled it in the air, and Laura, recognizing her cue, began to dress.

They'd been performing this ritual at least once every

couple of weeks for as long as Laura could remember. She completed the process as fast as possible, then stood ramrod straight in all her pink and flounce.

Aunt Jane nodded and gave a delicate clap of approval. "Now let me see you walk."

Laura pulled her shoulders back and pretended she had a book balanced on her head. She walked the length of her bedroom, pivoted, then returned.

"Oh, Laura, you're such a dream." Aunt Jane steepled her fingers beneath her chin. "Now come here and let me braid these ribbons into your hair."

Forcing a smile, Laura walked toward her aunt.

"Laura!"

She glanced up. A custodian stood across the stage.

"Jesus, wake up. I've been shouting at ya forever."

"Sorry," she mumbled. Not the first time she'd relived that particular fifteen-year-old memory.

He pointed to the back of the arena with his broom. "You got a phone call in the office."

Quickly, she finished soldering the speaker cable and unplugged the iron. She dusted her hands on her jeans and slipped her blue rabbit's foot from her front pocket. As she jogged off stage and through the empty, dark arena to the back office, she rubbed her thumb over the soft fur.

Picking up the dangling black receiver, she leaned back against the office desk. "Hello, this is Laura Genny."

"Hey, green eyes."

"Ed." They'd met five years before at a workshop he instructed in her third year of college studies. He'd been the one to hook her up with her current job as Sound Technician for the Nashville Arena.

"How's it going in Music City, USA?"

"Good. We've got an ice skating show scheduled in two days. I'm getting the place ready. Should be easy. No live music to accompany it. How about *Tourist*?" Ed had the perfect job as Head Sound Engineer for the international rock group.

"Funny you should ask. You sitting down?"

"Yeah."

"How would you like to sound mix for *Tourist*?"

"Wh-what're–*Tourist's* sound engineer? What're you talking about?"

"I've finally decided to open up my studio."

Ed had wanted to own his own recording studio for as long as Laura had known him. "Congratulations."

"Thanks. *Tourist* needs a new mixer. I thought of you first. I told the group about you, and they want to give you an audition."

Laura blinked. He'd talked to them already?

"Well, what do you think?"

Traveling with *Tourist* as their Head Sound Engineer was the opportunity of a lifetime. It's what she'd always dreamed of. "Where do I need to be, and when do I need to be there?"

Will Burns stood with his back propped against the wall, a water bottle teetering between his thumb and forefinger as he studied the scene in the room. The concert had ended two hours before, but the after party would go on into the morning.

The lead singer reclined on a sofa, his head thrown back and eyes closed, while a brunette's head bobbed between his legs. The keyboard player sat in a cushioned chair, cradling a topless redhead as he fondled her breasts. The bass player had one hip propped on a stool and each arm wrapped around a giggling blonde. The drummer meandered through the dozen or so other women, smiling and petting as he went along.

Will took a swig of his water. It tasted bitter going down. From across the room, brunette twins eyed him. One of them gave him a slow wink. The other linked fingers with the first and pulled her toward him. He held up his hand and shook his head. They both gave a pout and veered off toward the couch.

He'd bet his life an intelligent brain cell didn't exist in the whole lot. These women weren't here for intelligence, though. At the snap of a finger he could have a blowjob, a lap dance, sex, or anything else his heart desired. It nauseated him. There'd been a time when he took advantage, but it'd been years since he participated in the backstage romps of *Tourist*.

Why had he even bothered tonight?

"Hey, baby."

Will looked down at the hand slinking toward his crotch and grabbed it around the wrist. He pulled the manicured fingers away and looked into her drug-induced eyes. "What's your name?"

She swayed and smiled suggestively up at him. "Does it matter?"

"Yep, it does. I'm not interested."

The woman sniffed indignantly, pivoted unsteadily on her spiked heel, and staggered off. Alcohol fumes trailed her wake.

Eric, Will's best friend and fellow guitarist, was the only person not at the party. They'd known each other since high school band class. Will glanced at his watch. Eric would be back at the hotel by now dialing his wife's number. He'd been anxious to talk to his son before the concert.

"Will, man, my son rocks this world," Eric had bragged. "He had a soccer game today and scored ten points. He promised to stay awake until I call tonight. We've got to talk about the play-by-play action."

Will smiled a little as he remembered his best friend's excitement. Eric had the perfect life. Playing music for a living, happily married, a great father. What would it be like to love a woman and have her devoted to him, too? Those thoughts had intruded before, but they seemed more and more frequent of late. How would he ever attract a real woman with his lifestyle?

He peered through the smoky haze of the room. Familiar sounds surrounded him–sultry music, girlie giggles, raunchy language, clinking glasses. He sighed, scrubbed his fingers through his hair, and walked out.

Yep, this definitely wasn't what he wanted out of life.

Laura's plane touched down in Toronto so early the sun hadn't even come up. She slung her backpack over her shoulder, grabbed her duffel bag from the overhead bin, and made her way off the plane.

Ed stood in the terminal right where he'd promised he would be. If Laura had had a brother, she would've wanted it to be Ed. Bless his heart for getting up at such an ungodly hour.

"You had to be the last one off, didn't you, green eyes?" He grinned and grabbed her duffel bag. "How much luggage do you have in baggage claim?"

She stifled a yawn. "This is it."

Ed shook his head. "I forgot how light you travel."

Thirty minutes later they walked into the Toronto Marriott and rode the elevator to *Tourist's* reserved floor. She told Ed goodnight and closed the door to her king size room. Floral patterned curtains hung open to reveal the dawning Toronto skyline. Laura shuffled over and pulled them closed, then retrieved a roll of black electrical tape from her duffel bag. She tore off a piece and pressed it over the peephole in the door.

Seven years. It'd been seven years since she escaped Aunt Jane's home and still couldn't change clothes without thinking her aunt was watching.

Unsnapping her jeans, Laura pushed them down her legs, already feeling the sleepiness in her eyes. She glanced at her watch. Good. Five hours of sleep before they reported to work.

At one o'clock that afternoon, Laura and Ed stood in the tech box at the back of the Convention Center. She listened while he showed her new features of the MIDI system. The band members filtered on stage, laughing and joking with one another.

"Now don't be nervous," Ed reassured her. "Ready?"

Laura nodded and stepped in front of the mixing board. She picked up the house microphone and eased the volume up. "Check on mike one."

All the members of *Tourist* looked up at once, obviously taken off guard by the feminine voice echoing through the Center.

The lead singer stepped up to mike one. "Check."

Laura stretched her fingers across the board, positioned them on various sliding knobs, made a few adjustments, then said, "Check on mike two."

The keyboard player pulled his mike down and pressed his lips to the cushioned pad. "Check."

She continued through the rest of the stage microphones and then began on the instruments. Each time she turned to the EQ rack and boosted the bass, lowered the high end, or vice versa. She communicated with the guys on stage, asking them to play a specific chord or give feedback on the volume of the onstage monitors. She picked up on the reverberation from the right side of the house and made adjustments.

When sound check finished, she turned to Ed. "Well?"

Ed smiled. "I can honestly say you did every single thing I would've done." He opened the gate that led from the tech box. "Let's go meet the boys and see what they think."

Laura followed him to the stage.

"Yo, guys," Ed hailed. "Come meet Laura."

With reserved interest, she surveyed the famous men who

were making their way toward her. Silently, she put names to the faces she'd seen on album covers. All clean cut and dressed casually in jeans. Except for the drummer who'd over gelled his long hair, making it more stringy than stylish.

So, these were the musicians so many people idolized. They seemed ordinary enough to her.

Keeping her head high, she made eye contact with each of them and, as Ed introduced them, stepped forward to shake their hands. "This is Larry, lead singer, Jamie here plays keyboards, this is Keith, bass, and Lawrence, drums, this is Eric, one of our guitarists, and Will, the lead guitarist."

The inquisitive look in Will's dark eyes made her falter. One corner of his mouth lifted into a half smile. She took his outstretched hand, gave it a firm shake and nodded her head in greeting, then returned to her place beside Ed.

"You're a hell of a mixer," said the bass player. "As good as ol' Ed here. What do the rest of you guys think?"

The drummer sniffed. "I don't know. She's awful young. Probably not very experienced either."

Nothing she hadn't heard before. "You're right. I am young. However, I have confidence in my abilities. I'm talented, well trained, and respected by many in my field."

Crossing his arms over his chest, Will surveyed the tall, slender woman in front of him. He glanced down at her well-worn Nikes and smiled. He had on the exact same ones. He trailed up her long legs, noting her masculine stance, with each foot braced about two feet apart and hands clasped behind her back. She looked ready to take someone on in a fight. Her tucked in pale yellow T-shirt matched the highlights in her blond hair, and her ball cap sported *The Lakers*. A woman after his own heart.

Will studied her determined face as she squared off with the band's drummer. Sadness lingered there, behind those lovely green eyes. Had she even smiled yet?

"Tell you what," Will interceded, "Laura, you mix for us tonight, and Lawrence," he turned to the drummer, "if everyone's satisfied, we'll keep her. Ed'll be right there if something goes wrong."

The drummer grinned, pleased with the compromise. Laura gave her agreement in the form of a quick nod. Will bit back a smile. *So serious.*

She followed Ed back through the Convention Center, her long ponytail swaying with her movement. Will turned and picked up his guitar.

What will she look like with a smile?

Will woke at six the next morning and let out a loud yawn. His thoughts drifted to the concert the night before. It'd gone off without a hitch. Laura had done an equal if not better job than Ed, and the other *Tourist's* members thought so, too.

Officially, Laura was now the newest addition to their traveling family. The group had delivered the good news to her last night after the show. She'd looked at each of them, gave them a thank you, and said she felt confident everyone would be pleased with the new arrangement.

Will chuckled. She was something else.

After two good whole body stretches, he swung off the bed and padded into the bathroom. Minutes later he emerged, pulled on a pair of runner's shorts and a tank top, laced up his new Nikes, donned his disguise of dark glasses and a ball cap, and made his way down to the lobby. He exited the back of the Marriott and came to an abrupt stop.

Laura stood outside the hotel with a heel propped on a low wall and her leg stretched straight. Bending forward, she touched her nose to her knee and held it there for a few seconds. She reached her hands toward the sky and bent right, then left.

He stood, watching her stretch, fixated by her lean legs.

Like him, she wore runner's shorts, and with each movement, they gaped open at the sides to reveal her entire upper thigh and hip. "So, you're a runner, huh?"

Laura glanced up at him through her dark glasses. "Yeah," she answered and jogged away.

Will puzzled her retreating back. Women never brushed him off like that. He ran to catch up, surprised that her pace matched his own long-legged stride. "Do you run every day?"

"Pretty much."

"How far do you go?"

"Five miles."

Will nudged her arm playfully. "Me, too. What a coincidence, huh?"

"*Hmmm...*"

He gave her a sideways glance. The tip of her thick braid bounced against her rear end. A single bead of sweat sneaked out from under her ball cap and trickled down her cheek. "You're really tall. What are you, five-ten?"

She wiped the sweat with the back of her hand. "Five-eight."

Four inches shorter than him. He wouldn't break his neck for a kiss. "Where ya from?"

Laura's stomach tightened, as it always did when someone asked about her past. Aunt Jane's image flooded her mind. "Nowhere."

"Everybody's from somewhere."

"I move around a lot." Wanting to steer the conversation away from her private life, she asked, "How long has *Tourist* been together?"

"I've played for them for eleven years, but the band started a few years prior to that. How long have you been a sound tech?"

"Small gigs through college and full time for three years."

"Yep, I tried my hand at mixing once. I remember it was

in this bar back before I played for *Tourist...*"

Laura half listened to him ramble while she ran beside him. She turned her head a fraction of an inch to get a better look at him. Little black clumps of hair curled out from under his cap. It made him seem boyish and harmless. She couldn't remember the last time anyone had made such an effort to talk to her. Usually they mistook her quietness for iciness and found some excuse to end the conversation. Only Ed and Bizzy, her childhood friend, had taken the time to get to know her.

"So," Will interrupted her thoughts, "what instrument do you play?"

"What makes you think I play?"

"Most mixers do. Let's see...drums? No. Accordion? Spoons? I know. Jug blowing."

Jug blowing? Her lips twitched. "Guitar."

"Self taught?"

She nodded. The guitar had been the one emotional release she'd had as a child. Bizzy had kept one at her house for Laura to play when she visited. Aunt Jane had wanted her to learn a more "lady like" instrument...

"But, Aunt Jane, I don't wanna learn the flute," five-year-old Laura had whined.

Her aunt spun around, lips thinned and eyes narrowed, and charged across the living room. Laura gripped her flute and searched for a place to hide.

The older woman reached down, grabbed Laura by her upper arms, and lifted her to eye level. "Little Missy, I better never hear you whine again. Do you understand me?"

Laura stared unblinking at the beady blue eyes in front of her. When she didn't answer, her aunt gave her a hard shake. "Answer me, you little twit! Are you stupid or something?"

A tear slid from the side of Laura's eye. "I want my mommy," she whimpered.

Aunt Jane held her suspended in the air, glowering into her eyes. Then she released her, sending Laura into a sprawl across the hard wood floor.

"Your mommy?" She chuckled as if it was the most ridiculous thing her niece could have said. "Your mommy doesn't want you. Why do you think she gave you to me? She doesn't love you anymore. You were an awful daughter, and she never wants to see you again."

Laura covered her face with her hands and began to sob. Her aunt picked her up, and for a moment, Laura thought it was to comfort her. But when she opened her eyes, Aunt Jane deposited her in a closet, leaving her to huddle in the dark amongst the mop and other cleaning supplies.

"Laura?"

She'd stayed there for hours, smothered by the smell of pine oil and bleach, wishing she wouldn't have cried. It hadn't been worth it.

"Laura?" Will touched her arm.

She jerked back.

"You okay?"

"Yeah." She glanced around. They'd made it back to the hotel.

"You haven't heard a word I've said, have you?"

Laura pulled her rabbit's foot from her front pocket. Everything had been going fine. She'd been having a nice conversation and then something triggered the memory. Something *always* triggered a memory.

"Laura?"

"I'm going to finish my workout in my room. I'll um…catch you later." A little time by herself and she'd be fine again.

"I'll walk up with you if you don't mind."

"Suit yourself." She entered the hotel lobby and went straight for the stairs. When she noticed that Will followed, she turned to him. "You don't have to take the stairs because I am. It's a long climb to our floor."

Will took off his sunglasses and looped them in the front of his shirt. He stepped around her and opened the stairwell door. "I'm not. I always do it. It's good exercise."

Feeling foolish she'd assumed he was taking them because of her, Laura jumped the steps two at a time to their floor, conscious of the fact he climbed close behind her. Once they reached the top, she exited into the carpeted hallway and took a deep breath. Something about being so close to him made her jittery.

"Excuse me, Mr. Burns?" a maid hesitantly spoke from down the corridor. "May I have your autograph?"

Will let out a quiet sigh. On occasion the hotel workers would break the rules and ask for an autograph, or take a picture, or even worse, steal things from the rooms. A few years back a maid had taken some discarded items from his bathroom wastebasket. Why anyone would want some used Q-tips stretched beyond his imagination, but apparently people did.

Smiling at the approaching worker, Will reminded himself that if not for the fans, *Tourist* would be nothing. He took her outstretched stationary pad. "And who should I make this to?"

"My son, Jimmy, please. He's a huge fan." The maid glanced nervously over her shoulder.

Will scrawled his message across the pad, then returned it to the awaiting mother. He grinned at her huge smile and watched as she walked back to the cleaning cart.

He turned, intending to invite Laura to breakfast, and found an empty hallway. Not surprising. The quiet, elusive, new woman in his life probably wouldn't have accepted his invitation anyway.

Something had happened back there. She'd zoned out, seemed lost even when he finally got a response from her.

Laura was hiding something. And while he'd always felt indifferent about emotional attachment, this time he wanted to dig. Make her open up and share her scars with him. Almost as if he felt drawn to do so. She intrigued him.

She needed a friend, bad, and possibly a good hug or two.

Laura stood at the back of the Convention Center, preparing for the second and last Toronto concert. The doors opened in thirty minutes, and like last night, the concert was sold out.

She exited the tech box and trotted down the aisle, then climbed the ramp that led to the performance area. An amp sat stage left tilted on its side. The bass player would make a ruckus over that one. She walked toward it.

"I can't believe ice queen got Ed's job," a stage worker griped.

Laura paused and glanced past the tower of speakers. Two roadies stood talking. One looked familiar.

"How do you know her, anyway?" the other guy asked.

"We went to college together." The first one threw down a coiled cable and spit his tobacco juice into a cup. "I've been doing Ed's grunt work for years. Dude, I'm the one that deserves that job."

The second guy snorted. "Why d'ya call her ice queen?"

"Because she's real focused. All business." He grabbed his cup and spit again.

"Well she's the best looking techie I've ever seen."

The first roady shook his head. "Idiot. She's a lesbian."

"What?"

"Yeah. All the guys at school were always asking her out." He reached inside his mouth, scooped out the used snuff, and threw it into his spit cup. "We even had this bet of who could lay her first. The winner would get a case of beer." He took a swig of his soda, then let out a gurgly burp. "We all missed out on that sweet piece of ass."

Laura listened as both guys snickered. It wasn't the first time someone had made fun of her. Each time it hardened her heart a little more, made her reinforce the emotional wall she'd built around herself.

She spun around to head off stage and landed hard into Will's chest. He grabbed her arms to steady them both and searched her face with a focused expression that said he'd overheard every word.

"You okay?"

No, she wasn't okay. Twenty-five years old and she was still battling her childhood and the woman it had made her. How was she supposed to express that to someone, especially Will? She liked him, really liked him. He'd be repulsed to learn the things Aunt Jane had done to her. And then he'd pity her and be her friend out of obligation.

It had happened before, back in college. She'd shared one memory, one secret, with a boy she thought she liked. A friendship she'd hoped might turn into something romantic. And not only had he backed away, he'd told all his buddies. After that everyone had kept their distance, regarded her as some kind of a freak.

"Laura?"

"Sorry. Excuse me." She shrugged from his grip. "I need to get back to work."

Will stared as she hastily retreated to her tech box in the rear of the Convention Center. He'd heard every horrible word, and seeing the controlled anguish on Laura's face told him it hadn't been the first time she'd witnessed such malicious gossip.

He took a hesitant step. Should he go to her? What would he say if he did? Would she accept his words of comfort? Probably not.

The roadies sauntered on stage. Will pivoted on his heel. "Hey! We need to talk."

Two

Will and Eric lounged across from each other on *Tourist's* private jet. They were on their way from Canada to New York City, and Eric had been babbling about his son for the last thirty minutes. Will usually had an avid interest in his best friend's stories, but today Laura held his undivided attention.

She sat at the rear of the plane with a map of New York City sprawled across her lap. As Head Sound Engineer, Laura, along with the other lead production people, flew with the band members on their private jet. The stage equipment and road crew followed behind in several semi-trucks.

She chewed her gum and blew a huge pink bubble. It silently popped and disappeared back into her mouth. She made a few notes on a pad balanced on her knee, then returned to studying the map. Like every other time Will had seen her in the last few days, she wore a pair of jeans, a T-shirt, and a ball cap. With her lengthy legs and firm, little butt, she had the perfect body for jeans. But what would she look like with her hair down, wearing a sexy dress and heels?

"Then he said his project partner spilled milk all over it and they had to start again." Eric laughed. "Can you imagine?"

Will grunted in response.

Eric nudged him. "You're not even listening to me."

Cutting his attention back to Eric, Will smiled sheepishly. "Sorry, man. My mind's somewhere else."

Eric glanced over his shoulder in Laura's direction. He turned back with a cheesy grin. "Sooo, go talk to her."

Will blew out a long breath. He never felt apprehensive around women. What was wrong with him?

"Well, my, my, Will Burns, you're actually nervous. The last time I remember you being nervous about a girl was in ninth grade. You remember that cute little Suzie Pritchett who made your palms sweaty, don't ya?"

Will rolled his eyes. "How could I forget Suzie?" He took one last sip from his bottled water and set it aside. "Wish me luck," he muttered and made his way down the aisle.

Laura glanced up from behind her map as he approached. Another pink bubble came out and hung poised in the air.

"Hi," Will greeted her warmly. "Can I join you?"

She popped the bubble and placed her gum in a scrap of paper. "You're welcome to sit, but I won't be much company. I'm studying."

Not giving her a chance to change her mind, Will quickly stepped past her legs and took the seat beside her. "I've been to New York a lot. Maybe I can help."

"I want to visit Ground Zero and see all the major things you hear about on TV. And I want to eat in Little Italy. Italian's my favorite."

Italian's her favorite. Good thing to know. "So you want to hit all the sites like the Statue of Liberty, Empire State Building, Chinatown, and so forth?"

She nodded.

Will reached across and took the pad balanced on her knee. She jumped when his fingers brushed her leg. He kept talking, hoping to ease her skittishness. "So," he glanced over her list, "I know where all these things are. Let's see, you want to go to Grand Central Station." He leaned over her arm, pointed to a spot on the map. "It's right there. And as you can see," he trailed his finger to another spot on the map, "it's up some blocks from the Empire State Building. Convenient, huh?"

Laura cleared her throat. "I'm, um, more tired than I thought. I'm gonna try to get some rest before the plane lands.

Okay?"

"Oh...okay." He watched as she neatly creased the huge map and stowed it inside her backpack. She was retreating into herself, and he wasn't sure what he'd done to cause it. He thought things had been going smoothly. She pulled out her Walkman and slipped a CD in place.

"You don't mind if I sit here, do you?"

She smiled a little and shook her head. "No."

Will studied her profile as she put on her headset, leaned back, and closed her eyes. She had a cute little nose with just enough freckles to make her adorable. Those large, innocent, yet wary, green eyes made him want to protect her and earn her trust.

His gaze roamed over her face, clean and void of makeup. Someone cleared his throat. He glanced up to see Eric holding a piece of paper with STOP STARING! written on it. Will stuck his tongue out at him, then picked up the pad of paper Laura had used and began jotting down lyrics that had been going through his mind.

Laura inhaled a deep, calming breath, trying to make her heart slow to its normal pace. With a day's worth of whiskers, faded jeans, and tan cowboy boots, the man sitting next to her looked rugged, masculine, and in charge. He needed a leather vest, a rope, and a Stetson, and he'd look right at home on a ranch. She almost smiled at the image. Until a few days ago she'd rarely given a second thought to the way a man looked.

Their faces had been mere inches from each other while they looked at the map. He possessed the most unique, ebony eyes. So black, Laura couldn't discern where the pupil stopped and the iris began.

He'd brushed his arm across her breast when he leaned over to point at a spot on the map. An accidental brush, but it shot heat through her whole body, and she'd reacted the usual way–by freezing up.

From the look on his face, her actions had confused him. They'd confused her even more. But the fact that he insisted on staying beside her, even though she tuned him out, amazed her.

Will was doing crazy things to her insides. Something about him seemed non-threatening, comfortable. It was becoming increasingly difficult not to warm to his friendly demeanor. She wanted to reciprocate, flirt a little, but she didn't know how. Wasn't used to it. Generally, people acted polite to her, but it stopped there. Only Ed and Bizzy had made an effort to get to know her. Why? Because it was too hard. She required too much work, at least that's what a counselor had told her years ago.

Counselor. That had been a mistake. She'd seen an ad in her freshman year and signed up. A bunch of seniors taking a psychology class decided to do "counselor" work for extra credit. But she'd tried it, being eighteen and naïve, and was told by her assigned therapist that if she got drunk, she'd loosen up a little. Some advice.

Beside her, Will moved positions, and his arm bumped hers. Laura peeked at him through her right eye. He was scribbling on the note pad with a bright purple pencil, oblivious to her. She shifted away, closed her eyes, and let her mind drift…

Laura and Bizzy ran down the hallway toward Bizzy's bedroom. Aunt Jane had given Laura permission to spend the afternoon with her best friend. Never had she been allowed to spend four whole hours at Bizzy's house.

The two eight-year old girls lay side-by-side on the carpeted floor, coloring in Bizzy's new books. "I got some pencils for my birthday. Wanna see?" Bizzy grinned, displaying a missing front tooth, and tucked her springy black curls behind her ears.

Laura nodded, and Bizzy crawled across the carpeted floor to her dresser. She rummaged through the bottom drawer, pulled out some pink and purple iridescent pencils, then turned back. Her grin slowly faded.

"What happened?" she whispered, pointing to Laura's legs.

Laura glanced over her shoulder and saw that her yellow dress had ridden up her thighs, exposing the red welts slashed across the back of them. She scurried to her knees and smoothed her dress down, embarrassed that her best friend had seen the marks.

"Was it your aunt again?" Bizzy asked, crawling toward her.

Laura studied the crayons in her fingers. "I didn't want to eat liver. It made Aunt Jane mad."

Bizzy squeezed her neck. "We're gonna run away someday when we're big enough. I promise."

Laura nodded.

"Laura…Laura…Laura."

Her eyes flew open.

"Hey, the plane's landing. That must've been some dream. It took me forever to wake you up."

"Did I say anything?"

Will pulled back, obviously perplexed by her alarmed voice. "No," he ventured carefully. "You didn't talk in your sleep."

Laura looked away from his frown. Bizzy had told her once that she talked in her sleep. If Will heard her nightmares, it'd be too much…too awkward, too embarrassing. She reached inside her front pocket, latched onto the familiar rabbit's foot, and stood up. "Excuse me, I need to go to the restroom."

"Laura?"

The concern in his quiet voice made her stop and turn back. He leaned forward and propped his elbows on his knees. "I don't know what weighs so heavily on your mind, but everything's going to be okay. I won't pry, your business is your business, but you can trust me. I want you to believe that."

Never in her twenty-five years of living had anyone, but Bizzy, showed her such an open-armed, unconditional, extension of friendship. She stared at him blankly, not sure what to say or how to react.

"Thank you," she whispered, her heart banging so hard that her chest vibrated.

Will's eyes crinkled. "You're welcome."

A little dazed, Laura made her way down the aisle, feeling a smile forming on her face.

Laura stood motionless in the hotel's lobby with her backpack looped over both shoulders and duffel bag hooked in her right hand. Never had she seen anything so grand.

Gold accessorized and sparkled off the ashtrays, balcony railings, and elevator doors. The white marble floor gleamed from a recent waxing.

A couple of suited businessmen lounged in a corner off to the right. Linen and silk clad women stood in a tight circle talking in hushed tones, probably waiting to go shopping somewhere in New York. A young couple strolled by holding hands.

"It's magnificent, isn't it?" Will commented, coming up behind her. "Let's put our stuff down, and I'll show you around."

"I can't, but thank you anyway. I've got a meeting at Madison Square Garden in one hour." She turned and walked toward the check-in counter.

"You don't have to worry about checking in. Our manager does that for us. Come on," he motioned with his head. "I know what floor we're on."

Laura followed him across the lobby. Will pressed the

elevator's button, and when it dinged, they stepped inside. Glass-paneled doors slid closed, and she stood, confronted by her image.

She wiggled her toes in her scuffed Nikes and thought of the white, patent, leather shoes she'd been forced to wear as a child. God, how they'd hurt her feet.

Her well-worn faded jeans were unraveled around her ankles. The left knee had a tiny hole where she'd snagged it on the side of a speaker years ago. Aunt Jane had hated jeans and never allowed Laura to own a pair. It was the first piece of clothing Laura bought when she escaped her aunt's home. Jane would have a raging fit if she saw Laura's choice of attire now. Nothing pink and lacy about her.

Laura's gaze lifted to her gray T-shirt, which fit snug across her breasts. She reached up and loosened the material, unaware that her backpack had pulled it so tight.

Her black leather belt cinched her roomy jeans around her waist. Aunt Jane had called Laura's body scrawny.

Studiously she focused on her face and eyes, shadowed from her cap. Her aunt had told her that God gave her a simple, *ordinary* face. What would be considered extraordinary?

Laura squinted her eyes and conjured up an image of her face decorated with lipstick and eye makeup. Then remembering Will stood beside her, she shifted her attention to his reflection.

"How come you didn't let the bellman take your luggage?" he asked, wishing instead that he could tell her she was the most beautiful woman he'd ever seen.

He'd watched her survey herself in the glass-paneled doors of the elevator. It hadn't been done like women usually do those things, with aloof approval in the eyes. Instead, her expression had looked far away, locked in a long ago memory.

She switched her duffel bag from her right hand to her

left. "I'd rather handle my own stuff."

"We're on a year long tour and that's all you have?"

"I travel light." At the soft ding, she looked up at the lighted floor number.

Will let her step out first, then followed behind. He waved to the bodyguards posted at the elevator and stairwell. "Our manager tapes our name and key to our assigned room. Come on, let's find yours."

"Are guards necessary?"

He half laughed. "You have no idea what kind of crazy stuff fans will do to get into our rooms."

"Maybe...you can tell me about it some time."

Will smiled at the hesitancy in her voice. She'd given him a small invitation to further conversation.

They found her room located at the opposite end of the corridor from his. He took her key, and as he fit it into the lock, the door across from hers flew open.

"Good, Laura, you're here," the production manager rattled. "They want us at Madison Square as soon as possible. You ready? We can share a cab."

"Yeah, let me throw my things in here, and I'll be right out." Laura took her key from Will, gave him the sweetest, shyest smile he'd ever seen, and disappeared inside.

He watched her door close, her smile lingering in his brain. Never had a woman left him so dazed. He turned, strolled down the hall to his suite, and as he neared his door, he heard Laura and the production manager speaking.

Will glanced over his shoulder to see them waiting at the elevator, both of their heads bowed in deep discussion. Laura looked up at him then, and he held her stare from the opposite end of the corridor. She diverted her eyes and nodded at something the production manager said.

Will stepped inside his room and closed the door. Damp palms. Ninth grade all over again.

* * *

The alarm sounded at six the next morning. Laura turned it off and threw the covers back. The entire *Tourist* entourage had been given the day off. After a morning run in Central Park, she'd shower and have breakfast, then play sightseeing adventurer for the day.

She dressed and pulled her hair through a ball cap, left the hotel room, and walked down the carpeted hallway toward the stairwell. As she neared Will's suite, she slowed. Would he be awake by now or still in bed? Did he plan on running this morning? What would he do with his day off?

The door across from his flew open. Laura gasped and jumped back, landing with a thud against Will's suite.

"Baby, you were hot last night," the lead singer groaned, stumbling over the threshold with a giggling brunette straddling his waist. Her black panty hose dangled around his neck. A red leather mini-skirt rode high on her thighs.

She ran her fingers through his hair while he kneaded her butt. "Tell me you'll dedicate a song to me," she whined.

He pressed her against the wall and ground against her. "You come back tonight, and I'll think about it."

The little dark haired woman dug her spiked, black heels into his backside and made him moan. With a satisfied smirk, she shifted her neck to give his sucking mouth better access. Then she opened her eyes and caught Laura's stare. "Hey, honey, you like to watch? How about a threesome?"

Will opened his door. Laura fell backward onto the floor in front of him. "Larry, man, why do you have to do that crap in the hallway?"

Laura shot up from her sprawled position and bolted down the hall toward the stairwell.

"Hey, honey, where ya going? Things're just getting interesting," the brunette yelled after her.

"Shut up," Will snapped.

Laura fled down the stairs, her heart thumping, and face hot. She burst through the front doors into an overcast New York City morning. She closed her eyes and took some deep breaths.

"Hey." Will strode through the doors. "You alright?"

Laura bent into a hamstring stretch. "I'm fine."

Out of the corner of her eye she saw Will watching her. From her skittish reaction upstairs, she suspected he knew she wasn't fine. He sat on the concrete beside her a few seconds later and began putting on his shoes. He'd run after her, down the stairs and through the hotel, in his socks.

She levered the balls of her feet on the edge of the hotel's steps and leaned back to stretch her calves. One of Will's socks had a tiny hole. A dark skinned toe peeked out. She moved her gaze up his legs to his shorts, caught a glimpse of Bugs Bunny boxers.

"I'm sorry if I woke you," Laura mumbled, looking at his sleep-tousled hair.

Will knotted his laces and stood. "I was already up. Don't worry about it. How about running in Central Park?"

"That's where I'd planned to run."

He grinned. "Well, what a coincidence."

Laura tucked her T-shirt into her runner's shorts. "Aren't you afraid someone might recognize you?"

"Usually I wear a hat and dark glasses, but I was kinda in a hurry when I left." He started walking. "We'll see how it goes. It's early enough, probably not many people out at this hour."

"I can wait if you want to run back up to your room." The accommodating statement came out so naturally and quickly it startled her. She never made offers like that.

He laughed. "Come on, don't worry about it."

Laura hurried to catch up and fell smoothly in step beside him. They crossed over Madison Avenue and walked up Fifth.

They passed Saks, Liz Claiborne, Gucci, and Rolex, all closed at such an early hour. Workers in long white aprons swept and washed their storefronts. A little coffee shop advertised homemade bagels and Colombian brewed beans. Laura's stomach growled at the smell of fresh baked bread. It would be a nice treat after the run.

"Smells good, doesn't it?" Will asked.

"Yeah."

"I heard your stomach growl. Can you wait 'til we finish exercising?"

"I'll have to. I'll get sick otherwise."

Will stopped at the corner. "Well, there it is, Central Park. Kinda crazy there's a big park in the middle of the city."

The sky thundered. Laura looked up. "Looks like rain's coming."

"Not 'til later in the afternoon. We'll have plenty of time." They crossed Fifth Avenue and entered the south end of the park. "Let's go this way," he pointed, "toward the Wollman Memorial."

They started with a slow, warm up jog, then built their pace. Wide, paved trails held marked lanes for bikers, joggers, roller bladers, and walkers. Green lawns spread to trees, and beyond them, towered the New York City buildings. A retreat from the hustle and bustle.

A few minutes later he pointed to the left. In the distance sat a large, paved, circular area. A statue stood in the middle surrounded by a stone wall. A tall, slender, dark haired woman skated backward around the circle. Laura watched as the woman gracefully lifted her arms and leapt from the ground to spin in the air.

Will stopped their progress and jogged in place. "She's beautiful, isn't she?"

Laura looked over at him, surprised he found beauty in something so simple. "It looks like she's on ice."

"Yep, it does."

They watched the skater a few seconds longer, then picked up the pace again.

A few wet drops hit Laura's face and arms. She disregarded them, thinking it morning dew from the overhead trees. But when the splatters became more frequent, she looked up at the sky. Black clouds rolled across. "You said it wasn't suppose to rain until later."

Will chuckled. "I guess I don't make a very good meteorologist." He pointed to a white object in the distance. "There's a gazebo straight ahead. Come on." He took off with a sprint toward it.

Thunder boomed and rain began to fall in full force. Laura followed behind Will, squinting against the pellets hitting her face. With a splash, she landed in a puddle.

Aunt Jane never allowed me to play in the rain.

Laura looked for another and jumped in it, curling her toes in her squishy, wet socks. She glanced at the grass ahead and hopped from one muddy puddle to the next.

Look at me now, Aunt Jane.

Laura stopped and closed her eyes, tilted her head back. Rain splattered her cheeks. She took her hat off and let the water stream through her hair and along her scalp. Smiling, she inhaled the scent of fresh cut grass and turned a lazy circle.

A crack of lightning jerked her from her reverie, and in a quick flash she saw Aunt Jane, some twenty-five feet away, hidden in the woods. Laura held her breath, waiting for another bolt of lightning to illuminate the gloomy trees. It couldn't be Aunt Jane. There was no way she knew where Laura was.

I'll kill you if you ever run away.

Aunt Jane's venomous words ricocheted through Laura's head as another thundering streak lit up the sky. She stared hard into the woods, her gaze snapping from tree to tree, searching for her aunt...Laura had conjured up her image. That had to be it. Had to. She'd been thinking of her and created her likeness in the woods. It had happened before. It could happen again.

"Laura," Will called from the gazebo, alarmed at her sudden change in demeanor. One minute she'd been playing, and the next she'd been frozen stiff, staring off into the woods.

She ran up the grassy slope and ducked under the shelter.

"You okay?"

Laura nodded as she continued to scrutinize the thick clump of trees. While she studied the trees, he studied her. Couldn't make himself *not* look at her, in fact. The rain weighed her ponytail down and plastered it to her head. She hadn't bothered to wipe the wetness from her face or the tiny drops clinging to her lashes. Dripping wet, and she was still the most beautiful woman he'd ever met.

But her eyes weren't dancing like they'd been when she was playing. Her face showed no excitement, inquisitiveness. The pleasant curve of her lips had disappeared.

"Another minute and you would've been a piece of sizzled bacon," he joked, hoping to bring her good mood back.

She smiled a little at his humor.

"You should do that more often."

Laura switched her attention to him. "What?"

"Smile."

As soon as he said it, he wished he wouldn't have. Her face faded to an emotionless line. She didn't physically put space between them, but it felt like she had. Miles of it. He glanced at her lips, desiring beyond imagination to pull her close and kiss away the trouble, confusion, and worry in her eyes.

Instead, he reached out to smooth some wet, blond strands from her cheek, and she tensed. He paused his hand in midair, then slowly lowered it back to his side. Laura turned, folded her arms across her stomach, and stared out across the wet park.

Will studied her profile for a few seconds, then took a seat on the gazebo's bench. "I'm not like the other guys, if that's what you're thinking." When Laura didn't respond, he continued, "Ya know, what you saw back at the hotel. I'm not a partier, Laura, or a womanizer." He preferred his sexual encounters discreet and private. "I'd like for us to be friends, no pressure."

He'd never justified his actions to a woman before now, never needed to. And probably had taken that for granted. He'd smile, cut a few jokes, and women would warm right up to him. He'd throw them a signal or vice-versa and the game was on. It had always been easy, light-hearted, unemotional. Nobody ever got hurt.

Rain drizzled now and scattered sunbeams snuck through the tree limbs. A few joggers resumed exercise on the paths below.

"You ready to head back?" she asked without looking at him.

Will sighed. Why hadn't she responded to what he'd said? He pushed off the bench and deliberately walked out the other side of the gazebo, trying to give her space. "We'll circle around the other side of The Mall and head back that way."

They jogged in silence. The warming sun made the pavement steamy, birds fluttered and chirped, and Will replayed the gazebo scene over and over again in his head. Had he said or done anything wrong? Why was Laura so guarded? What could he do to get her to open up?

They crossed to Fifth and slowed to a walk, navigating the now crowded streets.

"Will?"

He glanced over at her, taken aback that she'd spoken, and

what he saw beyond her gave him a hard jolt. He grabbed her arm and took off in a run.

She tugged on his grip. "What are you doing?"

"They found me." He yanked her around the corner. High-pitched screams pierced the air. Will took another quick look at the crowd of fans running after them.

Laura followed his line of sight. "Oh my God," she gasped.

Will rounded the next street. "It'll get worse. Can you keep up?"

"Yeah."

"Let's go." He released her arm and took off in a sprint, weaving in and out of people and zigzagging the streets of New York. The hotel lay three blocks ahead.

He peeked over his shoulder. Good, Laura was keeping up. She sent him a reassuring nod. Energy and a hint of challenge flashed in her eyes. Will almost laughed. She was enjoying this little adventure.

The hotel sat a half block ahead. He turned, grabbed Laura's hand, and bolted into the lobby.

"Security!" he yelled.

The guards stepped forward and blocked the entrance as the mob crowded around trying to catch a glimpse of him.

Laura braced her hands on her knees and gulped in deep breaths. Will waved to those who had gathered outside the hotel's doors. The people jumped up and down, screaming and waving back.

He looked down at Laura. The exertion had reddened her face. Both their bodies gleamed with sweat. They'd slide right over each other's slick skin if they were naked.

"What were you going to tell me back there before we got mobbed?"

She straightened from her hunched position. "Your offer of friendship, I'd like that."

"Well, friend, would you like to spend the day together seeing the city?"

Laura hesitated, and he got the impression that if she accepted it would be a big step for her.

"Sure," she finally agreed. Then a camera flashed, and Laura spun in the direction of the bright light. "Damn," she hissed and dashed toward the stairwell.

Now her picture would be plastered all over tomorrow's paper. Or worse, on the front page of those gossipy tabloids Aunt Jane read.

Three

"Laura," Will yelled, chasing her into the hotel's stairwell.

Laura leaped the steps two at a time, ignoring the man behind her. What a fool she'd been.

If you ever try to run from me, I'll hunt you down. You won't live a day past our reunion. I'll make you suffer.

Aunt Jane had issued that threat many times over the years, and Laura didn't doubt for a second that her aunt would carry it out. She'd seen her close to that snapping point more times than she cared to remember.

Will grabbed her arm. "What's wrong?"

She pulled free. "Listen, I changed my mind. I'm gonna stay in my room today. I…I'm not feeling well." She needed to be alone, time to think.

"Liar. You feel fine. What was that all about in the lobby?"

"What?"

Will's jaw tightened. "You know full well what I'm talking about."

Laura turned and continued climbing, this time at a more subdued pace. "I don't like my picture taken, that's all." Maybe taking this job hadn't been such a good idea. It placed her too much in the public eye.

"Why?"

She needed to talk to Bizzy, see what she thought. Bizzy was the only person Laura could trust.

"Why?"

"None of your business." It was a bitchy response. She knew that. Maybe he'd leave her alone then. Move on. She was difficult anyway. Had too much baggage. Nobody liked dealing with baggage.

"Coward."

Coward? She whipped around. He took a step up, putting them at eye level, their noses and chests a mere inch apart. Challenge and defiance flicked in his eyes.

"The last thing I am," she gritted out, "is a coward." If only he knew the things she'd been through...but she really was a coward, for running. Did she really think she could hide from Aunt Jane forever? Maybe. But she had to face her past eventually.

One of his brows arched, as if her bristly demeanor meant nothing. "Prove it."

Laura narrowed her eyes. "I prove nothing to no one." She turned and continued up the stairs. She'd spent her whole life trying to conform to Aunt Jane's standards. Not anymore.

"Coward."

Slowly she came back around to face him, knowing he was baiting her. "What do you want from me?"

He looked up at her from five steps below. "I already told you. Spend the day with me. We'll wear dark glasses and hats. No one will recognize me. No cameras. Take a chance."

Take a chance. Bizzy had said those exact words to her during their last conversation regarding Laura's job offer from *Tourist*.

She pivoted, climbed the last two steps, then opened the door to their floor. *Take a chance*. "Fine."

"Be ready in thirty minutes," he called up to her, an obvious note of victory in his voice.

"I'll be ready in twenty."

Laura stood in front of her bathroom mirror braiding her wet hair. An hour ago she'd been standing under the gazebo with Will in Central Park, the most intimate moment she'd ever shared with a man. He'd wanted to kiss her, that much she figured out. Why couldn't she have reacted like a normal woman and received his kiss? He probably thought she was a freak.

She twisted a ponytail holder around the end of her braid, then flicked off the bathroom light. Will told her he wanted friendship, nothing else, no pressure. So today would be what? A friendship date?

Aunt Jane had arranged the one and only date Laura had gone on. It'd been in high school. Her aunt chaperoned. Timmy was his name. He had red hair and acne and was the son of Jane's prayer partner. He'd been pressured into the date, too, and felt as awkward as Laura. They went to a restaurant and saw a G-rated movie, both picked out by her aunt. It'd been a belittling and embarrassing experience.

Unzipping her backpack, Laura found her sunglasses. Those, paired with a hat, would disguise her from the cameras.

A knock sounded on her door. She walked across the room and opened it. Will stood in the threshold, handsome, freshly showered, and shaved. The smell of soap wafted in on a stream of air conditioning. With his bronze skin, khaki shorts, and white collared shirt, he looked dressed for an African Safari.

She swallowed. "Hi."

The pure, female appreciation Will saw in Laura's eyes did wonders for his ego. "Hi." About time she showed a little awareness of him.

"Give me one minute." She grabbed her shoes from beside the dresser and sat down on her bed.

Will stepped inside and closed the door. Laura's eyes snapped to his. Apparently, she hadn't expected him to come in. She looked ready to bolt. He stayed rooted to his spot and decided talking would relax her. "I called the lobby and found out one of the hotel employees took that picture, not a tabloid, in case that's what worried you." He'd been more than curious about her reaction, but knew better than to pursue it.

Relief softened her apprehensive expression. "Thanks." She bent down and loosened the laces on her shoes.

She'd gone head to head with him in the stairwell. No other woman had ever done that. Women usually fell all over each other to catch his attention. The fact that Laura seemed to be running in the opposite direction intrigued him. Frankly, it turned him on.

Will glanced over at her dresser. Neatly folded piles of T-shirts, jeans, bras, and underwear lined the top. He lingered on the underwear. Athletic, white, cotton. Nothing impractical like lace or silk for Laura.

He peered into the bathroom. Again, she'd lined her toiletries in a perfect little row: a brush, a comb, a bottle of lotion, a box of tampons, a toothbrush, a small travel-sized tube of toothpaste. No hair gels, mousses, or makeup, only the bare necessities.

Will looked back at Laura. "When you said twenty minutes, I thought you were kidding. Most women take an hour to get ready."

"I don't fuss a lot." She double-knotted her laces, then clipped a fanny pack around her waist. Inside she stuffed a wallet, camera, room key, and Chapstick. Now that made sense. He'd never grasped the concept of a bottomless purse.

Laura pushed up off the bed. "Ready?"

Her emerald colored tank top revealed slender, well-defined arms. Its color turned her eyes brilliant green. Tan shorts rode high on her thighs.

Will forced himself to look at her face and not those long legs. "You look very nice."

Her cheeks pinkened, and she quickly busied herself with the zipper on her fanny pack. He hadn't made a woman blush since...well, since ever. He wanted to fold her in his arms and rock her and jibber sweet nothings to her. "The hotel's surrounded by fans. So I've arranged for someone to pick us up and drop us off a few blocks away. I figured it'd be more fun to explore on foot and use the subway."

Laura nodded, but didn't look up at him. She checked the contents of her fanny pack, probably trying to hide her still flushed cheeks.

"I've got my handy dandy disguise, so we shouldn't have any problems." Will donned his dark glasses and Australian hat. "Do you recognize me?"

She glanced up. A smile tugged the corners of her mouth. "I think you'll be fine."

Will turned to open the door and stopped when he saw the black tape covering the peephole. He reached up to tear it off.

"Don't," Laura snapped.

Snatching his hand back, he spun to meet her panicked face. Why would she put tape on a peephole? She'd erect an emotionless barrier if he asked.

Instead, he calmly opened the door as if nothing had happened. "Let's get a move on. We have a lot to see today." He stepped into the hallway and heard her exhale a relieved breath.

"Young lady, you have sinned!"

Laura almost came off the bed at the sound of her aunt's fierce voice. She looked up to find Jane hovering in the bedroom doorway, a magazine curled in her fist, her nostrils flaring with each angry exhalation.

"Where did you get this?"

Fourteen-year-old Laura pushed up from her lying position to stand beside her bed. Her eyes darted from her aunt's face, to the magazine, then back to her aunt. Frantically, Laura searched through the details of her day. What had she done wrong now?

Aunt Jane stomped across the wood floor, arcing the

magazine high in the air. Automatically, Laura hunched her shoulders for the expectant blow. Her aunt swatted the balled up pages across Laura's cheek sending her head reeling to the right. She recovered from the blow and immediately focused on the floor. Making eye contact would only fuel the fire.

"You answer me this minute," Jane hissed and jabbed a pointed fingernail into Laura's chest.

Hesitantly, she lifted her head. Aunt Jane unrolled the magazine and shoved it under Laura's nose. She blinked and focused on the front cover, on the half-naked man sprawled across a couch. The girls in her class had been looking at it over the past week, giggling at the naked men. Laura had sneaked a peek too, curious what a penis looked like. How had it wound up in her backpack?

"I-I-I'm not sure how I got it."

Aunt Jane's eyes narrowed to tiny slits. "You may be a little slow, but you're not stupid. Now how did you get it?"

"Some girls at school were looking at it. I'm telling the truth. I don't know how it got in my book bag."

Jane rerolled the magazine and smacked Laura's legs with it. "Lies! Filthy, little liar! That's all you are."

She pinched Laura's ear between thumb and forefinger and led her out the bedroom and down the hall. Laura stumbled after her, clinching her jaw, knowing what was about to transpire.

Jane swung the bathroom door open and shoved her niece inside, then snatched a bar of soap off the sink. Laura backed up against the counter and gripped its edge. Aunt Jane slammed the door closed and came toward her.

"Open up," her aunt snarled, digging her nails into the back of Laura's neck. "You need your mouth cleaned from your lies."

Laura squeezed her eyes closed and opened her mouth. She tensed when the thick, waxy bar ground against her gums and teeth.

"Laura?" Will gently shook her shoulder.

With a jerk, Laura glanced right, then left, orienting herself. They were on the ferry, and The Statue of Liberty stood across the water in front of them.

"Hey." Will spoke softly, rubbing her lower back. "You okay?"

Laura stepped out of his reach, her heart pounding, and leaned against the ferry's railing. She slipped her hand inside her pocket and gripped her rabbit's foot. Closing her eyes, she took a couple of deep breaths. A few seconds. In just a few seconds she'd be okay again.

"Why do you do that? Why do you act like nothing happened?"

She fished her camera from her fanny pack and snapped off a few pictures. Something. She had to say something to get his attention redirected. "I need to get a picture of the Statue."

"You whimpered."

She whipped her gaze to his. *I whimpered?* They both wore sunglasses that hid their eyes, but Laura felt the unnerving sensation that he could read her thoughts, her mind. They faced each other for long, silent seconds, then Laura turned away first, busying herself with the camera again.

Please don't let him ask me any more questions. Please. It's too hard.

Will stepped toward her and placed his hand on her forearm. "Where do you go when you tune out everything around you?"

The warmth from his fingers permeated her bare skin. She studied the camera in her hand, wanting to share with him, trust him. The idea was too foreign, too strange, and scary as hell.

He rubbed his thumb across her skin. "When you're

ready, I want you to tell me about it."

Laura nodded. Will released her arm and propped his elbows on the railing next to hers. They stayed that way for the remaining ride, side-by-side on the upper deck, their shoulders and hips touching, watching the scenery. The air between them took on an affectionate, cozy, friendly feeling, and as time ticked by, Laura actually relaxed.

After the ferry ride, they rode the subway to Soho, where they wove in and out of tattoo parlors, piercing booths, tobacco shops, and tiny eccentric stores. Content to let Laura lead the way, Will found that his pleasure came from watching her explore and experience new things.

In Bob's 'Bacco Shop she picked up a foot tall pipe blown from blue glass and shaped like a mermaid.

A skinny man whom Will assumed must be Bob meandered over. "It's for the wacky tobakky."

Laura glanced up at him. "The wacky? Oh." She put the mermaid back down. "I see."

Will cleared his throat to keep from laughing, and when she turned around, saw that she was holding back her own smile.

"Ready to see Chinatown?"

He nodded and followed her from the store. When they stepped outside, they both shared a chuckle.

By nature she was a quiet woman, speaking when something truly fascinated her, which made him even more attentive and waiting expectantly for her sporadic comments.

In Chinatown they wandered the streets. On the corner while browsing a jewelry display, a police siren pierced the air. Not an odd sound for New York, but still people looked around, wondering where the action was.

An old Chinese lady rounded the corner, running, pushing a cart. Before he had time to register what was happening, the elderly lady ran right over Laura's foot.

"Hey," Will tried to stop the lady, but she was quick and the crowd was thick.

"It's okay," Laura said, half-laughing, obviously amused at the incident. "I'm not hurt. You suppose the police are after her?"

"Yep. Probably an illegal alien or pedaling stolen goods. You sure you're okay?"

"Oh, yeah. I'm fine."

Will knew a lot of women who would get offended or upset over such a thing. Or milked it for sympathy from him. Goes to show him what kind of stuffy women he'd been hanging out with.

"So what do you think of Chinatown?"

Laura shrugged her cute little shoulder. "Seems like a bunch of jewelry stores and restaurants to me. Oh, and crazy Chinese ladies, too."

Will laughed at that. "Ready for lunch?"

"Definitely."

By the time they found Little Italy, not an easy thing to do when given wrong directions, they were starving. They walked into the first restaurant they saw, she ordered a Jack and Coke, he a beer, and both veal piccata.

He picked up his mug. "Here's to more sightseeing in the Big Apple." They clinked glasses and took a sip. "So what do you think of your new job?"

"So far it's everything I'd imagined."

"Good."

She took another sip of her drink. "Do you have any brothers or sisters?"

Will nodded. "I do. I have a younger sister, Veronica."

"Really? I-I was an only child. I've always wondered what'd it be like to have a sibling."

An only child. Whether she realized it or not, she just

opened up to him a little.

"Tell me about her."

And so he did. Conversation during their lunch became one-sided as Will spoke of his childhood shenanigans. He tried to get Laura to talk, but she seemed content to sit, a pleasant smile curving her lips, listening to his stories. He loved her smile, but couldn't wait to hear her laugh. One that boiled up from the depths of her belly and bubbled over. It would be a beautiful sight.

As they finished their lunch, she insisted she pay for her own. It threw him for a loop. When he went out with a woman, he always paid. Not only because the woman expected it, but also because his father had taught him to.

"Laura, please let me pay for this. It doesn't feel right."

"Thank you, but no." She pulled cash from her fanny pack, counted it, and set it on the table.

It wasn't like he couldn't afford it. But she seemed determined. Then it hit him, "How 'bout you get this tab, and I'll get the next one?" That way it'd be a sure bet she'd go out with him again.

Laura scrutinized him through narrowed eyes, as if she knew he was up to something. He gave her his best, innocent look.

"Alright," she finally agreed and dug out some more cash.

They spent the rest of their day sightseeing, strolling along Broadway, seeing Times Square, visiting Ground Zero. She snapped pictures of the Empire State Building and Grand Central Station. The only complaint she made, which Will actually made first, was that her feet hurt.

Cheap date.

At ten that night he saw her to her room, then made his way to his own. Got a quick shower, slipped on a pair of Tweety Bird boxers, and flopped onto his bed. He stacked his hands beneath his head and studied the pattern on the ceiling, replaying the details of his day.

The ferry ride. Out of his whole day he treasured the ferry ride above all else. He would have been content to ride all day just for the opportunity to be so close to Laura. They'd shared an emotionally bonding moment, one full of comfort and warmth. And although she hadn't shared any of her secrets with him, he felt she took a step closer to trusting him.

He'd been attracted to Laura since the first day he met her, yet on the ferry the attraction hadn't existed. It had felt more like camaraderie, contentment. He'd never experienced that with a woman before now, or gone as slow. He'd never truly wanted to build a strong, lasting foundation.

Strange, the women he'd been around had always been hot, sexy, quick, no strings.

Strings!

Will bolted to an upright position. Getting involved with Laura would *definitely* involve strings. How did he feel about that? A little scared. But ready. The challenge would be convincing her she was ready.

"Tourist! Tourist! Tourist!"

In her wildest dreams Laura never imagined she'd sound mix for *Tourist* at Madison Square Garden. Exhilarated by the crowd's deafening roar, she looked out across the sea of bodies.

"Cue smoke and lasers," she heard in her headset.

Colored smoke shot up from hidden chutes, lasers beamed down from the ceiling, spotlights crisscrossed the crowd. Excited screams filled the air as the fans jumped to their feet, craning their necks, trying to catch a glimpse of one of the stars.

"Cue sound."

With her fingers already balanced on the sliding channel bars, Laura slowly slid them into place. Into her headset she answered, "Sound cued."

Hidden behind the smoke, the band began to play the opening number, then in unison, the six members of *Tourist* stepped through the smoke.

People jumped up and down screaming and flailing their arms. A woman in the first row fainted. Some eager fans pushed toward the stage, only to be stopped by security. Hand-made signs popped up all over the crowd proclaiming undying love for their favorite band member.

Good, raw music. No fancy dance moves. Just the six of them jamming out to songs the whole world loved.

Reaching over to the EQ rack, Laura adjusted the mid-range and cocked her head to listen for reverberation. Satisfied with the mix, she took a step back, folded her arms, and surveyed the stage.

Large television screens sat perched on either side showing close ups of the guys. Dressed in leather, silk, cotton, jeans, T-shirts, vests, boots, or sneakers, each had their own unique style. Only the drummer wore his hair long, and in Laura's opinion, he needed a pair of scissors.

Will's image flashed onto the screens. Her stomach did a slow roll. His eyes were closed as his head swayed from side to side, and he strummed the chords. Dark strands curled in spiky disarray all over his head. The top four buttons on his white, linen shirt hung open, offering a peek of chest hair. A silver necklace hung around his neck with an emblem on the end. Laura squinted her eyes but couldn't make out the design. She'd have to ask him about it later.

A group of women to the right of Laura stood with their arms linked, staring dreamy-eyed toward the stage, singing the words to the song. One woman had tears running down her cheeks. Laura studied them, puzzling their emotion. She couldn't recall the last time she'd cried. Nothing affected her that much.

"Laura, what the hell is going on?" a voice hissed through

the headset.

She placed her finger on the earpiece. "What's wrong?"

"Damn, woman. Haven't you noticed? Larry's mike's out."

"What?" Laura jerked her attention to the stage.

The lead singer stood a few feet away from his mike playing his guitar. To the audience nothing appeared wrong. He was jamming out instead of singing. But he had lyrics during this part of the song.

"There's a mike box stage left," she delivered in a calm, controlled voice. "Have a roadie grab cordless number two and make the switch."

She'd practiced making equipment swaps with her sound crew in case something like this happened.

Someone signaled the lead singer from off stage. He grabbed the bad mike and shoved it in his back pocket. While continuing to play, he strolled toward Will. Their heads came together as they sang into Will's mike, then the lead singer casually disappeared off stage.

Will continued with the lyrics while the mike swap took place. The lead singer stepped back onto stage and strolled to the center. He slid the new cordless mike into its stand and joined Will in finishing off the song.

That mike had worked earlier when she tested it. A perfectly good mike didn't go bad. Had somebody tampered with it? Why? Why would somebody purposefully screw up the equipment? It didn't make sense. She had to have made a mistake.

The technical crew had finished their work and retired for the evening. The semis were loaded and en route to the next city. The band members partied back at the hotel, while Laura sat on the floor backstage studying the mike that had gone bad.

Running her fingers over the screened metal head, she

gripped it tight and tested for looseness. She jiggled the transceiver end and discovered it durable. What had gone wrong? Mistakes rarely occurred under her direction.

She fished a screwdriver from her toolbox, quickly disassembled the mike, and found every single wire had been cut. Someone had tampered with the mike and sabotaged *Tourist's* concert. Who, though? It had to be one of the technical staff. No one else had access to the equipment.

"It's one o'clock in the morning. Why are you still here?"

Laura squinted up at Will through dry, tired eyes. She glanced past him into the darkness of the backstage area. They were alone. "What are you doing here?"

His mouth quirked. "I asked you first."

She threw the screwdriver back into the toolbox. "How did you know I was still here?"

"I got worried when you didn't come back to the hotel. I came out looking for you."

How had he known whether or not she was in her hotel room? Had he been watching her? Aunt Jane used to track her like that, following her on afternoon walks, calling school to make sure she hadn't skipped, parking her car outside Bizzy's house while Laura played. Jane would even do bed checks at night to assure Laura hadn't run away.

Cautiously, she regarded Will. "I'm a grown woman. I can take care of myself. There's no need for you to worry about my welfare." The words came out harsher than she'd intended. And looking at the confused, injured expression on Will's face, she knew she'd made a mistake.

He took a step back and defensively lifted his hands. "You've got some nerve, Laura. I was being thoughtful. I know you're a grown a woman. I don't know why you're peeved that I was worried about you. In case you haven't heard, that's what friends do for each other." He shoved his hands in his back pockets. "But hey, you want me to back off?

I will." He turned and started off. "See ya around," he threw over his shoulder, then disappeared into the darkness.

Laura stared out the cab's window as it navigated the streets back to the hotel. On the corner stood a man, shears in hand, snipping, and arranging flowers. At two in the morning, he looked as isolated and alone as she felt.

It was best she'd finally pushed Will away. Things were too complicated in her life. Imagine bringing somebody else into it. It was best...best that he move on.

Then how come it didn't feel like the best thing?

The cab pulled up to the hotel. Laura got out, paid the driver, then trudged inside. An attendant stood behind the counter, looking crisp in her uniform, fresh, and awake. Her pertness at this ungodly hour made Laura want to grumble.

Moments later, the elevator dinged, and Laura stepped out onto her floor. The bodyguards posted on their hall looked as awake and alert as the front desk lady. Laura acknowledged them with a slight wave and stifled a yawn.

She unlocked her room and stepped inside. A folded piece of red, hotel stationary had been slipped under her door. Her name was scribbled across the outside. The handwriting looked faintly familiar. She turned on the lights and retrieved it.

Four

The black and white TV flickered as The Three Stooges carried out their pranks. Laura and Bizzy lay curled up on a purple lounge chair, giggling, as Larry poked Curly in the eyes, then Mo slammed both of their heads together in disgust.

Laura had been at her best friend's house for three days. It was the first time she'd been allowed to stay overnight. Aunt Jane's work had sent her to Atlanta for training. They needed to send her away more often. The time with Bizzy had been the best three days of Laura's life.

Bizzy had received a moped for her birthday, and both of them had ridden it like crazy over the last few days. But this morning after breakfast they'd tried to climb a steep hill on Bizzy's property, slipped on some loose rocks and dirt, and slid all the way back down. Bizzy'd been driving, and Laura sat behind her. The moped fell on both girls midway down the hill, and the hot muffler had seared their tiny calves in matching locations. Bizzy's mom almost got ill when they'd tromped into the house displaying their red, bubbly-looking, six-inch long, twin injuries.

Now, with their legs bandaged and treated, they sucked on Popsicles, mesmerized by The Three Stooges' antics. Outside, a car horn sounded. Their smiles faded as they turned and held each others knowing stare. The car honked again. Quietly, Laura got up and threw away her Popsicle. Bizzy followed her out to the porch, they exchanged a quick hug, then Laura jogged down the steps and climbed into Aunt Jane's car.

Jane bobbed in her seat to big band music on the radio. Her manicured fingers strummed a beat on the steering wheel. She smiled at Laura, put her car in reverse, and drove off.

Laura eyed her warily, puzzled by her unusual good mood.

Aunt Jane chattered about her trip to Atlanta and surprised Laura by asking about her time at Bizzy's. They pulled into their driveway ten minutes later to find a van parked in their carport. A tall, light-haired man opened the driver's side door and stepped out. Jane sucked in a breath, and after a hesitant, surprised second, she scrambled to unbuckle her seatbelt and open her door.

Laura watched as her aunt raced across the driveway, the snug skirt of her business suit hampering a full stride, and leapt into the man's arms. They kissed while he twirled her in a circle. In the nine years Laura had been alive, she'd never seen her aunt be affectionate with a man, or with anyone for that matter.

The man lowered her to the ground and ran his fingers through her straw-straight, brown hair. Then the couple turned and stared at Laura through the windshield of the car. Aunt Jane arched her eyebrows and cocked her head, and Laura took that as her cue to climb out. Her aunt laced fingers with the man, and the two watched as Laura approached.

"That, my darling, is my sister's daughter," Jane announced.

The man smiled down at Laura. "Hello, my name's Gary."

"Hi." Who was this man? Why had he come?

"Gary and I met on the trip I just took." Aunt Jane hugged his waist.

Laura's gaze moved from one adult's face to the other, unsure of what to say or do next.

Gary cleared his throat. "Dear, are you babysitting your niece?"

Jane smiled sweetly at Laura. "No, Laura has lived with me since she was a small thing."

Dumbfounded, Laura stared back. Her aunt had never given her a sweet smile in her whole life.

Gary cleared his throat again. "I...didn't realize you had children."

Jane's smile faded. She turned to Gary. "I thought you'd be pleased to find out I have a child that you can be a father to. We have a future together, and I'm too old to give you children. You know I'm in my fifties."

Gary looked down at Laura. "Sweetheart, will you give us some private time?"

Laura nodded and walked to the house, and even though she knew she shouldn't, she crouched near an open window to see and hear what would transpire between them.

Gary pulled away from Jane. "I'm not sure how to say this in a nice way, so I'll just say it. I don't want children of my own, and I don't want to take care of another person's child. I never have. When we met in Atlanta, the way you talked, I assumed you didn't have children. I'm sorry, but I guess I should've asked."

Jane latched onto his forearm. "Please, Gary, don't do this. I'm a good catch. I'm impeccably groomed and well dressed. I'm attractive and certainly don't look my age. I'm outstanding compared to the other women in my church."

Gary gave her a puzzled smile, as if he didn't know how to respond. "Of course you're attractive."

Jane gripped his arm tighter and took a step toward him. "We don't have to keep her. I can put her in a home."

"You're not serious, are you?"

"Of course I'm serious."

Gary pulled his arm from her grip and pointed toward the house. "You can't throw her away like she's a rag doll or something."

"There're lots of good homes she could go to," Jane rambled in desperation, reaching for him. "Oh, Gary, we could be so happy together. I've prayed about you, and God gave me a vision. You're my future husband. The premarital

sex we had is justified. We have Heaven's approval."

"You're not the person I thought you were." He climbed into his van, started the engine, then looked at Jane through the open window. "You need help. There's something wrong with you." He pointed to his head. "You're mentally off."

Laura watched as Gary zipped down their driveway, then switched her attention back to her aunt. Jane turned from his retreating vehicle at the same time, caught her niece peeking out the window, and narrowed her eyes to two tiny slits. Laura spun and raced upstairs.

She made it to her room when she heard her aunt fling the front door open and slam it behind her. Laura tensed as she listened to Jane's feet pound up the stairs.

Backing away, Laura stared at her open bedroom door. Heavy footsteps stomped into Aunt Jane's room, paused, came back out, turned down the hall, passed the bathroom, and then Jane rushed into her room, wielding a long object high above her head. Laura fell backward onto her bed, immediately curled into the fetal position, and wrapped her arms around her head.

"You wretched excuse for a kid," Jane screamed and whipped the tree switch down across Laura's head. "You've ruined my life!" She struck her side. "You're a bastard child that nobody ever wanted, and I was a fool to adopt you!" She switched her legs. "It's no wonder your father didn't claim you when you were still in your mother's belly," Jane yelled and lashed her niece's body again, and again, and again.

Laura groped for her pillow, looking for something to shield her body. But her aunt had already flung it aside. Squeezing her eyes shut, Laura willed her mind to drift back to Bizzy's place, to the snack cakes they'd snuck at two in the morning, the dollhouse they made out of cardboard, and the flowered sheet they used as a tent in Bizzy's bedroom.

Aunt Jane's ire finally subsided, and she stood hovering

above her niece, heaving deep breaths. Laura didn't open her eyes. After a minute or so, she heard the older woman turn and shuffle from the room.

Laura stayed curled in a tight ball with her arms snaked around her head. A long time went by before she finally crawled out of bed and walked over to her dresser. In the mirror, she surveyed the puffy, red stripes that covered the right side of her body and head. She reached into the top drawer and pulled out a tube of antibiotic ointment. Squeezing a portion onto her finger, she began smoothing it along the raised, swollen sores.

Afterward she dug her rabbit's foot from its hidden spot under the carpet in the corner of the closet. Gripping it tightly, she sat in her window seat and stared out at the woods bordering their backyard.

Will shifted in his seat. He'd been in the same position for thirty minutes staring at Laura. She lay at the back of the plane, curled up on a couple of seats, sleeping. She had to be exhausted after her late night. They hadn't spoken a word to each other since their dispute after the concert. He wasn't pissed anymore, just frustrated, confused. Didn't know what to make of her.

Heaving a sigh, he glanced out the plane's window. How long did it take to get to Philadelphia anyway?

He stood and stretched, then walked to the bar to get a drink. After a long pull from a water bottle, he turned, leaned against the bar, and surveyed the sleeping occupants of the plane. Why did he have to be the only one awake?

Will's gaze drifted back to Laura. The ball cap she'd placed over her face to block the light had fallen to the floor. He tiptoed over to retrieve it and realized she was shivering. Quietly, he opened the overhead bin, found a blanket, then laid it over her body. He took the seat opposite hers and watched her sleep.

She lay facing him with her head cushioned by her backpack and her hands curled under her chin. He toyed with her ball cap a moment, then discreetly lifted it to his nose. Closing his eyes, he inhaled her shampoo and natural scent. Never in his life had he been so infatuated with a woman that he wanted to smell her cap.

A whimper, or more like a moan, came from Laura. Will opened his eyes and looked at her. She shivered. He knitted his brows, studied her more carefully. She shivered again. No, not a shiver, it was a flinch. He leaned closer. She flinched again. Then her chest began to rise and fall with quick, rapid breaths, like a panting animal. A low, wounded sound vibrated from her throat. His stomach lurched. Her right hand slowly unfolded, and her index finger made a clumsy, crisscross pattern on her cheek.

Will slid off his seat and knelt in front of her. He stroked his hand across her forehead and over her hair until she calmed. Then gently he ran his index finger along the line of her brows. Her lashes fluttered open. Tired, dazed eyes looked back at him. Will cupped her cheek.

"I'm sorry," she whispered.

"For what?" he whispered back.

"For last night. I got your note."

"Went by your room around eleven. Thought you'd want to go running this morning. When you didn't answer, I left the note and found you backstage."

"I realize that now."

He gave her a small smile. "Thank you for apologizing."

Emotion flowed from her eyes. Encouraged, he asked, "What were you dreaming?"

Laura closed her eyes. "Nothing. Just an old familiar nightmare."

Will took her face in both hands. "Tell me."

She pushed the blanket aside and sat up. "Excuse me, I

need to go to the restroom."

Still kneeling in front of her, he grabbed her hands. "You flinched and moaned. You were so distressed. Your finger made this crisscross pattern on your face. Let me in. What happened to cause so much pain?"

She diverted her face, closed her eyes, and swallowed. Will scooted in closer. "Hey," he whispered and waited for her to look at him.

Laura turned and searched his face. He hoped to God she saw trust, friendship, and kindness there. "I don't know what's going on, but have you ever considered talking with a therapist?"

"I'm not nuts."

"I didn't say you were. I've been to see one."

"You have? Wh-that's none of my business. Did it help you with your problem?"

"It did. And I'll tell you why I went. Years ago my grandmother died. I was very close to her. She and dad raised me and my sister. I had to go to counseling to deal with the loss. There's no shame in going to see someone professional. Certainly doesn't mean you're nuts."

"What happened to your mom?"

"Died almost thirty years ago giving birth to my sister."

"I'm so sorry."

Will accepted the condolence with a nod.

Laura's eyes lowered to his chest. "What's on the end of your chain?"

He hesitated, unsure about the change of topic, then reached inside his shirt and pulled out the necklace. Holding the pendant toward her, he told her the story. "When my sister, Veronica, and I were little, my grandmother took us mining in North Carolina. We worked all day panning muck from some river and never saw any gold. All of us were starving and decided to drive down the mountain to a restaurant we had seen that morning."

"Well," he chuckled. "Veronica had to pee so bad that Gramma pulled over on this curvy, mountainous road and told her to go behind a boulder. When she came back to the car, she was holding this lump of gray and white rock, and it had a gold line running through it. Gramma had it analyzed and discovered it was gold."

Will glanced at the emblem. "For Christmas that year, she had it broken into three pieces. Hers she carried in her purse and had necklaces made for me and Veronica. It's more sentimental than anything else. Gramma told us it would remind us of our good fortune and strong family bonds."

Laura took hold of the small lump encased in silver wiring. "It must be nice to have such wonderful childhood memories." She rolled it between her fingers. "I saw this during last night's concert and wanted to ask."

He watched her face as she examined the necklace, then she glanced up, and their noses bumped, making them both smile. Will took the seat beside her. He reached for her hand and settled it snugly between his palms.

"I think you're right about the counselor," she said some time later.

He lifted her fingers and pressed a kiss to her knuckles.

"I was having a nightmare about a whipping I received."

Will ran his thumb across the back of her hand. "Why did you get a whipping?"

"My aunt's boyfriend broke up with her because he didn't want any children."

"Is that who whipped you? Your aunt?"

Laura nodded.

"Why did you make crisscross patterns with your finger?"

She looked down at their joined hands. "Probably from the ointment I smeared on my welts."

Will clamped his teeth together. She'd been beat hard

enough to leave welts? How many times had she endured such pain over the years?

Long moments passed, and when she didn't say anything else, he lifted her hand and kissed it again. "Thank you for sharing that with me."

Laura stared unblinking into his eyes, as if she didn't know what to make of him. Then she gave him a tender smile that nearly broke his heart and turned her attention to the scenery outside the window.

The captain announced their descent into Philadelphia. Will squeezed her hand and released it. She slipped her fingers inside her front pocket and pulled out a tattered, blue rabbit's foot. As she continued to stare out the window, she rubbed her thumb along its surface. Will watched the movement from the corner of his eye, puzzling the significance of the charm.

Tourist's band members followed their manager through the corridors of the Philadelphia venue. The "Meet and Greet", a private backstage get-together requested by the sponsors, was set for six o'clock. The concert started at eight, the first of three held in the city.

Two oversized bodyguards dressed in black T-shirts and dark jeans accompanied them. Will walked beside Eric, listening to him tell a joke he'd heard on the radio. In front of them, the lead singer and keyboard player discussed one of the new songs planned for the evening show. The drummer and bass player brought up the rear, whispering about their sexual adventure from the night before.

Will glanced up as they came to a stop and nodded to one of the security officers standing off to the right.

Their manager turned to face them. "Okay, fellas, behind this door are the President of Coast Records, the CEO of Launch Enterprises, the Financial Advisor for LBC, the owner of this performance hall, the media, and many more." His lips stretched into a charming, professionally whitened smile. "Be on your best behavior, boys."

"Come on," the drummer whined. "We know the drill. We promise to be good and not molest their daughters until after the show."

The rest of the guys chuckled. Their manager shook his head. "You better be glad I love you boys. Lord knows the stuff I put up with." He opened the door, then stepped aside to let the men pass through in front of him.

Fifty people crowded into the green-carpeted room. White foldable chairs held half the crowd while the others stood along the back and side walls. A long table stretched across the front with six microphones placed at intervals.

Will walked into the room, lifting his hand in greeting. He took his place at the front table and surveyed the crowd staring back at them like they were pagan gods. He broke the awkward silence, "So, did anyone hear I got mobbed a few days ago in Central Park?"

The crowd laughed, and everyone started speaking at once.

"I wanted to ask you about that."

"It was in the papers."

"And on the radio and TV, too."

"Were you hurt?"

"You'd gone running, right?"

"Are you generally an early riser?"

"Had you eaten breakfast yet?"

"Who was the woman with you?"

When the lady in the back corner shouted the last question, a hush fell over the crowd. All the band members turned and grinned at Will, plainly relieved he was the one under scrutiny.

He kept his expression impassive. "Well, it's nice to know the paper, radio, *and* TV think I'm so newsworthy."

The crowd chuckled.

"Yes, I'm an early riser and enjoy running before I start my day. No, I hadn't eaten breakfast yet and don't until after my run. I wasn't hurt, and the woman? A fellow runner, that's it."

"Where did you meet her?" someone in the front asked.

"At the hotel or out in the city?"

"Is she younger than you or older?"

Will nudged Eric's foot under the table, trying to tell him *help!* He knew who Will had been with that day.

Eric must have got the hint because he leaned forward into his microphone. "Hey! Have I bragged about my kid yet?"

The crowd laughed, and the attention effectively switched to Eric, who everyone knew loved to talk about his son. He glanced Will's way and delivered a quick, knowing wink.

Will relaxed back in his chair. Rumors, bad media, or pressure were the last thing he and Laura needed.

The band completed a last minute sound check. The house was set to open in ten minutes. Will hurried around the corner onto the stage where he'd left his hat. Laughter, chatter, and squeals filled the air from the crowd waiting outside the Philadelphia performance hall.

The drummer sat behind his gear, idly tapping a rhythm on the snare, staring off into space. Will grabbed his hat from under a riser as he studied the drummer. The other guys had already gone to their dressing rooms to prepare for the evening show.

Will followed the drummer's line of sight out into the venue. Laura stood at the soundboard, midway to the back of the house, coiling cables. He turned his attention back to the drummer, noted the interest etched in his eyes, and walked across the stage. "Hey, the house is about to open. What are you doing?"

The drummer pointed his chin in Laura's direction. "Enjoying the scenery and contemplating flirting. I usually go for big hair and tits, but the natural look works for her." He gave a snort. "Wouldn't ya love to get her in bed? It's the quiet ones that scream."

Will ground his jaw. He'd heard the guys talk trash about a lot of women over the years, but he never expected Laura to be on the receiving end. None of the guys, but Eric, knew Will had an interest in Laura. He wanted to keep it that way.

The drummer let out a slow, low whistle. "Check it out. That's a real woman for ya."

Will glanced over his shoulder to see Laura carrying a sub woofer down the aisle.

The drummer set his sticks down and stood. "That speaker's got to weigh fifty pounds, if not more. Turns me on watching her maneuver it."

Will's teeth clamped together so hard he thought he felt a tooth crack. Pivoting back to the drummer, he summoned the most lighthearted voice he could. "You don't want to waste your time with a techy. She's not a play toy. There'll be plenty of girls around tonight after the show."

Laura grunted.

Will turned around just as she crawled under the stage pushing the sub woofer in front of her. He hurried across the performance area and down the steps. "What are you doing? We hire roadies to do stuff like that."

"I'm perfectly capable."

He squatted down and peered between boxes of backup equipment. "I know you're capable, but you could hurt yourself. That thing's heavy."

Laura emerged from behind a clump of speakers. "I'm fine."

Will straightened and moved out of her way. "Have a roadie do that next time, please."

She stood and brushed her hands on her jeans. "If I need something done, and I've got the time to do it, then I do it."

He folded his arms across his chest and gave her his best disapproving look.

She copied his stance.

Will bit back a grin.

A smile tugged at the corners of Laura's lips.

The drummer walked to the end of the stage and looked down at the two of them. "Hey, Laura, I was telling Will how sexy you look hauling all that heavy equipment around."

Laura glanced up at the drummer, then back at Will. The humor faded from her expression. "House opens in one minute. You guys need to clear out." She turned and walked down the aisle back to her soundboard.

"Nothing fazes that woman," the drummer said. "I think I'll make it my mission to get a reaction out of her. What do you think, you in?"

Will glared up at him. "No, I'm not in. She's not a gambling experiment. Find something else to do with your free time."

Five

On stage, Jay squatted at the back of a speaker pretending to adjust some wires. Peering down the length of the Philadelphia performance hall, he confirmed Laura was still playing her guitar at the mixing board. She'd been cautious all day with the technical workers, overseeing their every movement. With the microphone mishap in New York, everyone understood.

Glancing first over his right shoulder, then left, he stood, pulled the tiny scissors from his front pocket, and strolled over to the onstage monitors.

Pretending to drop something, he leaned down, picked it up, and cut the monitor wiring all in one motion.

"Yo, Jay, wanna join me for a smoke?"

Jay spun around and shoved the scissors into his back pocket. He winced. "S-sure. Go on out, I'll be there in a second."

He licked his dry lips and cut his gaze toward Laura. She still existed in her own world, oblivious to him. With his luck she'd be the Head Sound Engineer for years, and he'd never get a shot at the position.

Jay tilted his head back and looked up at the stage lights, imagining himself behind the mixing board in charge of the whole show.

He wanted it and would do anything, *anything*, to get it.

Tourist fans jammed behind the barriers, screaming and reaching for the six band members as they pulled up to the performance hall after their promotional luncheon.

The band's manager stopped the guys from exiting the

limousine. "Listen up. Wave and smile, but no autographing. We've got a packed afternoon with sound check and rehearsing our new song."

He ushered them out of the vehicle and into the venue. The guys filed off in different directions to use the bathroom, have a smoke, or relax. Rehearsal didn't start for fifteen minutes.

Will made a beeline for the sound area and Laura. When was the last time he had a jittery stomach over a woman? Thirty-three years old and he felt like sixteen again. And all over a shy, beautiful lady that turned him inside out.

He came to a stop a few feet from her, staring at the picture she made. Laura's khaki-clad legs stretched to eternity in front of her with her heels balanced on the edge of her mixing board. The guitar she cradled looked ten years old. She'd pulled on a gray sweatshirt, probably to ward off the chill in the theater.

With her eyes closed, her slim fingers moved deftly over the strings. Will didn't recognize the loving melody, but the emotion in it had settled her face into a peaceful, content expression.

Then it hit him. That music. He'd heard it before. Something about it seemed familiar. He listened to the bars more closely, trying to place it...

"Is my music that awful?" Her voice had a certain dream-like quality to it. He hadn't heard it quite like that before. Amazing how the right piece of music could settle someone's soul.

"What is that? Usually I can peg a piece of music, but you've stumped me."

Laura wedged the pick under one of the strings. "It's been rolling around in my mind for days now. I'm not sure where I got it." She slid off the stool and laid the guitar back in its case.

"Well, whatever it is, I like it. Did your guitar just get here?"

She nodded and snapped the case closed. "I had a colleague in Nashville send it to me. Did you have a good lunch?"

"Yep. Did you eat?"

Laura propped her hip against the stool and folded her arms across her stomach. "The sponsor had some food laid out backstage."

"I brought something for you."

"Thanks, but I'm not hungry."

Will shook his head and closed the small distance between them. "That's good, because it's not food." He reached into his back pocket and pulled out a Philadelphia patch. "I noticed your duffel bag has patches sewn all over it. I figured you'd want one from this city, too."

Laura stared at the tiny, cloth patch lying in his outstretched hand. She didn't reach for it, and he wondered if he'd made a mistake. Will studied her face, trying to read her expression.

He started to take his hand away. "If-I thought-it's okay–"

She placed her hand on top his, effectively stopping his stammering. Sliding the patch from his fingers, she lifted bewildered eyes to his. "Thank you."

A cloth patch, small and insignificant to most, but she reacted as if it was her first gift ever. It made Will want to shower her with silly, little trinkets and big, expensive whatevers. "You're welcome."

The guys began to filter on stage. Laura tucked the patch in her front pocket and glanced at the performance area.

"Good luck mixing the new song," Will said, then trotted, or rather it felt more like floated down the aisle.

"That's a silly grin you've got," Eric teased as Will came on stage.

He didn't realize he *had* been grinning. "I'm telling ya, there's something about that woman that makes me all..." he waved his hands around looking for the right word.

Eric laughed. "I know, man, my wife does the same thing to me." He clapped Will's shoulder. "Welcome to the world of love."

Will's grin faded. "L-love? Jeez, man, I wasn't quite ready to give it that word."

"Hey, don't let a little four letter word freak you out."

He reached for his guitar and strapped it on. "I'm going to have to think about that one."

"Well don't think too hard about it. You'll ruin some of the fun of letting things happen naturally."

"Okay, guys. Ready?" Laura's voice echoed over the house mike.

The band signaled her with a wave.

"Check on mike one."

The lead singer stepped up to his microphone. "Check."

"Check on mike two."

"Wait a minute, Laura," the lead singer yelled out through the house. "I can't hear myself in my monitor."

"Okay, hang on a minute."

Will heard Laura on the radio to the backstage monitor mixer. "Jay, make sure the lead monitor is up."

"It's up," Jay responded.

Laura grabbed the house mike again. "Okay, now try."

"Testing one, two, three. Testing." The lead singer shook his head.

Stepping over the barrier that surrounded her area, Laura jogged to the stage. She walked over to the bad monitor and knelt down to examine it. "Looks like it's been cut." She held up some snipped wires.

"First my mike and now my monitor. What the hell's going on?" the lead singer demanded.

Laura stood and looked him in the eyes. "Someone is tampering with our equipment. I examined your mike in New York after the mishap. The wires on the inside were shredded."

"Well it's your job," the lead singer pointed a finger at her, "to make sure that crap doesn't happen. We never had these problems when Ed mixed for us."

"It's my job," she calmly responded, "to make sure this equipment gets set up, and I mix your show to the best of my ability. I cannot be everywhere at once and act as security for all the equipment."

"Well whoever's messing around with our stuff either has it out for you, or me. Now," he took a step closer to her, "I'd say it's you because this wasn't going on before you showed up."

"Lay off her," Will interrupted. "She can't help it if someone's messing around with our stuff."

The lead singer pivoted toward him. "You stay out of this."

"Gentlemen," Laura spoke in a soft, but commanding voice. "I'll replace this monitor, and we'll continue with sound check. Afterward, I'll speak with security and have them pay closer attention to our workers." She turned and walked off stage, not giving either of them a chance to respond.

From up on his pedestal, the drummer chuckled. "And then she exited leaving an icy path in her wake." He dramatically shivered. "I feel like I'm on a soap opera. I can see the headlines now, 'Sabotage Plot on Rock Tour'."

"Shut up," Will and the lead singer snapped in unison, then turned and glared at each other.

Laura stepped out of the shower and wrapped a towel around her head. She eyed the Pennsylvania patch sitting on the bathroom counter top. Will had noticed the state patches sewn on her duffel. He'd understood what meant something to her, went out, and bought it.

Aunt Jane had given her gifts over the years, but they were always what Jane wanted her to have, not what Laura wanted. Whether a fluffy dress, hair ribbons, or a porcelain doll, Jane had given her what she thought a "perfect" girl should have. She'd never known, or cared, about Laura's *real* likes and dislikes.

She glanced up at her naked reflection, turned left, then right, peeked over her shoulder for a rear view. What if she stood like this in front of Will? Would she be unselfconscious and confident of what belonged to her? Or would she be shy and inhibited and want to cover up?

You'll go straight to Satan if any boy touches your body.

Laura shook her head, casting out her aunt's voice.

With your scraggly body, you'll be lucky if any man wants you.

Laura tugged the towel off her head. "Go away," she hissed.

Don't you lock that door, young lady. If I want to see you naked, I'll see you naked.

She grabbed the comb off the counter and yanked it through her hair.

There's nothing special about you.

"Shut up," Laura screamed and threw the comb at the mirror.

She stomped out of the hotel bathroom and over to her suitcase. She picked up her T-shirt, roughly shoved it over her head, then tore it off and threw it across the room.

"You know what, you stupid, crazy aunt?" she yelled. "I'm *not* going to put on any clothes! You are *not* barging in this room! You are *not* telling me what stupid dress to wear! You are not *ever* going to comment on my body again!"

She paced over to the window, jerked open the curtains,

and stood stark naked, raggedly breathing. From the twentieth floor she stared down at a dark, twinkle lit Philadelphia. "And I locked the door and there's nothing you can do about it," she finished through gritted teeth.

A knock sounded. She spun around. "What?"

"It's Will."

Laura took a deep breath and quickly pulled on her shorts and T-shirt. She walked over and opened the door. He stood there dressed for bed in pajama bottoms, a white T-shirt, and socks. His cuddly look soured her mood even more. "What do you want?"

Will cocked a brow at her tone of voice. Her flushed face looked annoyed, and her wet hair hung in long, partially combed clumps. Her recent shower made the air moist with the smell of soap.

And she wasn't wearing a bra. "I wanted to see if you had any problems with the show tonight."

Still holding on to the doorknob, Laura propped her other hand on her hip. "After the monitor mishap? No, nothing else."

"Good." Will peered past her into the hotel room. "I heard voices."

"The TV's on."

He had a clear shot of the TV from where he stood. "No it's not."

Laura sighed. "Is there something you needed?"

Will shifted and propped his shoulder against the doorframe. He smiled and decided to have infinite patience with her obvious foul mood. "Thought I'd visit for awhile."

"I'm not in a good mood and don't feel like being around anybody."

"That's okay, I've got enough of a good mood for both of us."

"Wiiilll," she warned.

"Lauuurrra," he warned back.

She clinched her jaw, pivoted on her heel, and headed back into the room. Will felt like punching the air over the triumph.

He stepped over the threshold and closed the door. Once again, black electric tape covered the peephole. Turning, he glanced in the bathroom, saw her towel heaped on the floor with a comb on top. A few blond hairs wound through the teeth. Not at all her usual neat, tidy self.

With casual ease, he strolled the rest of the way in, then plopped down in a corner chair. Laura had busied herself packing for tomorrow's flight, methodically folding and situating her clothes.

He watched her in silence for a few moments. "You want to talk about it?"

"No."

Will propped his elbows on the arms of the chair and steepled his hands in front of him. He tapped the pads of his fingers together as he contemplated her.

Should I sit here and say nothing? Should I talk about lighthearted stuff? Should I try to get it out of her? She's in just enough of a feisty mood that I may be able to get her to talk.

"Why do you put black tape over the peephole?"

Laura's hands stilled. "None of your business."

"Are we friends?"

She looked up at him through cautious eyes. "Yes."

"Well, that's good, because in my book friends talk to each other."

"I hardly know you."

"You know me well enough, and you also know we're on a year-long tour together and stuck with each other whether we like it or not. Now," he firmed his tone. "Talk to me."

Laura straightened from her hunched position. Every

muscle in her face clinched into a hard line.

"Oh, no you don't," he warned. "Don't you dare start putting up walls. Talk to me."

"Fine." She charged over to the door, yanked the tape off, and faced him. "You want to know why I put this on my door? Because my aunt used to get a kick out of watching me dress and undress. I even found a hole in my wall that she used to look through when I didn't know about it."

Laura stomped over and waved the tape in his face. "And you know why she did it? Other than being a pervert, she said God wanted her to watch over me at all times. Girls did things behind closed doors they weren't supposed to. It was her job to make sure I didn't do them and stayed holy." She flung the tape in his lap. "To this day I still can't dress or undress without remembering or thinking she's watching me."

Will kept eye contact with her as she loomed above him, nearly ready to explode. He'd known her childhood hadn't been pleasant. His gut told him this was only the beginning.

What do I do? What do I say?

He wanted to pull her into his arms and hold her, but felt like she wouldn't let him.

Laura's shoulders slumped then, and she sank down on the edge of the bed. Her defeated posture broke his heart.

"I can't believe I yelled at you." She gave him a weak smile. "It felt good to let loose a little."

"I bet it did. Thanks for sharing."

She shifted her attention to the windows. "I've arranged to see a counselor in the next city. I'm so tired of carrying my childhood around with me. I want to be a normal woman."

Will pushed out of the chair and knelt in front of her. He slid his arms along the sides of her legs, loosely cradling her. He looked at the side of her face and waited for her to turn back toward him. When she finally did, he whispered, "You are normal. You have some awful stuff to work through, that's all."

He tightened his hold around her legs and scooted closer. She stiffened, clearly uncomfortable with his nearness. He stood and backed away, recalling the article he'd read that morning. Abuse victims needed space. Sometimes physical contact overwhelmed them, put them on edge, brought back bad memories.

"Laura?" He waited, but she didn't lift her face to his. "Have you always dealt with your memories alone?"

She looked up at him then. "My friend, Bizzy, has been there for me."

Will sat beside her on the bed, leaving enough space so as not to crowd her. "Well I know I'm not Bizzy, but I want you to know that you can tell me anything. Please don't ever feel ashamed of your childhood."

Her tensed body relaxed a little. She turned sideways to face him. "I didn't expect Will Burns, rock star, to be you."

He chuckled and turned to face her. Their knees touched as they sat companionably on the bed. "So what did you expect from Will Burns, the rock star?"

Laura shrugged a shoulder. "I don't know. I guess sex, drugs, and rock n' roll." She waved her hand toward the door. "Like the rest of the guys."

"Sex, drugs, and rock n' roll, huh? Well, I've definitely had sex." She blushed at that statement. "But I've always been private about it. Not in the hallways or backstage like the other guys. As far as drugs go?" He flicked his hand in the air. "I've always hated drugs. I have gotten drunk a time or two, though. And the rock n' roll? Well, hell, that's what I do for a living."

Laura smiled. "I like you Will. You're fun to be around."

He leaned forward and gave her a quick peck on the cheek. It startled her, but she didn't freeze up. "Well, that's good, because I like you, too. Now," he stood, "time for both of us to go to bed." He walked to the door. "Sleep well,

Laura."

"Good night, Will. Thanks for everything."

He paused in the open doorway, unsure of himself for the first time in his life and scared out of his mind that he'd screw up somehow. "You're welcome. That's what friends are for. See ya tomorrow."

Laura studied the oil painting hanging on the wall. A foggy, London scene straight out of the 40's with an old car ambling along and a man dressed in a top hat and coat strolling across the canvas.

"Miss Genny? Doctor Masters will see you now."

Laura glanced from the painting to the receptionist's desk. She took a deep, fortifying breath, then followed the secretary into the doctor's office.

Doctor Masters sat behind his desk, bent over a file scribbling something. The secretary exited the room, quietly clicking the door closed behind her.

"Welcome, Miss Genny. Do come in," he invited in a British accent.

Laura stepped further into the room. She hadn't expected him to be English, or so young.

He stood and extended his hand. "I'm Bill Masters."

She shook his hand, glad to find it warm and dry. "Laura Genny."

He pointed to some chairs in the corner. "Let's have a seat over there."

Laura followed him to the indicated sitting area. Shelves lined his walls displaying books, certificates, portraits, and knickknacks.

"Would you like to take a minute to browse my shelves?"

Embarrassed that he'd caught her snooping, Laura quickly shook her head and took a seat in one of the leather chairs. He didn't look like her image of a Psychologist–little, balding, and thick glasses. With blond hair, tan skin, and blue eyes, Bill Masters looked like he should model for *GQ*.

"I don't look much like a doctor, do I?"

She cleared her throat, embarrassed again by his perceptiveness. "I was just thinking that."

Masters chuckled. "My wife says I look like a surfer dude."

Laura couldn't help but smile at his friendly demeanor and poor attempt at a "surfer dude" accent. He lifted a picture frame off a side table and handed it to her.

"Is this your family?" Laura asked, studying the photo of a stunning dark-haired woman holding a Chinese toddler.

"Yes, my wife, June, and our daughter, Chi Chi."

Laura handed the picture back. "Chi Chi?"

Masters smiled as he settled the frame back on the table. "Her real Chinese name is about a mile long, so we shortened it for ease. We adopted her five years ago."

"Oh." Laura looked at the picture again. Chi Chi's big, sweet grin sported a missing tooth. "I was adopted, too."

He relaxed back in his chair and crossed his legs. "Tell me about it."

"Well, from what I understand, when my mother got pregnant, my father left. She kept me for a couple of years, then gave me to her older sister to raise."

Have you ever seen your mother or father since then?"

"No."

"Tell me about living with your aunt."

Laura glanced over to the open window in his office. "That's why I'm here, Doctor Masters, to try and figure out how to let go of my childhood, or bury the memories, or whatever I need to do to move on in life."

She turned back to him. "I suffer from horrible nightmares and flashbacks. I need to release them. I want to be a normal woman."

Masters nodded. "I'm good at my job, Laura. I'm confident you and I can sort through your past, make sense of it, and put aside the stuff that doesn't matter anymore."

Laura sighed, relieved to hear his determined tone of voice. "That's good. I'm ready. I'm *really* ready to move on."

"Let's start with your earliest memory," he said, grabbing a notepad and pen.

She looked toward the window as her mind reeled back through the years. After some moments, she told Masters a vague memory of a blond-haired woman, who Laura assumed to be her mother, combing her hair. She recalled a playful scene in the park on a swing, again with her mother. Then Laura began to describe a house ruled by religion where discipline had been done in the name of God. She detailed Aunt Jane's use of a belt, tree switch, isolation, cleansing rituals with soap, prayer, withholding basic needs of food and water.

Laura spoke for forty-five minutes, pausing at increments to gather her thoughts or respond to questions from the doctor. At the end of her allotted time, a sense of serenity had settled her soul.

Masters clicked his pen closed. "I feel this has been an extremely productive session."

She'd had her reservations about seeking help, hadn't been sure anyone *could* help her. It didn't feel that way now. "I don't think I've ever talked that much in my whole life."

He chuckled.

"Thank you, doctor. This went better than I expected. I'm glad Will encouraged me to come."

Masters eyes brightened. "Will? As in Will Burns?"

Laura nodded.

"My secretary told me you work for *Tourist*. We're huge fans. We've got all their CD's at home."

"You going to the concert tonight?"

He perked in his chair. "Oh, yes. We've had tickets for six months."

"Where're you sitting?"

A grin split his face. "Gold circle."

"That's right in front of my area. After the concert, come back to the mixing board. I'll take you backstage to meet the guys."

Masters' jaw dropped. "Are you serious? June and Chi Chi are not going to believe this."

Laura smiled and glanced at her watch. "I've got to be at the Trans World Dome in thirty minutes." She'd left Jay in charge of set up.

"Of course."

"I'm on the road full time, and you're here in St. Louis. How are we going to do our counseling sessions? By phone?"

Masters got up and circled around to his desk. "Do you have access to a computer and privacy?"

"Yes. There's a laptop I can take into my hotel room."

"Good. We're going to video conference." He pulled a box from a drawer and took two small cameras from it. "These will be hooked to both of our computers. At our scheduled time, we'll dial in and have our session."

Laura walked over to his desk and took one of the cameras. "Technology is something else, isn't it?"

"Yes, it is." He offered her his hand. "Very nice to meet you, Laura. I look forward to seeing you tonight after the concert."

Sitting cross-legged on the floor behind the soundboard, Laura spliced a cable, then soldered a new connector. Will watched her perform the task, smiling at her concentrated expression. "How did it go with the therapist?"

She jumped.

"Sorry, didn't mean to startle you."

"That's okay." With her shoulder, she smoothed some flyaway hairs from her face, then went back to her soldering.

He squatted down beside her. The scent of melted copper wafted toward him.

Laura clamped the new connector with a vice. "It went wonderful. I can't begin to describe how light I felt walking out of Dr. Masters' office."

She seemed relaxed, comfortable, very approachable. Her usual barriers were nowhere around.

Laura set the hot soldering gun aside. "I never realized I'd feel so good after talking." She smiled slightly. "I hate talking. Or at least I thought I did. Thank you so much for pushing me toward seeing him."

"You're welcome. I'm glad it went so well. How are you two going to meet with him here in St. Louis and you on the road full time?"

"Video conferencing. Technology is something else, isn't it?"

"*Hmm.*" Her flyaway hair had come back. Will reached forward and smoothed it behind her ear. She didn't flinch or move away. Encouraged, he stroked her earlobe with his thumb. She allowed the physical contact for a few wonderful seconds, then diverted her gaze to his chest. He withdrew his hand.

"Doctor Masters and his family will be at the show tonight. I told them I'd bring them backstage to meet you all." She glanced up at him, as if suddenly realizing that might be a problem. "Is that okay?"

Will wanted to pull her into his arms and squeeze her. "Of course it's okay."

He couldn't help it. He had to touch her again, feel her warm skin. He stroked some pretend hairs away from her face, then stood. "Well, I'll let you get back to work."

Laura swallowed what Will thought looked like a huge

nervous lump and grabbed the wire she'd been working on.

He loved knowing he made her usual controlled self a teensy bit jumpy.

Cocking her right ear toward stage, Laura listened closely, then reached with her left hand to adjust the mid-range on the equalization rack. Satisfied with the mix, she took a step back and propped her hip on the stool behind her.

The St. Louis crowd had been subdued all night, no broken barriers, or women fainting, or people sneaking into the restricted areas.

Dr. Masters had stopped by before the show to introduce his family. Little Chi Chi's wide-eyed enthusiasm had been contagious. Laura invited the tiny Chinese girl past the barrier into the technical area, where she'd examined and asked questions about all the lit up buttons and knobs.

Laura had never felt at ease around children, and truthfully, she was scared to death she'd slip up and treat them like Aunt Jane had treated her. But Chi Chi had brought out a warm, nurturing sensation in Laura that left her craving more. What kind of mother would she be?

With a quick glance toward stage, Laura zeroed in on Will, and her stomach did a slow roll. He'd dressed for rock-n-roll in a pair of black leather pants, a black T-shirt, and a black leather jacket that hung to his knees. With his dark, spiky hair and tan skin, he looked very, very sexy.

What if she and Will had a child? Not that they would ever reach that point, but what if? What would that child look like? He/she would be tall, definitely. Would the baby have black hair like him or blonde like her? Maybe his black hair and her green eyes.

Laura switched her attention from Will back to the soundboard. She stretched her fingers across the sliding bars, then transitioned them into the last song of the evening.

Funny, she'd never imagined having children or picturing what they would look like until now. Until meeting Will.

* * *

"That was incredible!" Dr. Masters shouted over the crowd's noise.

Laura turned from her work, held up a finger to signal him to wait, then responded to a question that came through her headset. With things taken care of for the moment, she stepped over some cables and unlatched the protective gate that surrounded her area.

She motioned his family inside. "Were your seats good?"

"Oh, much better than expected," June said.

"You ready to go backstage?"

"Yes," Masters and his wife cheered in unison, then turned and laughed at each other.

Laura smiled down at Chi Chi. "I think your parents are star-struck."

Chi Chi giggled and slipped her fingers inside Laura's hand. She looked down at their connection, marveling at how protective that tiny hand made her feel.

The little girl tugged on her arm until Laura leaned down. "Can I meet Will Burns?" Chi Chi whispered into her ear.

Of all the things Laura had expected to hear, that was not it. She gave the child a conspiratorial wink, then led the family down the aisle toward the backstage area.

"Hey, Don," Laura greeted the bodyguard on post.

"Evening, Miss Genny," he replied, his voice so deep it sounded almost inaudible.

"I'd like to take some friends of mine backstage to meet the guys."

"Sure thing. Still need to pat 'em down, though."

He quickly frisked Dr. Masters and his wife, then bent to Chi Chi, who broke into a fit of giggles, making everyone, including the bodyguard, laugh. Laura led the family through the backstage hallways. Fans lined the walls, waiting for admittance into the group's private area. Many of the women had dressed provocatively in some feeble attempt to catch the eye of a rock star.

Laura signaled the officer guarding the restricted zone.

He unlatched the rope gate to admit them into *Tourist's* private area where the dressing rooms and lounge were located.

Will's door sat third on the right. Laura tapped on it, then turned to the Masters' family. "He may still be changing, but we'll try our luck anyway."

"I'm not still changing so your luck is running strong." Will laid his hand on her shoulder and gave it a light squeeze.

The family in front of her wore matching star-struck expressions. She glanced over her shoulder at Will, fresh out of the shower with wet hair. "Will, I'd like to introduce you to Dr. Masters, his wife, June, and their daughter, Chi Chi."

Will kept one hand on Laura's shoulder while he greeted Dr. Masters and his wife, then he squatted down in front of Chi Chi. "Well, well, well, you must be at least five or six."

"Five," she said, flashing him a toothless smile.

"My niece is just a little older than you."

Chi Chi giggled and wrapped her arms around Dr. Masters' knee. He reached down and urged her forward. Hesitantly, she stepped out from behind his protective leg and shook the hand Will had extended to her.

Baffled, Laura watched the exchange between the rock star and tiny Chinese girl, the first time she'd seen Will around children. How gentle and at ease he seemed. And he had a niece?

Will invited everyone into his dressing room for a visit, then took the family around and introduced them to the rest of the band. The fans began to trickle in to the lounge area, and Will suggested they end their evening. Laura agreed. What went on backstage after a show was no place for a child.

Watching them navigate the crowded hallways, making their way to the exit, Will saw Chi Chi reach up and grab Laura's hand. She looked down at the tiny girl, smiled, and said something. Chi Chi giggled, then looked over her shoulder at Will. He sent her a two-finger wave, which made a grin light up her face. Cute little thing. She'd be a knockout some day.

What would it be like to have a child of my own?

Six

Pacing the room was doing Laura no good. Having lost interest in the television, it now provided background noise. Her guitar lay in the corner, placed there with frustration a few minutes after she'd picked it up. The Dallas scene outside her hotel window bored her, people and cars coming and going.

She straightened the clothes on top of the dresser to keep her hands busy and glanced at the clock. Maybe she'd misunderstood the time of Bizzy's arrival.

The phone rang. Laura leapt across the bed to answer it. "Yes?"

"Miss Genny, you have a visitor in the lobby."

"I'll be right down."

Laura hung up, quickly straightened the covers she'd just wrinkled, then shot out the door. She waved to the bodyguards on post and jogged down the stairwell to the first floor. And there, leaning against the counter, stood Bizzy, her childhood friend. As usual she'd struck up a conversation with a complete stranger, and they were laughing and talking as if long lost buddies. Laura had always envied that part of Bizzy, that magnetic, bubbly, outgoing side of her that drew people in.

Laura started toward the counter. Bizzy turned from the stranger and caught sight of her, let out an ear-piercing squeal, and took off across the lobby. Everyone got quiet when the commotion started. Laura hunched her shoulders, mouthed, "Sorry," to the onlookers, and accepted her friend's larger-than-life embrace.

Bizzy gripped Laura's shoulders and held her at arm's length, surveying her face, hair, and clothes. "You look fantastic!"

"You're supposed to say that. You're my best friend."

Bizzy waved her hands in the air as if swatting at annoying gnats. "Yeah, we're best friends, but I still wouldn't have a problem telling you that you look like crap. I'm serious, Laura, you look happy."

She *was* happy. For the first time in her life she felt as if her future had hope. Yes, Aunt Jane was still out there somewhere, but Laura had actually gone days, *days*, without looking over her shoulder, expecting her past to catch up with her.

Shoving her hands into the back pockets of her jeans, Laura nodded toward Bizzy's suitcases. "Let's get your bags and go upstairs."

The two women each grabbed a suitcase and headed toward the elevator. Bizzy talked non-stop about her trip from Mississippi. As usual, she spared no details in her descriptions. She told Laura all about the nice old man she'd met in the airport, the little kid who sat behind her and kicked her seat, the young woman who shared her row on the plane and had bad breath, the taxi driver that reminded her of their high school's custodian, the boy who worked the luncheon counter making extra money to send his sister to college, the toilet in the airport that electronically flushed on its own, and the lipstick Bizzy had forgot to pack. Laura listened to every detail, content to let her friend ramble on and on.

They exited the elevator and rounded the corner of *Tourist's* private floor. Bizzy came to a sudden stop. Laura looked up to see Will standing at the end of the hallway, leaning against her door, watching her.

"Oh, Judas Priest, is that Will Burns?" Bizzy whispered.

Laura nodded.

"Do you know him?"

She started walking again. "Of course I know him. Have you forgotten what my job is?"

"Yes, I know what your job is," Bizzy replied sarcastically. "I didn't expect to see him standing right here in the hallway, though."

Laura stopped and turned to Bizzy. "I don't think I've ever heard you try to speak quietly before. This whispering of yours is amusing me."

Bizzy saucily propped her hand on her hip. "What're you saying, that I'm a loud mouth or something?"

Laura almost smiled. "Not at all."

Bizzy shoved her shoulder. "Okay, Miss little head sound whatever, lead the way." She stepped aside, and with a dramatic swoop of her hand, signaled Laura to continue walking.

Will watched the two women approach him, amused at their sisterly bantering. It was good to see Laura happy and in such a carefree mood. If anyone deserved it, she did.

"Will, this is my friend, Bizzy."

He extended his hand. "Pleased to meet you."

Bizzy laughed and pumped his hand. "Wow, I'm star struck. I can't believe I'm actually meeting Will Burns."

With her playful grin, sunken dimples, and springy black curls, she resembled a baby doll he'd given his sister decades ago. "Well, it's nice to finally meet you. Laura has spoken a lot about you."

Bizzy waved her hands in the air. "Oh, all good I'm sure."

"My friend, the self conscious hermit."

Bizzy giggled and bumped her hip against Laura's. "Oh, grumpy butt, now what fun would it be if I were a hermit? Now," she rubbed her belly and looked around, "where's the nearest restaurant? I'm starving."

Laura shook her head. "She's always starving. I'd swear she has a hollow leg."

Will tucked some hair behind Laura's ear. He'd been doing that a lot over the last few weeks, casual affectionate touches. To his delight, she'd become relaxed and used to them. "Actually, that's why I'm standing beside your room. I came to see if you wanted to get something to eat, but since Bizzy's here, I'll let you two catch up."

"I think it'd be fun if we all went to dinner together." Laura looked at Bizzy. "What do you think?"

Bizzy's confused gaze moved slowly from Laura to Will, then back to Laura.

"Bizzy?" Laura ventured.

"What?"

"Do you want to?"

"Want to what?"

"Do you want to go to dinner with Will?"

"Um, sure. Let me throw my bags in your room."

She followed Laura into their hotel room and dropped her luggage on the extra bed. Will dashed into the bathroom and grabbed some tissue for his runny nose. When he emerged, Bizzy was staring at him.

"The desk clerk recommended a good pizza place two blocks down. Sound good?" He looked at Laura, who nodded, then turned to Bizzy, whose face had transformed into a suspicious narrowing of the eyes.

Will smiled at her what-are-your-intentions-with-my-best-friend look and opened the door. "Ladies, shall we go?"

"Hey, don't forget your disguise." Laura tossed him his hat and glasses.

He put them on, held the door open for Bizzy, then Laura, tugging flirtatiously on her hair as she passed by.

The walk to the pizza parlor went much quieter than expected. Bizzy's usual hyper-self had disappeared. A subdued, courteous, little lady replaced it. Will tried engaging her in conversation numerous times, but after her monotone yes/no answers, he finally gave up. For the first time ever,

Laura carried the conversation. Two of the most important people in her life weren't getting along, and not only was it stressful, but irritating as hell.

They arrived at the restaurant. Laura knew she had to do something or the friction would go on through dinner. "Will, do you mind getting us a table? We'll be right in."

He nodded and headed inside. Laura turned to Bizzy. "What's wrong with you?"

"Nothing."

"Good grief, I know something's wrong with you. You barely spoke a word the whole way here."

Bizzy silently studied Laura's face. "Well, first of all I'm shocked you and Will Burns are so casual together. I've never seen you this comfortable around anybody else but me. He tucked some hair behind your ear, went into your bathroom and blew his nose, invited you to dinner like it was some normal everyday thing. And your peephole doesn't have black tape. You didn't flinch when he touched you or even bat an eye when he entered your hotel room."

"I'm confused. Doesn't that make you happy for me?"

"Of course, I'm happy for you. It's just," Bizzy threw her hands in the air, "unexpected. Are you two dating or something?"

"We're not dating. But I can tell you that I'm very attracted to him."

"Who wouldn't be? The man's gorgeous."

Laura's face grew warm. "We're friends. He's been really nice to me."

"He's a big time rock star. I don't want you to get hurt."

"He's not like that. Wait until you get to know him."

Bizzy pondered Laura's eyes, then glanced over her shoulder at the pizza place behind them. Looping her arm through Laura's, she spun them both around. "Come on. I've got a handsome rock star to get to know."

Will inconspicuously watched them through the window. He couldn't hear them, but did his best at reading their body language. Bizzy struck him as the type to stomp back to the hotel in a rage of temper. But when they turned and walked toward the door, arm-and-arm, smiles on their faces, he released a slow breath.

The women approached his booth. Laura excused herself to the restroom. Bizzy sat down across from him and buried her nose in the menu. He signaled the waitress.

"Can I get y'all something to drink?" the waitress drawled.

Both Will and Bizzy pointed to Laura's spot in the booth. "She'll have a Jack and Coke," they said in unison, then looked at each other with puzzled smiles.

Laura slid into the booth next to Bizzy. "What're you two smiling about?"

"Oh, nothing." Bizzy looked up at the waitress. "I'll have whatever beer you've got on tap."

"Me, too, please." Will turned his menu around and pointed to a selection. "Does this sound good to you two?"

Both women leaned forward to read the items that came on the House Special. Laura's V-neck, cotton shirt gave him an unexpected peep of her bra and breasts. He told himself to look away, but didn't.

Bizzy plopped back in the booth. "That sounds yummy. What do you think?"

"Anything would do at this point. I'm starving. Hey, I saw a jukebox by the bathrooms. Any requests?" Laura stood and fished three quarters from her front pocket.

"We're in Texas. Give me something country western," Bizzy twanged in her best attempt at a hick accent.

"As long as it's not that stupid *Tourist* group, then I'm game," Laura teased.

Will growled and playfully pushed Laura away. When she made it to the jukebox, he turned his attention back to

Bizzy, who was tapping her finger on the table, studying him. He gave her an inquiring cock of the brow.

She took a deep breath. "Laura's like a sister to me. I love her. I've known her my whole life. I don't know how much you know about her, but I'd hate to see her unhappy ever again. Please don't screw around with her. She's not somebody to have a fling with."

Will folded his hands on top the table and looked into Bizzy's sincere face. "I know a little about Laura's childhood. I know it's not been easy for her. I can only imagine what kind of image you have of a rock star. Please understand I would never intentionally hurt her. She's a very special friend."

"Is that all your intentions are? To have a friend?"

Shifting in his seat, he looked across the restaurant to where Laura still stood at the jukebox, then back at Bizzy. "Right now we're friends. If it went somewhere else, I wouldn't be unhappy."

Bizzy peered deep into his eyes as if looking for hidden secrets, then she pointed her finger at him. "You injure her emotionally or physically, and I swear I'll make you regret your whole life."

Will nodded. "Fair enough."

She spread her arms along the length of the booth and fixed him with a sweet, mischievous smile. "Now, tell me about yourself."

Will began telling her about his childhood. He spoke of growing up in Michigan and fighting the horrible winter snowstorms. He told her about his younger sister, Veronica, who lived in Florida and had recently married. He described his Native American grandmother, who died a few years ago, who he still desperately missed. He talked a little about his profession and how he had come to play for *Tourist* eleven years ago. He told her about his love of sports, the enjoyment he got out of running. He described some of his experiences while on tour in Asia, Australia, and Europe. And sometime during the middle of his spiel, Laura came back to join them.

The waitress set the extra large pizza on their table. Bizzy stuck her nose at the rim and inhaled. "That smells delicious." She grabbed the first slice and took an oversized bite. "So what's it like to be famous?" she asked around a full mouth.

Will slid a piece off the silver platter. "It's interesting. I never dreamed I'd play in such a famous group. It just kind of happened. All I knew was that I loved playing the guitar. I figured if I made some money at what I loved then I'd be a happy man. I never imagined I'd be leading the life I am."

He took a bite, then glanced at Laura, who was quietly chewing her pizza, listening to the two of them carry the conversation. "Being so well known has its ups and downs. Privacy, of course, is what I have sacrificed the most. Any time I want to go out, I have to hide under a hat and glasses."

Bizzy licked some sauce from her thumb. "What happens when you don't wear your disguise?"

Wanting to bring Laura into the conversation, Will prompted, "Tell her about that time we went running in Central Park."

Laura took a sip of her Jack and Coke. "When we were in New York, Will and I went running one morning. He thought no one would be out to recognize him at such an early hour. And no one did, until we returned to the streets from the park. It was crazy, really. One person saw him and told another, who told another, and another, and another. Before we knew it a mob of people were running after us. We dodged in and out of streets, trying to make it back to the hotel. We did, luckily, but I think those people would have run us over. Not that they intended us harm, they were just excited to see someone famous."

Bizzy narrowed her eyes at Laura. "Sounds to me like you enjoyed the thrill of the chase."

Laura shrugged a shoulder and smiled a little. "It was adventurous."

Will chuckled. "So, what about you, Bizzy? What kind of life have you had?"

Bizzy wiped her mouth and leaned back. She patted her stomach, looking very much like a satisfied feline. "Oh, it's awfully hum-drum, but I'll bore you anyway. Laura and I grew up in Tupelo, Mississippi. We met in kindergarten." Bizzy looked over at Laura. "Ya know, I still remember the first day we met. Do you?"

Hoping to learn more about Laura's childhood, Will quickly encouraged, "Tell me about it."

Bizzy smiled. "Well, I'd been in kindergarten for half the year, miserable because I hadn't made any friends. I remember one morning Mrs. Knoble, our teacher, made an announcement that a new girl had moved to Tupelo and would be joining our class. Well I'm thinking, thank God! Because I had yet to make friends, and let's face it, I'm the kind of person that thrives on being social."

She waved her hand in the air. "Anyway, so I'm sitting there like a little angel coloring or something, and our classroom door opens. All I remember thinking when I saw Laura is that she looked prissy and rich. Her aunt had dressed her in some hideous pink and white lacy thing, and her hair had these long ringlets. Ya know, like Nellie Oleson on *Little House on the Prairie*."

Will smiled at the picture of Laura in a prissy little dress with long ringlets. Certainly not the image she maintained now. He glanced over at her, but she wasn't smiling or laughing at the memory. She'd gone very still.

"The day wore on," Bizzy continued, "and I kept my distance, scoping her out and trying to figure out her story. By the end of the afternoon, I'd pretty much written her off as a snob because she stayed to herself and didn't say a word to anyone."

Will's heart ached at the sad little picture Bizzy painted of Laura's first kindergarten day.

"Then she walked right up to me and said, 'My name's Laura Franks. Will you be my best friend?'"

"What did you say?" Will asked.

Bizzy reached over and grabbed Laura's hand. "I took her hand and told her to come meet my old best friend, Frog, which was a stuffed animal in my backpack. I told her I'd rather have a real best friend anyway." Bizzy waved her hand in the air. "And the rest, they say, is history."

"That's a sweet story, ladies." Will grabbed his beer and lifted it to his lips. He paused, lowered it back to the table. "Wait a minute. Did you say Franks?" He looked across the table at Laura. "I thought your last name was Genny."

Bizzy's smile faded. "Shoot."

Seven

"Here's your ticket. Y'all can pay here when ya ready." The waitress slid the bill to the middle of the table and meandered off toward other customers.

Will and Laura reached for it at the same time.

"I've got it," Will said.

"No, please. Let me."

Grabbing the bill, he removed his wallet from his back pocket. "I said it's on me."

"Don't be ridiculous. Tell me what our part is. I'm treating Bizzy."

Will glared at Laura. "I said it's on me."

He counted out the money, set it on the end of the table, then folded his arms across his chest and studied Laura's bent head. She'd focused her attention on her lap, looking very much like a child who'd gotten into trouble. He was the reason why.

Will shifted his gaze to Bizzy, who shot daggers back at him. Frustrated, he grumbled, "Lift your head and look at me. I'm not your Aunt Jane, and you're not in trouble."

Bizzy straightened. "Hey, why don't you ease up?"

Will rolled his eyes to Bizzy. "Listen, why don't you–"

Laura stood, reached into her front pocket, and pulled out her hotel card key. "Bizzy, I'll meet you in our room. I want to talk to Will."

Bizzy stared at the outstretched key a moment, as if contemplating whether or not she should do what Laura asked, then slid across the booth and took it. She shot Will a warning look and walked from the restaurant.

The Aunt Jane comment had been uncalled for. He was a

jerk for making it. And the way Laura had backed away and Bizzy came to her defense made him feel like a dominating creep. Enough, though. Laura's secretive past and emotional barriers had him knocking his head against a wall. To have just found out that she'd changed her name and had been hiding it from him...*enough.*

"Let's go for a walk." Laura led the way across the pizza parlor to the exit door.

Bizzy had been coming to her rescue her whole life. When they were little, it'd been Bizzy who hid Laura from Aunt Jane during her tirades. In high school, Bizzy told the kids to back off when they made fun of Laura's shy, quiet ways, calling her ice queen, mute girl, or stone maiden. Bizzy had been Laura's backbone for as long as she could remember. Way past time she started taking control of her own life.

Laura and Will walked in silence for a few moments while she gathered her thoughts. She glanced up at the star-filled, October, Dallas sky. It would have been romantic under other circumstances.

Reaching inside her front pocket, she clasped onto the rabbit's foot. "I changed my name from Franks to Genny because I ran away from home at seventeen. I didn't want my aunt to find me, and so far, I've been lucky. You and Bizzy are the only two that know, so I'd appreciate your confidence in the matter."

"Would you have told me if Bizzy hadn't slipped at dinner?"

"I would've told you in time."

He stopped walking and turned to face her. "I'm sorry I was an asshole back there. Your secrets frustrate me. I know you're dealing with a lot. I'm trying to be patient, but by nature I'm eager."

Laura took a deep, calming breath. "Thank you."

"For what?"

"For being my friend. For having incredible patience with me."

Will's eyes traveled leisurely over her face. One corner of his mouth lifted into a half smile. "You're very beautiful."

The unexpected comment sent her stomach dancing. Laura reached up to pull her hat further down, then remembered she wore no hat. She crossed her arms and looked down at the sidewalk beneath her feet. "Are-are you ready to head back?"

"No." Will lifted her chin with his finger. "I gave you a compliment. You're supposed to say thank you."

Laura switched her gaze to his shoulder. "Thank you," she mumbled.

He dropped his finger from her chin. "Why did you do that?"

She took a step back. "Do what?"

"I gave you a compliment, and you got nervous and clammed up on me. I thought you'd smile or something."

Laura rubbed the pads of her fingers up the center of her forehead. "I'm sorry. I'm not good with compliments."

Will took a step forward. "Why?"

She shrugged, but she knew why. Dr. Masters had discussed it with her during their last session.

"Why, Laura?"

"There's a lot you don't know about me." A lot she was too ashamed to share. She started walking back toward the hotel, her pace quick, hoping Will would drop the subject.

"Laura," he called, but she kept walking. "Laura," he tried again, jogging up behind her. He grabbed her arm. "Would you stop? Talk to me, please."

Laura looked down at his grip, then back up at his frustrated face. "Please remove your hand from my arm." Her voice came out more acidic than she meant it to.

Quickly, as if he'd touched a hot iron, Will dropped her

arm and took a step back. "Sorry. Did I hurt you?"

"No. Takes a lot more than that to hurt me."

His eyes flicked, and in that moment Laura saw pain. A pain that he felt for her, and she knew without a doubt that she wanted to take a risk, tell him more, and deepen their bond.

"My aunt," she began, then stopped.

Will gave her a small, encouraging smile.

She started walking and began again, "My aunt had some sort of sick infatuation with me. One minute she'd compliment me on my pretty hair or per-perfect breasts, and the next minute she'd insult my skinny body or splotchy freckles. She used to spend thirty minutes every day combing my hair to perfection and putting the right amount of ribbons or braids or curls in it."

"When I bathed," Laura cleared her throat, "she'd watch me shave to make sure I got every unsightly hair. Biblical reasons stood behind it all. Something about ungodly vanity and my body being a temple."

"Did she sexually abuse you?"

"No. She was a voyeur. Doctor Masters says that's the reason I'm overly protective of my body. He says I wear hats because I'm hiding under them."

She stopped walking and fastened her attention to the toes of her shoes. "I've been trying a few things he suggested, like not wearing my ball caps and dressing with the curtains open. He says it will help me realize my aunt isn't in my life anymore, and I don't have to hide my body from her or anybody else."

Will leaned back against a street lamppost. In her peripheral, Laura saw him studying her. What was he thinking? Did he feel disgust, pity, anger? She shuffled her feet, uncomfortable with his scrutiny.

"Laura, I really hate your aunt." He reached out, took her hand, and pulled her a little closer. "I know there's a lot of stuff about your childhood you haven't told me. When you're ready, I want you to share more. Your past is nothing to be ashamed of, especially around me. You have unconditional friendship with me, okay?"

She chanced a quick look into his eyes and saw warmth there.

"Your aunt had some weird fascination with you, and the stuff she did to you wasn't your fault. She's a sick woman, mentally." He squeezed her hand. "Now, I'm going to make a deal with you. Every time I give you a compliment, you accept it for what it is and say thank you. Don't think there's some underlying meaning, and don't get tense. Let's start right now." He gave her hand a playful tug. "Laura, you're a very beautiful woman."

She smiled at his silly game.

He loudly cleared his throat in an obvious show of waiting for her to respond.

"Thank you." Thank God he'd lightened the mood.

He grinned with satisfaction. "Good start. But we'll try again later until you get it right."

A movement beyond his shoulder grabbed her attention. She glanced past him. A tall, skinny woman with shoulder length, straight hair stepped back into the shadows. Laura froze. *Aunt Jane?*

"Laura, what is it?"

She stared hard at the buildings lining the sidewalk, studying the dark storefronts, searching for any movement.

Will stepped to the side and followed her gaze. "What is it? What do you see?"

"A-a woman. Over there. Aunt Jane."

"What? Where?"

Couldn't be. No way Aunt Jane knew where she was. Impossible. Then the skinny woman shifted out of the shadows, and Laura saw her digging through her purse.

"Is that her?" Will asked, already heading toward her.

"No!" Laura shouted it so loud, the skinny woman looked up from down the street.

Will turned back, and Laura shook her head. "It's not her. I'm sorry." She covered her face with her hands. "I'm sorry. I do that sometimes. I think I see her, but I really don't. I'm so sorry."

He wrapped his arms around her. "Stop apologizing."

"It makes me feel like an idiot."

"It's because we were talking about her. That's all. It's not her." He pressed a kiss to her temple.

Laura concentrated on inhaling, then exhaling, inhaling, then exhaling, slowly, calming her rapid-fire heart.

It's okay. Aunt Jane can't hurt me anymore. Aunt Jane isn't in my life anymore. Aunt Jane doesn't even know if I'm alive.

She repeated those sentences over and over in her head. As she felt the muscles in her body relax, other things began to enter her senses. Will's warmth. His arms around her. His clean, soapy scent. The fact that he'd been rocking her, slightly, the entire time. The only other person that had ever hugged her was Bizzy. But Bizzy's hugs weren't anything like this...all encompassing, soothing, protective.

And Bizzy never smelled this good.

Will pressed another kiss to her temple and stepped back. "Better now?"

Nodding, Laura took her hands from her face.

"Do you play?"

"What?"

He pointed down the street to a neon sign. "There's a pool hall. Do you play?"

"Yeah, I can play."

"How about a friendly competition?"

"Alright."

"What are we wagering?"

She hadn't thought about actually wagering something. It'd always been money that she bet in college. Somehow money didn't seem appropriate with Will. Then it dawned on her, "I know. If I win, you have to switch rooms with me at the next hotel. I want to stay in one of those fancy suites you guys are always treated to."

He gave an affirmative nod. "Fair enough. And if I win, you have to give me a kiss."

A kiss? He wants a kiss? Laura worked her throat, trying to swallow, but couldn't produce any saliva. Okay. She wanted a kiss, too. Bad. But the last time she'd kissed anybody was that guy back in college. That had been a fumbled attempt at best. What if she'd forgotten how?

"O-okay." She headed in the direction of the pool hall, very aware of her stiff leg muscles.

Will followed her, wanting to laugh at her stunned reaction. A kiss. He'd actually made a wager for a kiss. He had it bad for this woman.

Smoky, dimly lit, and smelling like beer, the pool hall epitomized a typical bar. A barbeque pit occupied one corner. Small tables sat scattered about. A horseshoe shaped bar took up the middle. Three pinball machines stood against the back wall. Four pool tables formed a line, each spaced a few feet apart.

The male dominated clientele looked like they'd gotten off shift work from some nearby plant. Two of the four pool tables were occupied. Will led Laura to the furthest one. He slid some quarters into the table's slots. "What do you want from the bar?"

Laura started racking the balls. "Corona with a lime."

She placed every striped and solid in a specific spot, then spun the eight ball for a tighter break. He lifted his brows at her technique and was even more surprised when she began to study the cue sticks. Slowly, she rolled them across the table, probably looking for a bowed shape or any other oddity.

She glanced up. "Corona with a lime."

He nodded and headed toward the bar. While waiting on their beers, he leaned against a stool and watched her. She chose two sticks and chalked the tips. Satisfied with that, she strolled around the table studying the green felt. She squatted down to eye level and scrutinized it from that angle.

Will rejoined Laura with the beers. She took a bottle, squeezed a lime into it, toasted his, and then took a swig. "So, do you want to play eight ball, nine ball, snooker?"

He cocked a brow. "I have a feeling you know more about this game then I think you do."

Laura shrugged a shoulder. "I've played a few times. So, what'll be?"

"I only know how to play eight ball."

"Good choice. That's a good betting game. And I've got a hotel suite to beat you out of."

"Okay, fancy pants, don't go thinking you've already won. I've got a kiss on the line, in case you've forgotten."

Her face turned that sweet, blushed color. She reached into her khaki pant's pocket and pulled out a quarter. "Call it." She flipped it into the air.

"Heads."

Laura snatched it on its descent and turned it over onto her forearm. They peered at it. Tails. She slanted him a sly look, and Will grunted his disappointment.

Shoving the quarter back into her pocket, she spun on her heel and pulled the rack from the balls. Positioning the cue ball a little behind the line and to the right, she leaned over, slid the stick back and forth a few times between her thumb and forefinger, then executed a clean break. The loud cracking noise attracted the attention of the other pool players. They all turned to watch.

A solid red sailed to the rear corner pocket. Laura circled the table, grabbed her hair and pulled the length of it over her shoulder, then lined up for the next shot. How was he supposed to win with all that hair in his way?

The solid yellow went in the side pocket. A light round of applause followed. Amused, Will turned to the group of onlookers, some sitting on stools, others leaning on their own pool sticks, some standing around, all engrossed in Laura. He turned back around in time to see a solid blue shoot across the table into a corner pocket. When the green one missed, a depressed sigh came from the crowd.

Jumping from his stool, Will headed toward the cue ball. "Looks like you've got some fans."

She made no response, just continued studying the table with her poker face. He succeeded in sinking the purple striped ball, but missed on his next try.

Laura stepped back into place and leaned over for her next shot. Will stood behind her, a perfect location to stare at her round little fanny. But when her cue stick came back for the shot, he yelped and jumped out of the way, narrowly missing a jab to his groin, and quickly found his stool.

The solid green ricocheted off the side and zipped into the opposite corner. Like the crowd, Will reacted with awe at her technique and showmanship.

Straightening from her crouched position, Laura went to take a swallow of her beer. Her focus never left the table. She set her bottle down, circled, squatted to study the solid purple. She stood, placed the cue stick behind her, and rested her backside on the edge of the table. Slowly, she slid the stick back and forth across her fingers, and then the cue ball slammed into the purple, sent it from one end of the table to the other, back again, and spiraling down a front corner pocket.

The crowd shot to their feet with cheers as Laura rounded the table for the winning shot, the eight ball. Will thought it looked easy enough. She pointed to the side pocket to signify where the eight would go, then hunched over, lined it up, and gave it a soft tap. The eight rolled a few inches and plopped into its appointed hole.

More applause followed, and as people dispersed back to their original spots, Laura placed her cue stick into its wall-mounted holder and walked over to stand in front of Will.

"Guess you're out of a suite in the next city."

He hooked his thumbs through her belt loops and pulled her into the space between his legs. "Well, Miss Genny, looks like you're a woman of many talents. Where did you learn to play pool like that?"

"I put myself through college with government grants, a couple of jobs, and gambling on the weekends at local pool halls."

Will twisted her hips. "Ah ha, you little sneak. You could have let me in on that secret prior to our bet."

Laura's eyes lit with mischievousness. "And give up a deluxe suite? I don't think so."

"I guess I'll have to wait for that kiss then."

"Guess so."

He laughed and squeezed her hips, then jumped off the stool. "Ready to go?"

She nodded and followed him out the door and down the street.

"Your hair looks nice tonight. I like it down." Will glanced at her through the corners of his eyes. "That was a compliment. What are you supposed to say?"

"Oh," she let out a nervous chuckle. "Sorry. Thank you."

He laughed and bumped his shoulder against hers. "What a pitiful thank you. I can tell this compliment business is going to take some practice."

Laura smiled. "Will?" she said a few seconds later.

"*Hmmm*?"

"I came real close to botching that game."

"Why is that?"

"Because I-I wanted to lose the bet."

Will stopped walking. "Laura, are you flirting with me?"

She covered her face with her hands and nodded. He grinned, pried her hands from her face, and kissed her on the cheek, delighted with her playful flirtation. Linking fingers with her, he led her back to the hotel, arms swinging, chatting about the latest movies.

They'd made significant strides in their relationship tonight. Hopefully, nothing would happen to stop the progress.

It was after midnight when Will and Laura returned to the hotel from the pool hall. They agreed to meet in the morning for a run prior to reporting to the Dallas Convention Center for concert preparations.

As they passed the other musician's rooms, sounds of clinking glasses, music, voices, and giggling filtered through the walls. Laura eyed one of the doors. Would Will rather be partying with them than hanging out with her? The women who attended those parties seemed a lot less complicated than she was.

"Looks like we're here." Will stopped at her door.

"I had a good time," Laura whispered so the bodyguards on post wouldn't overhear.

"Me, too," he whispered back.

They stood, staring at each other. She looked into his dark eyes, becoming more lost as the seconds passed. He focused on her lips and took a step closer, reached up and cupped her cheek. One of the bodyguards loudly cleared his throat.

They both blinked and glanced down the hall. Some of the partygoers stumbled from a room.

Will looked back at Laura, obviously disappointed but trying to smile anyway. "I'll see ya in the morning."

She nodded slightly and watched him walk away, half expecting him to go join the party. But he unlocked his door and disappeared inside. Turning, Laura knocked softly on hers. She'd given Bizzy her only key.

"Well, I thought you'd vanished off the face of the earth," Bizzy said, swinging open the door.

"I'm sorry. Will and I had some things to talk about."

Laura headed into the bathroom, and after brushing her teeth wandered over to her duffle bag and pulled out a blue T-shirt and red plaid boxers. She took a deep breath and with her back to Bizzy, quickly changed clothes. When Laura was done, she put her discarded items in her laundry bag, then chanced a glance at her friend, who stood rooted by the television, staring at her.

Hesitantly, Laura ventured, "What are you looking at?"

"I-I can't believe you did that."

"Why? Was there something wrong with it?"

"No," Bizzy quickly responded. "God knows I've gotten naked plenty of times in front of you. You took me off guard, that's all. You usually lock yourself in the bathroom to change."

Laura fingered the cord on the laundry bag, trying to decide how to ask what she really wanted to know. "Bizzy…wh-what did you think of my body? Ya know, just now when you saw it?"

Bizzy just stared at her.

"It's okay," Laura quickly went on. "I didn't mean to make you uncomf–"

"Hey," Bizzy interrupted quietly. "It's fine. I don't mind the question. In the many years we've known each other, I've never heard you fuss about your hair, or face, or body, or clothes. You've never asked those typical questions like, 'Does this make me look fat?' or 'What shoes should I wear with this outfit?' I've always thought you have the perfect body. You're tall and slender, and you have those fantastic long legs."

"Really?"

"Really." Bizzy crossed the hotel room and settled on the bed beside her. "Tell me what's going on. I like the changes you're making, but what brought them on?"

"I've been seeing a counselor."

"I knew there was something different about you. You seem more relaxed, not so guarded. I'm proud of you for seeing a professional. I wondered when you'd finally take a step like that." Bizzy hugged her. "You're an incredible woman, Laura, and I'm glad you're a part of my life."

"Thanks."

Bizzy flopped back on the bed. "Tell me all there is to know about that dark, handsome rock star we spent the evening with, and then I'll fill you in on my love life."

Laura smiled and lay down beside Bizzy. She began sharing everything she could remember. The talks they'd had, the traveling they experienced, the funny stories he'd told. She showed Bizzy the trinkets he'd given her, and when Laura finished, an hour had gone by and the clock read one-thirty in the morning.

They called it a night, but Laura slept restlessly, her dreams filled with Aunt Jane. In the morning she dialed Will's number, canceled their running date, then went straight to the Dallas Convention Center.

By mid-morning she was immersed in her work.

Eight

Standing, foot propped against the wall, Jay studied Laura as he flip-flopped ideas for tonight's Dallas show. He'd let the last one go by without a mishap, figured it looked more realistic if a "Laura mistake" happened every couple of productions, not every single one. Trying to figure out what to tamper with was becoming way too fun.

Shoving his long bangs out of his eyes, Jay pushed off the wall and headed toward her. "Hey, Laura, I'm looking for the midi rack. Have you seen it?" He wasn't looking for anything, other than an excuse to get close to her and the mixing board.

Distracted with her work, she didn't even look up at him. "Last time I looked it'd been unloaded off a semi and was sitting backstage."

"Oh, okay." Nonchalantly, he leaned over the back of the mixer and unplugged one quarter-inch cable. The one, in fact, that controlled the speakers to the right side of the house.

Laura glanced up just as his hand retreated. "Did you need something else?"

Jay shook his head and shuffled away, heart pounding, wondering when she'd discover the mishap. Hopefully, not until tonight's show had started.

Curled up in a tight little sleeping ball, Bizzy lay sideways in one of the Convention Center's hardback chairs. Her hand balanced a Styrofoam coffee cup on the armrest. Will approached her and gingerly took the cup from her fingers. She tightened her grip around the coffee and opened her eyes.

"Sorry, thought you were sleeping."

Bizzy yawned and sat up in the chair. "No, just resting."

Will took the seat beside her. "Long night at the slumber party?"

"Hardly. Laura kept us up with her nightmares."

He ran his fingers through his hair. "Jeez, I hate hearing that."

"I'd stay clear of her for a little while," Bizzy cautioned. "She's in a pisser of a mood."

"Where is she?"

"Last time I saw her she was down there," she waved her hand, "under some equipment, doing some tomboy techy-thing."

"Funny. Never thought of her as a tomboy."

"Compared to what she used to be she's a complete tomboy."

"And how was that? Ya know, what she used to be?"

She took a sip of her coffee, studying him over the rim. "Normally, I'd skirt around a question like that, but," she gave him an approving look, "I've decided I like you and what you're doing for Laura."

Will rolled his eyes. "Thanks, I'm glad I have your blessings."

"No problem." She smiled cheekily, then slowly grew serious. "Growing up, Laura's aunt always had her dressed in some pink, yellow, lace, ruffly concoction with curls or braids or ribbons in her hair. Laura was forbidden to do anything considered "boyish," like sports or eating with her hands, and she attended a charm school once a week."

"Charm school?"

"Yeah, ya know where they teach stuff like dancing and eating fancy. Anyway, all the kids at school hated her because they thought she was a priss. They mistook her shyness for snobbishness and made fun of her clothes. I hated them for her. I knew what was really going on."

Bizzy took another sip of coffee. "I'll never forget the first time she put on a pair of jeans." She smiled faintly and fixed her gaze to a spot in the distance. "It was the night I helped her run away from home. Her aunt had locked her in her bedroom for some reason. Laura and I had already planned to meet at two in the morning. Being locked in her room didn't slow her down. She popped the screen out of her window and jumped two stories to the ground. I'd left my bike in the woods at the end of her driveway, and she showed up at our meeting point weather beaten from the rain and scraped up legs from her jump to freedom."

"I'd gone shopping for clothes," Bizzy continued, "but neither one of us knew her size because she'd never worn pants. So I tried my luck and bought size six long jeans. Luckily, when she slipped them on they fit. She balled up her dress and threw it into the surrounding woods. I gave her the keys to my car, she gave the bike to me, we hugged, and drove off in opposite directions."

Bizzy turned to Will. "Two weeks later she sent my keys back to me in the mail with a note, telling me where she'd left the car and that she'd contact me once she got settled."

Will tried to swallow a lump that had built in his throat. Unsuccessful, he reached for Bizzy's coffee. "Mind?"

She shook her head and handed it to him. After downing the last of the hazelnut-flavored brew, he leaned forward, rested his elbows on his knees, and studied the cement below his tennis shoes. How had Laura done it? How had she survived such a childhood? How had she turned out so sweet? How come she wasn't a raving lunatic? God knew she had every right.

Bizzy rubbed a soothing hand across his back. "I know it's hard to believe what she came from, and I know it makes you mad. Believe me, I spent my whole childhood pissed off at Aunt Jane and the raw deal that Laura had been given in life. But she's an incredible woman, definitely one that's worth the time and patience that it takes."

Will glanced over his shoulder at Bizzy.

She smiled back at him. "I'm happy you're in her life."

He handed the empty coffee cup back, then gave her a peck on the cheek. "Thanks. I'm glad she had you to help her through the bad parts." He stood and looked toward the stage. "I think I'll go fiddle with some lyrics I've been working on." Will took a few steps and then turned back. "By the way, what's Bizzy short for?"

"You don't want to know." She scrunched up her face. "Believe me, my nickname's better."

"Come on. Tell me. I promise to keep it a secret."

Bizzy gave him an irritable, indulgent look. "Beatrice Elizabeth."

He barked a laugh. "You're right, Bizzy's better."

"Oh," she growled and threw her empty cup at him.

Will dodged the cup, chuckling, and jogged toward the stage.

Laura checked and double-checked the equipment, assuring no one had tampered with it. In thirty minutes the band would report on stage to practice for the evening's show. Her mood had lifted since her rough night and early start. Will had stayed out of her way and let her do her work, which put her at ease. She hated being around him when she felt cranky.

The lighting technician stood beside her, going through some last minute staging changes with *Tourist's* manager.

Laura thumbed through her collection of CDs, picked *Spyro Gyra*, and slid it into the player. When the music filtered through the house speakers, the manager glanced up at her with an approving smile, then he paused and straightened from his hunched position. At the same time, Laura jumped off her stool and glanced at the mixing board.

No sound!

No sound from the right side of the house. This couldn't be happening, not again. Quickly and efficiently, she scanned the knobs and sliding bars, confirming they were set appropriately. Then she rounded the mixer and studied the back, tested each connection. At the end of the quarter-inch plugs teetered the loosened cable that controlled the right side of the house.

Laura pulled the cable out and studied it, then peeked into the female end on the back of the board. Nothing looked irregular. She tested the tip for sturdiness, pushed it back into place, and immediately, The Dallas Convention Center filled with music.

Spinning around, she scanned the stage, uneasy, feeling as if someone might be peering out from a shadow, watching her discover the mishap.

"Something wrong, Laura?"

Laura turned to look at *Tourist's* manager. "No sir. Everything's taken care of now."

She busied herself checking all the other connections, conscious of the fact the manager watched her every move. He knew all about the sound mistakes that had happened since Laura had taken the job. He probably thought she was negligent. She hoped his intuition told him otherwise, because something was going on, and she'd end up taking the fall.

"I'm going to miss you," Laura murmured, hugging her friend close. Bizzy sniffed and squeezed back.

"Alright, alright, alright." Bizzy waved her hands in the air. "I'm getting all weepy." She turned to Will and extended her hand. "It was so nice to meet you." Will brushed her hand away and pulled her into a bear hug. She squeaked and hugged him back, then turned to Laura. "Now I don't want you to worry. No one knows that I came to see you, well except for Mom, but you know things are safe with her."

Laura nodded. "Tell your mom I said hello."

"I will."

The two friends stood staring and smiling at each other, and a moment later Laura asked a question she'd been curious about since Bizzy's arrival. "Is Aunt Jane still holding prayer vigils for my safe return?"

Bizzy sighed. "Yes. Whenever she's there."

"What do you mean?"

"She's been gone a lot."

Laura stilled. *Gone a lot?* "Where?"

"Not sure. Probably with her job. She's still working at the insurance place." The airport announced the departure of flight one-four-nine-zero. "That's my flight." Bizzy hugged her again. "I love you, Laura." She looked up at Will, pointed to her best friend. "You watch out for her, okay?"

"Count on it."

Laura and Will stood in the terminal waving Bizzy off. When she disappeared down the corridor, they turned and started in the opposite direction.

Gone a lot. Aunt Jane rarely traveled. She didn't like it. How many times had Laura experienced that sick feeling in her stomach, that ill taste that her aunt was near? How many times had Laura imagined her standing there, watching her?

Paranoia. Pure and simple. But even as Laura told herself that, she scanned the airport.

Will reached under her hair and lightly squeezed the back of her neck. "You okay?"

She nodded, enjoying the warmth of his fingers. "Ya know, your disguise reminds me of Clark Kent."

"If we were near a phone booth, I'd whip in, spin around, and emerge in blue tights. You'd be my Lois Lane, and we'd fly off together through the night."

"Ah, and if I had kryptonite you would be my slave forever."

He growled and pulled her close to his side. "The images you invoke are going to require a cold shower."

Laura almost missed the step onto the escalator. Will followed her, scooting in close to give the people behind him more room. He slid his arm around her stomach to hold her snugly in place. She closed her eyes and told herself to breathe.

He ran his thumb along her ribs. "Relax," he whispered against her ear.

She glanced up at him with a reassuring smile.

"Don't you two make the cutest couple?"

Will looked over his shoulder. A pink-faced, jolly woman stood behind him. "Thank you."

"How long have you two been married?"

He smiled at her inquisitive, chubby face and turned sideways to better talk with the older lady. "Few months."

"A few months?" the woman sang, joyfully clapping her hands, making a perfumey scent waft around them. "How lovely for you both. Newlyweds, oh, how lovely. So tell me, dear, are you on your honeymoon?"

"No ma'am. We're visiting Dallas."

"Well, Dallas is my home town. You'll absolutely love it here."

"We already do. Don't we, sweetie?" Will prodded Laura's side, signaling her to play along. She smiled and nodded in agreement.

"Oh my, watch out dear. The escal–"

"I got her." Will gripped Laura around the waist and walked off the escalator. He lowered her the few inches to her feet.

She straightened her shirt. "Why did you do that?"

"You mean the marriage thing?" He grinned. "Because it was fun."

A smile tugged at the corner of her mouth. "It was

mischievous."

Will looped his arm around her neck and pulled her toward the exit door. "Yep, it was that, too. So tell me, how did you like being married to Will Burns, international rock star?"

She shook her head as if he was a helpless cause. "Why don't you check that ego of yours at the door."

He chuckled.

A camera flashed. Laura inhaled sharply and spun around, looking for the photographer. It flashed again.

Will grabbed her hand and pulled her out the exit door. "It's okay. It was a man taking a picture of his wife." Though he suspected something else.

He'd seen the camera, up on the balcony, and it had been a man taking a picture of a woman. Only the camera hadn't been focused on the woman. It had zoomed in on Will and Laura, one story below.

Nine

"Where were you today?"

Laura looked up from her high school English homework. Aunt Jane stood in her bedroom doorway, feet braced apart, scowling.

"At school," Laura answered. What had she done wrong now?

"Liar," Jane spat and stomped over to Laura's desk. "I'm going to ask you again. Where. Were. You. To-day?" She enunciated each word as if Laura had just learned to speak English.

Quickly, Laura ran through the events of her day, desperate to figure out what she'd done to make her aunt so upset. Then she remembered. "Are you talking about fifth period?"

With a satisfied, smug sneer, Jane crossed her arms over her chest and stared down her nose at her niece. "You didn't think I'd find out, did you?"

"I didn't do anything wrong," Laura quickly responded. "I swear. Our gym teacher was absent so we were given off campus passes for fifth period."

"I know, and that's not the point. You're not supposed to leave the campus." Jane poked her in the forehead. "Period. Where did you go and what did you do?"

Laura searched her aunt's face imploringly, hoping to placate her. She knew all to well what it was like when Jane's temper blew. "Bizzy and I went across the street to the Dairy Shack for ice cream. That's it. I promise."

"Were there any boys with you?"

Laura forced a nervous lump down her throat. "Bizzy's

cousin, Sam."

Jane pursed her lips and scrutinized her niece. "Come with me," she commanded softly, then walked from the bedroom.

The quiet directive put Laura on edge. "Where are we going?"

"Come with me," Aunt Jane repeated in that same eerie, soft tone.

Laura followed her aunt out the bedroom, down the stairs, across the porch, and into the passenger side of the car. She buckled her seat belt and gripped the edge of the leather seat. Where were they going? To the Dairy Shack so Jane could verify her story? To the high school so her aunt could tell them never to issue her another off campus pass? Maybe to Bizzy's so Jane could tell her that Laura didn't have permission to leave school again. Going to Bizzy's wouldn't be that bad. She'd understand.

When they pulled into the emergency room of the county hospital, Laura glanced over at her aunt. "Why are we here?"

"Come with me." Again, that redundant, matter-of-fact voice. Laura almost preferred Jane's turbulent temper to the quiet commanding statements.

Laura followed her aunt inside the hospital.

"Have a seat over there." Aunt Jane pointed her niece toward the waiting area and walked to the receptionist's desk. She exchanged some hushed words with a nurse behind the counter, then meandered over to the magazine rack and chose something to look through. Laura watched her every move. What was going on? Had Aunt Jane hurt herself?

Exactly thirty-one minutes and fifteen seconds went by. Laura knew because she'd watched the clock tick off the time.

A man dressed in scrubs pushed through the admitting doors and walked toward them. "You requested to see a doctor. May I help you?"

Jane stood and motioned him to a corner of the waiting room, obviously for some privacy. Laura wedged her hands under her thighs and watched her aunt talk to the doctor in a hushed tone. She looked worried and kept glancing in Laura's direction as she explained something to the doctor. Aunt Jane even dug a hanky from her purse and dabbed at her eyes with delicate little sniffs. Laura couldn't recall a time she'd ever seen her aunt cry.

The doctor didn't seem particularly sympathetic to Jane's plight and in fact looked bored. He said a few things to her. Aunt Jane responded with the same pleading body language. He said a few more things to her, and then Jane started getting prickly. Laura recognized the telltale signs of her aunt losing her patience: the clamped jaw, speaking by moving only her lips, beady eyes narrowed.

The young doctor closed his eyes and seemed to be counting to ten. Laura grimaced. She knew all to well what he was going through. He opened his eyes and glanced across the waiting room at her. Then he turned back to Aunt Jane and shook his head no.

Her chest puffed up like she was about to bellow obscenities. Instead, she balled up her hanky, crammed it in her purse, and charged back across the waiting room. Automatically, Laura scooted back in her chair as she watched her aunt storm toward her. Jane grabbed her by the arm, jerked her to her feet, and continued right on out the exit door, dragging her niece behind her

Laura glanced over her shoulder at the doctor and sent him an apologetic smile. He had a concentrated frown on his face as he watched them leave.

The exit door closed behind them, leaving them in the ambulance zone. Aunt Jane mumbled something about going to every hospital in the surrounding counties until someone did what she wanted.

The exit door opened again, and the doctor shot through it. "Wait," he called out, jogging toward them.

Jane pondered him with a haughty lift of the chin. "What do you want, Doctor?"

He looked at Laura, then back at Jane. "Come on back inside. I can help you out."

Aunt Jane gave him an imperious nod and followed him back inside the emergency room. Laura started toward the waiting area, expecting her aunt to go with him through the admitting doors, but Aunt Jane grabbed her arm and pulled her along.

When they got to the admitting doors, the doctor stopped and held up his hand to Jane. "She comes the rest of the way alone."

More confused now than before, Laura stared at the young doctor. Why was she going with him? She wasn't sick or hurt.

"Very well. I'm sure there's some paperwork I need to fill out." Aunt Jane reached up. Laura instinctively flinched. Her aunt let out an annoyed sigh, then awkwardly patted her niece's head. "Go on with the doctor. Everything will be alright."

The doctor led Laura through the admittance doors, passed a few examining tables, pulled back a curtain, and motioned her to sit. Laura stiffly climbed up on top the table while the doctor rolled a chair over for himself.

Extending his hand, he gave her a sunny smile. "Hi, Laura. I'm Doctor Brock."

Laura shook his hand, knowing full well hers was cold and clammy from nerves. He must have noticed because he rubbed her hand between both of his dryer, warmer ones.

"Don't be nervous. I'm going to take good care of you." He released her hand. "Do you know why you're here?"

She tried to use her voice, but ended up shaking her head instead.

"Your aunt wants us to make sure you're not pregnant."

"What?" Laura croaked. "Why? I didn't do anything wrong. I went for an ice cream with Bizzy, that's all. I promise."

The doctor nodded his head. "I know, sweetie. But she still wants us to do a pelvic exam on you."

A pelvic exam? God, how humiliating. "Can't you do a urine test for pregnancy?" she mumbled.

"Yes, we can. But she also wants assurance that you're still a virgin."

Squeezing her eyes shut, Laura fought back a wave of nausea. "I am a virgin," she whispered. "I've never even kissed a boy." She opened her eyes. "I promise. Please don't do this."

Reaching over, he laid an assuring hand over her tightly clasped ones. "I don't want to do this, but if you don't let me perform this exam, she'll drag you all over this state until someone does."

Staring into his compassionate eyes, Laura knew she would have to do this. There were no other choices. No one to call, nowhere to run, Bizzy certainly couldn't help her. Laura took a deep breath, straightened her spine, tried to clear her mind, then delivered in her best brave voice, "Tell me what to do."

The doctor squeezed her hand. "Good girl. I'm going to leave and get a nurse. You take off your clothes and put on that gown behind you. You can leave your bra on, though." He gave her a bolstering look. "We'll do this as quick as possible, okay?"

Laura nodded. He pulled the curtain back and disappeared. She slid off the table and quickly changed clothes. Outside she heard whispers.

"This is the biggest crock of crap I've seen," the doctor spoke furiously, his voice muffled by the curtain. "Her aunt

says she's some kind of wild child, skipping school and running around. I'm here to tell you that beautiful little girl in there is about as sweet as they come. I'm so angry I could smash my fist into something, preferably that aunt of hers."

"Well, did you tell her aunt this is an emergency room, not a family clinic," a woman whispered back.

"Hell yeah, I told her that. I refused to help her. But she swore up and down she'd drag that poor kid around all night until someone did the exam."

Laura heard the woman heave a sigh. "Is she her legal guardian?"

"Yes. Now listen, we're going to take as long as needed to make this girl feel comfortable, okay?"

"Okay."

Laura climbed on top the table. A few seconds later the doctor pulled the curtain back and stepped inside. "Laura, this is nurse Donna. She's going to be assisting me with the exam."

Clutching her gown, Laura stared at the large, happy looking woman.

Nurse Donna patted her leg. "Hi, Laura. I don't want you to worry about anything. You've got the best doctor and nurse team in the whole county examining you."

"Okay, I have few quick questions before we get started." Doctor Brock flipped back the top of his chart. "When was your last period?"

Laura switched her gaze to her lap. No one had ever asked her such a personal question. "Two weeks ago," she answered.

"What method of birth control do you use?"

"Nothing."

"Are you sexually active."

"No."

"Are you allergic to anything?"

"I don't think so."

"Okay, that's done with." He laid the clipboard aside. "Laura, have you ever had a pelvic exam before?"

"No."

"Let me tell you what we're going to do. First off, you're going to scoot your bottom all the way to the end of the table and put your feet in these stirrups. Then you're going to lie back and spread your legs." Her face caught on fire. "Now don't worry about that part," he interjected quickly. "We'll put a sheet over you and cover you completely. I'm going to insert this device," he held up some silver thing that looked like a medieval torturing tool, "into your vagina and open it up a little."

"It's not painful," Nurse Donna added. "You'll feel a little pressure, that's all."

Dr. Brock clicked his pen and slid it into his chest pocket. "Alright, that's it. Any questions?"

Laura shook her head.

"Laura, look at me please," the doctor requested quietly.

She raised her eyes to his.

"We're going to do this as quick as possible. There's no need to be embarrassed. Nurse Donna and I have performed many of these exams over the years."

Laura appreciated his attempt at reassuring her, but just wanted to get the whole thing over with.

Doctor Brock pulled out a sheet and laid it across her legs. "Go ahead and scoot down, put your feet in the stirrups, and lie back." He remained standing while the nurse helped Laura get in the right position. "Now I'm going to take a seat and pull the sheet back a little."

Laura's legs started to tremble.

"I'm going to put my hand on your knee first so you can get used to my touch."

She jumped when he touched her knee.

"Now I'm going to touch your inner thigh."

She didn't jump that time, thank God.

"Now I'm going to insert that silver tool I showed you and open you up a little."

Humiliated, Laura closed her eyes and turned her face away from where the nurse stood. She concentrated on the future and what her life would be like away from Aunt Jane. Laura imagined being an adult and sharing an apartment with Bizzy.

"All done." The doctor lowered the sheet and stood. "Did I hurt you?"

Laura opened her eyes and cleared her throat. "No."

"Thank you, nurse Donna. I'd like to have a private moment with Laura, please." The nurse walked from the examining room as he helped Laura sit up. "I need to ask you something, and it is imperative that you tell me the truth." He waited until Laura looked him in the eyes. "Does your aunt abuse you?"

Frozen and empty inside, Laura held steady for a long time, but didn't answer. What did she say to a question like that? Where would she be sent if people discovered her aunt's cruelty? Foster care, a home? Laura had no family, no alternatives.

Finally, Doctor Brock sighed and reached inside his pocket. "I'm going to do something that I've never done before." He pulled out a business card and wrote on the back of it. "This is my home number. If you need any help at all, with anything, I want you to call me, night or day, no questions asked." He handed her the card. "Put that in a special place where no one can find it but you."

Laura looked at the card in her hand, then back up at the doctor. "Thank you."

His lips curved into a slight smile. "You're welcome." He lifted the curtain to leave. "When you get dressed, come on out to the nurse's station, and I'll walk you out."

Laura changed clothes and tucked his card into her sock. She emerged from the examining room. All the nurses looked up at her with matching, pitying expressions. She hated that. Doctor Brock walked toward her, a warm smile on his face, and led her out to the waiting room. Aunt Jane stood the minute she saw them.

Doctor Brock handed her a file. "Here's the report you requested."

Jane yanked it from his fingers and quickly scanned it. She slammed her hand over her heart in a dramatic gesture. "Oh, thank God," she breathed.

The doctor's upper lip twitched in disgust. "I think it is despicable what you put your niece through."

Aunt Jane pierced him with a sharp glare. "Well, thank you doctor for your professional opinion. I'll take my niece home now."

Fluttering her eyelids open, Laura stared at the shadowed ceiling, orienting herself. She was lying on her back, in a bed, in a hotel room…no, not a room, a suite. Will's suite to be exact, she'd won the pool hall bet.

A chill ran through her body, and she realized the bed covers sat in a heaped pile on the floor. She must have kicked them off during the dream.

Her knees were bent, spread wide in a pelvic exam position. Groggily, she closed them, then swung her legs over the side of the bed and grabbed her rabbit's foot from the nightstand. She sat staring at the Seattle skyline.

Doctor Brock. Someone she hadn't thought about in a long time. She'd called him, the night she ran away from home, almost a year after he'd examined her. He vowed he would help her, no questions asked, and true to his word, he had. He met her at a gas station with an envelope of money. He didn't want it paid back, but Laura had repaid him with interest.

Will's suite, correction, her suite, had a spectacular view of Seattle. For two in the morning, the city seemed to sparkle and bustle with activity.

Sliding off the bed, Laura put her rabbit's foot down, and padded into the kitchenette to rummage through the cabinets. She found some crackers and cheese, a bag of macadamia nut cookies, and espresso ground coffee.

Knowing she'd be awake the rest of the night, she started the coffee brewing, then meandered through the archway into the living room. She flicked on the television and scanned the channels, hoping to find a Bogie movie.

When the phone rang, she nearly jumped a foot in the air. At such a late hour, a wrong number probably, but she answered it anyway. "Hello?"

"Hey, you sound awake," Will mumbled in a voice made gravely by sleep.

She smiled. "I am awake."

"Everything okay?"

"Yeah. I've got the munchies and a craving for a late night movie. How did you know I was up?"

"I'm not sure. I woke up a few minutes ago and felt that maybe you were awake, too. Strange, huh?"

"Yeah." She listened to him rustling the sheets of his bed and imagined him straightening the covers.

"You gonna go back to sleep?" He sounded more awake now.

"Probably not. I'm not really tired."

"Want me to come over and keep you company?"

Her stomach did a slow roll. "Are you sure? Sleep's more important."

He chuckled. "I'll be there in five."

Laura hung up the phone and rushed into the bathroom. She splashed cold water on her face, swished mouthwash around in her mouth, then finger combed some flyaway hairs. She hurried into the bedroom, yanked off her boxers, pulled on a pair of long pajama bottoms.

A knock sounded at her door.

She opened it. He closed his eyes and with a silly grin, inhaled. "I smell coffee. You read my mind."

Would this man never seem unattractive to her? Even in sweatpants, a T-shirt, and regular old athletic socks, he was the sexiest man in the world. "I've got lots of food, too. You hungry?"

"I could munch." He followed her in and shut the door.

"How do you take your coffee?"

"Cream." Will pulled a stool from the island that separated the kitchen and hopped up. He reached for a cookie.

Laura handed him a mug. "What are you smiling at?"

"You. It's fun watching you putter around the kitchen making something for me."

"Making coffee's no big deal. I'll make you dinner sometime. You'll really be impressed then."

"I'd like that," he said and held her gaze until she glanced away.

She cleared her throat and turned out the kitchen light, then walked into the living room with a plate of crackers and cheese. "You ready to watch a movie?"

"Yep." Will grabbed the bowl of cookies and jumped down off his stool.

Laura sat the food down on the coffee table and curled into a corner of the couch. She folded her legs under and propped a pillow beneath her arm. Will snatched a blanket that had been tossed over an easy chair and took the other corner of the couch. After getting settled, he grabbed some crackers and munched.

The television provided the only light. Its flickering cast odd shadows across the walls and furniture. Laura kept her attention fixed to the TV set, but knew Will's was glued to her.

"Tell me about the dream."

She glanced over at him. "How did you know I had one?"

"Messy bed, late night. I put two and two together."

She studied Will, *really* studied him, the man, not the rock star image he portrayed. His outward appearance appealed to her, yes, but his heart attracted her the most. He offered it in such an open, honest way that it staggered and humbled her. She wanted to be that open with him, unconditionally.

Will pulled his blanket aside. "Come 'ere."

Laura hesitated.

"Talking. That's all we're going to do, lay here and talk." He gave her a tender smile and beckoned her with his head.

She put her coffee down and crawled across the couch, positioned her body beside his.

He wrapped his arms around her and squeezed. "You're all toasty warm."

Relaxing a little, Laura rested her head and hand on his chest. Will pulled the blanket around the two of them and tucked it in tight. She let out a soft breath, relishing the content, warm, safe feeling of his arms cradling her.

He reached up, ran his fingers along her forehead and through the hair on the crown of her head. "Tell me about it."

Laura closed her eyes and listened to the steady rhythm of his heart. He ran the pads of his fingers up and down her arm in long, soft strokes. A few minutes later, she told him about the dream.

When she finished, he said nothing. He'd stopped stroking her arm, though, and in fact had tightened his hold so much that her ribs hurt.

"You're hugging me too tight," she wheezed.

Will loosened his grip, but said nothing. Minutes ticked by. Still, he said nothing. What was he thinking? She wanted to ask, but didn't.

She started to pull away, and he tightened his arms. "Don't get up. Please. Stay beside me and let me hold you."

Laura gazed into his eyes, and odd enough, she saw pain there, coupled with a need for comfort. She reached out and touched her fingers to his cheek. The first time she ever voluntarily, affectionately touched anyone in her life.

They stayed in that position, her eyes holding steady to his ebony ones. Time suspended as their souls communicated mutual hope. And then she ran her thumb over his stubble.

Ten

The sun slipped through the balcony's blinds, flicking rays across Will's lids. He slit open his eyes and absorbed the beauty of a dawning, Seattle morning. Laura lay in his arms, or more like half-on, half-off him, with one leg and hand thrown over his body. The combination of her softness, weight, and warmth felt incredible. Wonderful. Awe-inspiring. They'd fallen asleep wrapped around each other, lulled by the rhythm of their hearts and slow, steady breaths.

He raised his head and peeked down at her face still nestled into his chest. She was sound asleep. Good. She needed it. He placed his nose on the crown of her head and inhaled...ah, uniquely Laura.

The television played morning cartoons. They must have fallen asleep with it still on. Their coffee cups, cookies, crackers, and cheese remained on the coffee table, with the cheddar looking a little oily and suspicious.

Careful not to wake her, Will reached up and rubbed his eyes. A pen and pad of hotel stationary sitting on the coffee table caught his eye. He stretched his fingers, snagged the corner of the paper, slid it closer, and began scribbling some lyrics that had popped into his mind the night before.

Some time later Laura stirred and nuzzled her head into his chest. She could do that all day as far as he was concerned. His stomach growled.

"Morning," she mumbled in response.

Will hugged her closer and kissed the top of her head. "Morning."

"You're hungry."

"Yep."

Laura pushed the blanket aside and swung her legs around. She grabbed a couple of cookies off the coffee table, handed one to him, and took a bite out of hers.

He jammed the whole cookie in his mouth. "Seeb 'el?" he managed around a full mouth.

She glanced down at him, smiled sleepily, and took another bite. "That was the best sleep I've had in a long time."

"Well, of course. You were snuggled in the arms of a big time rock star."

Laura shook her head as if she didn't have a clue what to do with him. Then her gaze fell on the notepad. "What's that?"

He snatched it away. "Lyrics."

She reached for it. "Let me see."

Will put the pad against his chest. "No peeking."

She slanted him a challenging look and made another grab for it.

He slapped her hand away. "No."

Laura poked him in the ribs, and Will jackknifed to a sitting position. She tugged on the pad. He tugged back. She tugged again, harder, and Will let go, sending her flying to the carpeted floor. She looked up at him in surprised shock. He bit back a smile. She lifted the pad to chance another peek, and with a growl, Will propelled off the couch on top of her.

Sandwiched between the couch and the coffee table, he planted his knees at her sides and pinned her arms to the floor. She let out a soft laugh. He pried the pad from her grip and flung it across the room. She got an arm free and jabbed him in the ribs again. He jumped and flattened his body along the top of hers.

"Okay, smarty-pants, you want to play rough?" Will wrestled her arms above her head, clamped her wrists together, and with his free hand tickled her ribs. "Uncle, say uncle."

Laura squirmed and scrunched her face into a determined line. "Not on your life."

"Better yet, say Will is the most wonderful man in the whole-wide world."

She laughed and shook her head. "You're a big bully."

Will leaned down close to her ear. "Oh, my heart's breaking you poor little defenseless woman."

"That's it!" She gave a hard twist right, then left.

He gave in and rolled off, and the two lay facing each other, legs intertwined, laughing, breathing heavy. Will smoothed her tousled hair from her cheeks. He wished he had a picture of her flushed face and smiling eyes, it wasn't often that he saw her so carefree.

Disentangling their legs, she pulled herself up and sat on the edge of the couch. He continued to grin like a fool while she straightened her twisted clothes.

"Scooby-Doo?" she asked.

"*Hmmm*?"

Laura pointed to his feet. "Your socks have Scooby on them."

He pulled his foot up and looked at the bottom. "Ed gave them to me for my last birthday."

"Ed. That's a name I haven't heard in awhile."

Will owed Ed every thanks in the world. Because of him, Laura worked for *Tourist*. "I love cartoons. I think I've got on Miss Piggy undies. Wanna see?" He looped his thumbs in the band of his sweatpants and pretended to push them down.

She shot off the couch. "No!"

He chuckled. She gave him an exasperated look and walked into the kitchen. Will switched the television to the news, and together they cleaned up their mess from the previous night. Neither said a word as they worked companionably, listening to world events in the background. After things had been put back in order, they agreed to meet for a morning run before Laura reported into work.

* * *

Jay had worked under Laura for four months now. When Ed left, Jay assumed he'd be given the Head Sound Engineer job. After all, he'd been next in line. And still was...next in line to Laura, though.

Playing second wheel was not his life's ambition. His little sabotage games had filled everyone's mind with doubts concerning Laura's competency. The stage workers were either for her or against her, but management was definitely disgruntled.

Jay smiled, confident that one last huge mishap would get her fired. Of course, that would make him the new Head Sound Engineer.

Jay saw Laura disappear under the elevated stage carrying her toolbox. He knew what he needed to do. He'd been thinking about it for weeks. Making his way backstage, he jumped a pile of cables and came to a stop in front of the main power supply. Imagine, all the power blowing during a show. The crowd would go insane, the performers would be pissed, and the band's manager would be forced to act to insure nothing that drastic ever happened again.

Bye, Bye, Laura.

Brilliant idea if he had to say so himself. The generator would kick on, but that'd be easy enough to hinder. No one ever checked it because total power failure was unheard of, until now.

"*Tourist! Tourist! Tourist!*" the crowd chanted.

Laura scanned the sold out, Seattle stadium. Even the seats behind the stage were packed. Who in the world would pay to watch the back of someone's head for three hours?

The usual backstage chatter rattled in her headset.

"Cue the guys in ten minutes."

"There's a riser missing stage right. Where the hell is it?"

"Damn! Someone tape down these cables before I bust

my head open."

"Close the loading dock doors! Some fanatic creep'll wander in."

"Hey, man, those are my cigs. Where'd ya find em?"

Someone was always looking for a cigarette right before a show.

"We want Will! We want Will! We want Will!"

Laura swiveled on her stool and looked behind her. A few rows back bounced four, big-busted, braless women, all in tight, white T-shirts each with a letter of Will's name printed on the front. They jumped up and down and waved their arms, their boobs bouncing with each exuberant hop.

The lights dimmed, and the crowd screamed their heads off. Laura slid the house channels up. Will and Eric stood with feet braced apart, one on each side of the stage, elevated on platforms, playing in unison with the drummer. Smoke and white lights shot up from the floor illuminating each member of *Tourist* in their spot.

The lead singer stepped up to his mike. Laura opened his channel on the board. He sang one line of lyrics, and the entire stage ground to a sounding halt. Lights and smoke still worked, but speakers and mikes went out. At first the band members didn't realize what happened and continued to play, which, in such a huge place, sounded like little toy acoustical instruments. The crowd booed, hissed, and yelled profanities. Laura blocked out the confusion as she checked every connection within her reach.

The voices in her headset yelled and shouted her name. The band members put down their instruments and walked off. The crowd became even more disgruntled and began pushing and shoving toward the stage.

Laura grabbed her toolbox, jumped over the barrier to her area, and ran along side of the crowd toward the backstage entrance. The security officer saw her coming and opened the gate. She dashed through it. The tech workers rushed at her, wanting an explanation.

She held up her hands for quiet. But with the crowd's noise out front, she had to yell anyway. "Listen up. Everyone calm down. Go to your assigned area and check all the connections. Don't just look at them either, put your fingers on them and assure yourself that they are firmly in place. No one speaks into this headset unless you're telling me that you've completely finished checking your area."

The workers charged off in different directions. She darted down the back hall toward the sound generator. Why hadn't it kicked in? With complete power failure the lights should've gone out, too, but they still worked. Only the sound was gone. She pushed a box out of the way, flicked the button on her flashlight, and squatted down in front of the generator. A severed wire dangled from the back. Exactly what she'd suspected. Laura pulled the strippers and electrical tape from her toolbox and spliced the cut wire.

"Laura," Jay's voice came through her headset. "You're not going to believe this. It looks like someone unplugged the main power source to the sound equipment."

"I believe it. I'm at the generator. Someone cut the wires. Let's not waste any more time. Plug in and I'll get back out to my station."

"Good show tonight, guys," the band's manager congratulated them.

"Yeah, once we got sound," the drummer sneered.

Will ground his teeth together.

The manager scanned the five *Tourist* members sprawled out in his hotel suite. "First, I want to thank you for meeting with me at such a late hour. I wouldn't do this if I didn't feel it necessary. As you know, we have another show tomorrow night, and I want to get this problem taken care of before then.

We had a huge mishap tonight and can't afford to have it again.

He lit a cigarette and took a drag. "Laura's a fantastic sound engineer but someone's sabotaging her work. At first I thought the screw-ups were intended to hurt the reputation of *Tourist*, but now I'm confident they're directed toward her. These things weren't happening before she got here. I recommend we replace her. We don't need the bad publicity or the loss of ticket sales over the rumors of a bad show. I can't make this decision without you. What do you guys think?"

Will straightened in his chair. They couldn't dismiss Laura. What would he do without her? "The only other person who knows how to mix our show is Ed, and there's no way we can get him here by tomorrow night."

The manager flicked his ash into a nearby tray. "I called Ed a few hours ago. He's agreed to help out until we get things figured out."

Will stood, shoved his hands in his back pockets, and walked to the window. "But what if the mishaps continue to occur even after Ed takes over?"

"I don't know," the manager answered. "I guess we try and figure it out from there. All I know is we didn't have these problems until Laura arrived. Maybe if we get rid of her, whoever's doing this will stop."

"Well maybe we should beef up security and install cameras to catch the person who deserves to be fired, not Laura." Will knew his voice sounded desperate.

"Okay, that's an option," the manager agreed. "But don't you think rumors will spread and everyone will know about the cameras?"

Will threw up his hands. "But that's a good thing because everyone will be on their best behavior."

The drummer twirled his drumstick in the air. "You're only fighting for her because you're in her pants."

Will jerked around. "Shut up, you son of a bitch. You

have no idea what you're talking about."

The drummer smirked. "What? Are you gonna tell us you're in looovvve with her?"

Will charged across the room.

Eric stood up between the two of them. "Cool it you two." He looked Will in the eyes. "I have an idea. I say we give Laura time off, bring Ed in to cover, and hire an investigator to find the guilty person. We'll be the only ones who know about the investigator, and we can bring him on as an assistant or something as cover."

"That's not a bad idea," the manager added.

The other band members nodded and mumbled their approval.

Will crossed the room to the door. "I'm going to be the one to tell her."

Standing in Laura's room, Will stared at her and waited for her response. He'd told her everything in one long rush of breath.

She moved to her duffel bag, unzipped it, and began placing clothes in it at a methodical, steady pace.

Will followed her movements with his eyes, then unable to control his patience, snapped, "Well?"

"It's a smart move on management's part. *Tourist* can't afford to have the kind of problems that you've been having since I arrived."

She sounded too logical. "But aren't you pissed?"

"No."

Irritated with her rational demeanor, Will paced the room, searching his brain for a solution. She zipped her duffel and tossed it onto the floor.

He spun on her. "I don't understand you."

"I'm sorry."

"What are you sorry about? You're the one who's getting screwed out of all this."

She leveled a tolerant look on him. "Don't you think I realize that? I learned a long time ago that you can't get upset over what life deals you. It's a waste of energy. The way I see it, I'm going on a little vacation, the investigator will nail the guilty party, and when I come back to work, my job will be even better. Now, you need to step back, take ten deep breaths, and lose the impatient tone in your voice." She pushed past him and walked into the bathroom.

Will jammed his fingers through his hair and plopped down in one of the room's two chairs. Maybe he'd feel better if she'd rant and rave and shout or something. Not Laura, though, count on her to be unemotional and removed from the situation. Didn't she realize it might be months before they saw each other again? Clearly, it either hadn't occurred to her or didn't faze her. Okay, fine. If she could adopt such a mature attitude, then so would he.

Who was he kidding? He'd miss her terribly. Their morning runs, seeing each other at the venue, dinners together. Will sighed and dropped his chin to his chest. "Where are you going to go?"

"I think I'll rent a camper and do some sightseeing," she called from the bathroom.

Great. Then she'd be stranded, God knows where, with a flat tire or maybe a busted radiator. The person who stopped to help her would be on the ten most wanted–

Will jerked his head up. "I have an idea." He pushed out of the chair and rushed to the bathroom door. "I've got a log cabin in Tennessee. It's secluded on a hundred and forty acres. There're lots of valleys and hills and green pastures. There're a couple of creeks, and I've got great toys like a dune buggy, four-wheeler, motorcycle, and some bicycles. What do you think?"

Laura's eyes twinkled. "I think that sounds like fun."

He danced in place. "Great!" If he couldn't have her with him, at least he'd have peace of mind she was safe at his cabin.

Eleven

Laura stood atop the tallest mountain on Will's Tennessee property, looking out over rolling, tree-laden hills burnished red and yellow from the last remnants of fall. She had no idea where his land stopped and somebody else's began, but with one-hundred-and-forty acres, she suspected it encompassed a lot.

A small town sat wedged into the hills in the distance. She'd gone down to it a few times since her arrival one week ago. It contained a grocery, a post office, two restaurants, and a small school. Laura hadn't realized such quaint little towns still existed in the States.

How did Will find this place?

A dog barked. The sound echoed along the ridge. Laura turned, hoping to see Jake, the black lab that had befriended her the first day she arrived. Shielding her eyes from the early morning sun, she glanced down at Will's cabin nestled in the valley below. A thin line of smoke snaked from the chimney. The log cabin wasn't at all what she'd imagined. Small, with one open area for living and a loft bedroom, half of it was built into the slope of the ridge, while the other half extended out with stilts.

Rubbing her hands together, she breathed into her cupped palms. Warm, moist air flowed across her chilled nose and cheeks. The weatherman said it was colder than usual for November, and flurries might appear in the next day or so.

She stamped her boots to get the circulation back into her cold toes, then climbed into the dune buggy she used when exploring his property. As she descended the ridge, she thought of Will and how much she wished he could share this beauty with her.

It had only been six days, but it felt like six weeks. Laura missed him terribly. More than she thought possible. His cabin didn't have a phone. He'd told her as much before she left *Tourist*, but the reality of not being able to hear his voice hit her around the second day. Which is why she found herself constantly scanning the radio for any of their songs.

A small creek ran across the driveway leading to his house. Laura slowed, having learned that the frigid water would splash her from beneath the buggy's sparse steal frame. She spotted Jake when she pulled under the stilted house.

He nudged her hand as she climbed from the buggy. "You're a good boy," she cooed, rubbing his ears. "What do you feel like for breakfast? How about left over burger from last night?"

Aunt Jane never allowed animals in their home. Laura put all those childhood years of wanting a pet into spoiling Jake.

She walked up the stone steps leading to the front door and grabbed a towel that she'd left there for him. She wiped down his legs and feet and let him in the house.

"Will probably doesn't want you in his house, but I won't say anything if you don't."

Jake's nails clicked on the hardwood floors as he pranced over to the fireplace and plopped down. Laura smiled at his arrogance and pried off her boots. After fixing Jake a bowl of food, she wandered over to the bank of windows that overlooked the rolling valley. As she stood there, thoughts of Will occupied her mind again.

Is he as lonely without me as I am without him?

Life sucks.

Will blew out a frustrated breath and dropped his chin into the palm of his hand. He stared at the white fuzz outside his window as *Tourist's* jet flew through a cloud on the way to

Phoenix.

Laura had been excited about seeing Arizona. Now she wouldn't get the chance. He'd bring her back someday. Anything to see her eyes light up, the way they did every time she saw a new city. She loved to travel.

Two weeks. It'd been two *long* weeks since he'd seen her.

Tourist's schedule had been non-stop, but that hadn't made time go by any quicker. His cabin didn't have a phone, so he hadn't talked to her either. He'd sent her four letters, two a week, and hoped that was the right amount. Not too many to smother her, not too little to make her think he'd forgotten her.

He hadn't received a letter from her, which didn't mean she hadn't sent one. It took a while for mail to catch up with the group. She'd left a message, though, a few days after she settled into his cabin. She'd called his hotel, but the front desk clerk hadn't put her through because she thought Laura was a crazed fan. Luckily, the clerk took a message, which he got later that day, saying that Laura found the place as described and thanking him.

That was it. Nothing else. If he could just see her smile, for a second, he'd be okay again. Not being able to communicate with her was driving him nuts.

Will blew out another breath and shifted in his seat.

Eric, who sat in his usual spot opposite Will, looked up from his magazine. "You're starting to annoy me. If you're going to keep breathing like that, then go somewhere else."

Will shot his best friend a snarly look and glanced around the plane. Ed lounged in the back where Laura usually sat. His head was bowed as he studied something in his hand. Will continued watching him, thinking he looked forlorn, then Ed twisted his fingers, and Will saw that he held a blue rabbit's foot.

Will straightened in his chair. Why would Ed have Laura's rabbit's foot? Maybe she'd given it to him for good luck. No, she never let that thing out of her sight. Lots of people carried a rabbit's foot. Ed happened to be one of those people.

Curiosity winning out, Will pushed himself up and walked down the aisle to the back of the plane. Ed slid the rabbit's foot into his front pocket and glanced up.

Will saw the sorrow and devastation in his eyes and lost all thought of the blue foot. "Hey, you okay? You look like someone stole your last lollipop."

Ed chuckled half-heartedly at the humor. "Memories."

Will sat down across from him. He and Ed were friends, but they'd never shared anything personal. That didn't stop Will from offering, "Anything you want to talk about?"

Pressing the pads of his fingers into his eyes, Ed sighed. "Do you know I have a sister?"

"No."

"Her name was Sandra."

Was? Will sensed something horrible coming. "That's a pretty name."

Ed smiled sadly. "Twenty years ago today she disappeared from my mother's garden and was never found." He turned his head and peered out the small window. "Everyone was so excited when she was born. My parents tried for ten years after they had me to have another baby. Sandra was the light of all our lives. She had all this wispy-white, baby fine hair and big green eyes. She was always happy. I remember tickling her little belly and she'd giggle."

Ed heaved another sigh and closed his eyes. "One day when she was five, my mom had her in the garden. The phone rang, mom ran inside, and when she came back out, Sandra was gone." He swallowed. "We lived in a little two bedroom house in Oregon. Our nearest neighbor lived a mile away. Search parties combed the woods around our home. Nobody knew if she wandered off or had been kidnapped. Weeks went by. Months. People gave up hope."

Ed opened his eyes and gazed wearily at Will. "My parents didn't have a lot of money. They couldn't afford investigators and media and stuff like that. Finally the local police told us we needed to face the fact that Sandra was probably dead." Ed shook his head. "You know what, though? I never felt it." He rubbed the heel of his hand over his heart. "In here she's still alive."

Even if Will could have found his voice, he didn't know what to say. This was the kind of horrible tale that he heard about on the news. He'd never met someone who had lived through it. "I don't know what to say. I don't think 'I'm sorry' is the appropriate phrase."

"There's nothing to say." Ed shrugged. "What can be said?"

"Is there anything I can do for you?"

"No, I'm fine. Thanks for listening." Ed closed his eyes and leaned his head back.

Will stayed rooted to his spot, Ed's story spiraling through his head. He thought of the blue rabbit's foot again, but didn't want to bother Ed.

Laura entered The Piggly Wiggly, grabbed a basket, and headed toward the produce section. She'd been coming to this grocery for three weeks now, but people still eyed her suspiciously, as if she was an alien, dropped off by the mother ship to suck the life out of everyone.

Giving a soft reassuring smile to one of the stockers, Laura rounded the pet aisle. She passed up the squeaky toys and went straight for the bones. Jake's favorite. She grabbed a rather large rawhide one, then took her place in line at the register.

Three people stood ahead of her. A hearty woman with pudgy legs jammed into galoshes, a teenager in skin-tight jeans and teased hair, and an old farmer dressed in overalls and a John Deere hat. His manure smell told Laura he'd walked into the grocery straight from a pasture.

"Oh, Momma," the teenager twanged. "I wanna see 'em in concert so *baaad*."

Laura glanced at the magazine the teenager pointed to. *Tourist* was featured on the front. Dressed in a pair of faded jeans and tight white T-shirt, Will stood with the other band members, his guitar hanging nonchalantly in front of him. She fought the urge to sigh and continued staring at the cover.

The teenager snapped her gum. "They's comin' ta Knoxville. You know thaaat?"

Her mother paid the kid at the register and shuffled toward the exit. "I told ya, honey, ya ain't gonna see a concert 'til ya eighteen."

"But *Mooommaaa*," the teenager whined as she followed her mother out the door.

Laura grabbed the magazine and paid for her groceries.

She drove Will's Jeep to the post office next, hoping to find another letter from him. One from Bizzy had been delivered instead. Laura ripped it open and scanned the paragraphs filled with Bizzy's usual prattle and hometown gossip. The last paragraph, though, said Aunt Jane had suffered a heart attack and was in the hospital. Laura read and reread that paragraph, thinking she should feel sorry for her aunt, but unable to work up any emotion at all.

She's getting what she deserves.

It was a bitter thought, but Laura continued to think it all the way back to Will's property. As she pulled through the creek, Jake barreled down the ridge, his black body darting tree stumps and leaping downed limbs.

Laura climbed from the Jeep and waved his bone in the air. "Got something for you, Jake."

He raced to her side, panting, eyeing the bone with

dancing, black eyes. She laughed at his wagging tale and hanging tongue and tried to make him sit before giving him the treat. He cocked his head and barked. She gave in with a shrug and handed him the bone. She'd teach him to sit later.

After making a cup of hot chocolate, Laura bundled into her coat, grabbed the magazine, then settled in the creaky porch swing. Jake lay curled at her feet, chewing on his rawhide bone. Snow flurries filled the valley. Laura sighed longingly.

If only Will was here.

Okay, first I'll say, "hi," and then I'll ask Laura if I can kiss her.

No.

I'll say, "hi," and kiss her without asking.

No.

I won't say, "hi." I'll just kiss her.

No.

Maybe I should wait until tomorrow to kiss her.

No.

Hell, Will had never put so much thought into a kiss in his life. He'd walk in the cabin and do whatever felt right. There. Settled.

Strumming his fingers on his knee, he bounced his leg and stared out the window of the utility vehicle. Four *long* weeks.

His driver hesitantly climbed the narrow, gravel road leading to the cabin. Will rolled his eyes. They were in a Land Rover. What was the guy's problem?

Will leaned up from the back seat. "Let me out when we round that corner up there. I don't want my friend to hear the engine. This is a surprise."

"Yes, Mr. Burns. Will you be needing a ride back to the airport?"

"No. Thanks anyway."

The vehicle rolled to a slow stop. Will jumped out, and

while the Land Rover navigated back down the mountain, he grabbed his suitcase and made his way toward the cabin, hoping Laura wouldn't see his approach.

He came to a stop outside the front door, closed his eyes, and took a couple of deep breaths.

Okay. Don't screw this up. It's going to be okay. It's just a kiss. Just a kiss? Hell, who was he kidding? He'd been waiting for this kiss his whole life. Or at least it felt like it.

As quietly as possible, he turned the knob. Her guitar music filled the air. That same mesmerizing piece that she'd played the first day her guitar had arrived on the tour.

Will clicked the door closed and lowered his suitcase to the hardwood floor. It hit him then. The lyrics he'd been working on matched her music perfectly. How could that be? He'd started those lyrics months before he met her. Granted, he hadn't written notes, only words, but the two merged in his mind in perfect harmony.

Realizing her music had stopped, Will looked up at the loft. Laura stood on the landing, staring down at him, wearing the sweetest, loveliest smile he'd ever seen. His heart thumped twice, hard, then started racing. She turned toward the stairs and slowly descended, keeping her eyes leveled on his the entire time.

She reached the bottom step and stopped. They stared at each other from across the living room for long seconds. She looked more beautiful, more enticing than he remembered. Will reminded himself how to walk and quickly covered the short distance between them. She came off the last step to stand toe-to-toe with him on even ground. Their smiles faded as he held her alluring gaze.

He reached up with both hands and lightly ran his fingers up her cheeks and into her hair. She was wearing it down, just like he liked it. He rested his palms on each side of her face and tilted it up. Searching her expression, Will looked for any hint of doubt or hesitance, knowing it would kill him to pull away, but for her he would. He saw trust in her eyes, though, and desire, too.

Reassured, he lowered his mouth to hers. She closed her eyes and parted her lips. Will pressed a slow, soft kiss at the corner of her mouth, then leisurely moved to her top lip where he left another. He brushed his lips to the other corner and lingered there for a few seconds, then slid down to her bottom lip. He sucked the fullness into his mouth and bit down lightly on its release. He placed one last gentle kiss on the same corner he'd started at and lifted his head.

Laura's lashes fluttered open. Will smiled, rubbed his nose affectionately against hers, and stepped back.

Her butt landed hard on the bottom step. She gave her head a quick shake and looked up at him through dazed eyes.

Clearly, the kiss came off exactly as he'd hoped. Pleased, Will grinned and held out his hand. "Hi."

Twelve

Five kisses. Will had given her exactly five kisses, like a sampled piece of fine chocolate.

He was standing in front of her, hand extended, grinning devilishly. She took his hand, and he pulled her up. "I've never knocked a woman off her feet before."

Leave it to Will to say something like that. "I see your ego is still larger than life."

He chuckled. "Something smells good. Chili?"

"You interested?"

Will swept his arm to the side. "Lead the way."

Laura crossed the living portion of the great room and entered the kitchen. She grabbed two bowls from the cabinet and spooned chili from the crockpot.

He took a seat at the small four-seater table. "It looks like you've settled in nicely."

"This place is incredible." She set the bowls and spoons on the table and poured two glasses of milk. "What are you doing here? You're scheduled for promotional work this week."

"You've been keeping up with my schedule, huh?"

Laura's face grew warm as she settled in the seat across from him. "Something like that."

Will took a bite of his chili. "It's promotional work, no concerts. I asked for some time off."

She glanced up at him. "Oh?"

He smiled. "I wanted to see you."

"Oh." Her stomach did a slow roll.

They stared at each other for a few seconds. A dog barked, snapping them back to reality. Laura wiped her mouth.

"That's Jake. Want to meet him?"

"Jake?"

"My dog. Well, actually, a stray black lab. But we've sort of adopted each other." Jake barked again. Laura walked to the door and glanced back at Will. "Mind if he comes in?"

"No, not at all."

She grabbed Jake's towel and let him in, wiped down his legs and paws. He pranced over to the fireplace and plopped down.

"I can see he's made himself quite at home."

Laura gave him an innocent, little shrug, and settled back at the table.

Jake slept sprawled in front of the crackling fire. Outside, frozen tree limbs fell from their trunks, producing a hollow, popping noise that echoed through the valley.

Will relaxed on the couch, sipping a glass of Merlot, patiently waiting for Laura to join him. She'd been keeping busy every since he'd arrived. He suspected her constant puttering came more from nerves than anything else. Hell, he felt nervous, too. This vacation would give them days, and nights, of uninterrupted private time.

Will glanced over his shoulder into the kitchen. She wiped a counter that she'd wiped ten minutes earlier. "Laura, stop cleaning and come sit with me."

She paused in mid-wipe and raised her head. He gave her what he hoped was a reassuring smile. She tossed the rag in the sink, grabbed her wine, and turned out the kitchen light, leaving only the fire to illuminate the room.

With glass in hand, Laura sat on the couch cushion furthest away from him. "I got your letters." She took a sip.

He'd indulge the distance she'd put between them for a little while. "Yeah? I got yours, too, finally." Will put his hand over his heart and gave her his best, hurt expression. "For a little while there I thought you forgot all about me."

Her eyes widened. "No. I didn't forget about you."

Will scooted across the couch and took her hand. "I missed you, Laura, a lot."

"I missed you, too...a lot."

Will took the wine glass from her and set it on the coffee table along with his. He turned back to her. Flickering shadows danced across her face. Would he ever get enough of her? Looking at her, hearing her, talking with her, her scent, her taste.

"You're beautiful." When she didn't respond, he prodded, "Say thank you, Laura."

Her lips curved. "Thank you. Will?"

"*Hmmm*?"

"I'm really nervous."

His heart flip-flopped. "Me, too."

"Yeah?"

"Yeah."

He placed a feather kiss to each tip of her long, slender fingers, then closed his eyes and pressed her palm along the length of his cheek. He shifted her hand and with his tongue traced a small circle in the center. Laura caught her breath.

Will opened his eyes at the erotic sound she made. He ran his hand along the back of her neck and pulled her forward, placed a lingering kiss to her right cheek. Slowly, he brushed down to her mouth and lightly rubbed his lips back and forth across hers. He ran his tongue along their seam, then moved over to her left cheek and pressed a kiss there. Will slid back down to her lips, and this time when his tongue ventured inside, she met it, her tip tentatively touching his. She tasted of wine.

"Give me your tongue," he spoke against her lips.

"What?" she breathed.

"Give me your tongue."

This time she gave him better access. He grabbed her tongue and circled it with his own, sucked it into his mouth, pulsed it in, then out in a slow, sensual rhythm. She moaned and dug one hand into his thigh, the other into his side, pulling him closer.

Will slipped his arm around her back and slid her down to the couch. He stretched his body on top of hers and trailed his lips across her cheek to her neck. Tugging down the turtleneck portion of her green sweater, he nibbled a line as far down as the sweater allowed, then growled impatiently, "Next time wear something that doesn't cover your neck."

Laura let out a shaky laugh. Will moved up to her ear where he breathed a warm, moist sigh. She gasped and dug her fingers into his sides. He tightened his grip around her back and pressed his body harder against hers.

A foul odor wafted across his face. She must have smelled it, too, because she opened her eyes and blinked a few times. They both turned their heads to the side. Jake's chin sat propped on the couch, right next to theirs, watching them make out. Will cocked a suspicious brow. Jake put on his best, innocent face, looked from Laura, to Will, then back to Laura.

"I think he's got to go out."

Will looked down at her, lying beneath him flushed and well kissed. He shot a scowl at Jake. "Likely story."

A smile tugged at the corners of her mouth. Will moaned his disappointment, pressed one last kiss to her lips, then rolled off the couch.

"Morning sunshine." Will tickled her toes.

Laura pried her left eye open. He stood at the foot of the loft bed, grinning cheekily. She pulled the covers over her head.

"I've got fresh coffee," he whispered enticingly.

She pushed the covers off her face and sniffed. As if out

of thin air, a cup appeared under her nose. Laura wiggled up to sit in bed, grabbed the mug, and took a couple of welcoming sips.

"Did the couch sleep okay?" she asked on a yawn.

"Yep."

"What are you so happy about this morning?"

He pushed her legs aside and plopped down beside her on the bed. "Nothing special. Life in general."

She took another sip, then glanced up at the skylight above the bed. "Looks like it's going to be a pretty day."

"Yep. And that's a perfect lead into what I want to ask you. What are you doing today?"

"I have an appointment with Dr. Masters this afternoon, but that's it."

"Dr. Masters? Where do you do that? There's no phone jack here at the cabin."

"The local library. They have a private computer room hooked to the Internet." Laura flashed him a proud smile. "I haven't had a flashback in a month."

He gazed at her tenderly. "I'm happy to hear that."

Will's admiration sent a stream of warmth flowing through her body. Four weeks since her last nightmare. That's how long she'd been at the cabin. This place was good for her.

She lifted the mug to her mouth and took another sip. "So, what did you have in mind for today?"

He leaned forward, challenge flashing in his eyes. "Ever been four-wheeling strapped to the roll bar of a Jeep?"

"Uh...no. Sounds dangerous."

"Not really, but it takes two people. Can I talk the adventurous side of you into it?"

He looked like a little boy excited to play with his toys. How could she resist him? "Sure. Sounds like fun."

"Alright!" He bounced off the bed. "Can you be ready in ten minutes?"

Laura threw the covers aside. "I'll be ready in five."

"My kind of woman." He dropped a kiss on her mouth and bounded down the stairs.

She smiled, enjoying his silliness and the easy affection between them.

Laura stood in the frosty pasture, her hands planted on her hips, staring hesitantly up at Will. She looked cute snuggled in a coat with a scarf wrapped around her neck and earmuffs secured over her head.

"Are you sure about this?"

He looked down at her from his perch on back of the Jeep. "Yep. Now get in and stop wasting time."

She sighed, sending a rush of frosty breath into the air, and climbed behind the wheel. She buckled her seatbelt, started the engine, and slowly pressed the accelerator.

After a minute of going the same, boring speed, Will urged impatiently, "Come on, speed up."

Over her shoulder, Laura gave him a mischievous look, then slammed her foot on the gas pedal. They shot forward in the field. The Jeep gave a hard lurch right, and then left, as it bounced over uneven ground. Will flung his arms in the air, hooting and hollering. He glanced down at Laura. Her face had taken on a thrill-seeking gleam.

After ten minutes of weaving back and forth across the open field, Will yelled for her to stop. "Let's switch places."

She shook her head. "I'm fine driving."

"Oh, come on," he teased. "Don't be a sissy."

Laura slanted him a look. "The last thing I am is a sissy. Now strap me in."

Will bit back a grin. She took his place behind the roll bar, and he helped her clip security straps to a special belt fastened around her waist. He drove slowly at first so she'd get the feel of it, then picked up speed. After a few minutes, he glanced up at her. Laura had a white-knuckled, death-grip on the roll bar, but her face held a mixture of concentration and excitement.

"Put your hands in the air," he yelled over the engine. "You're strapped in, you'll be fine."

In the rearview mirror, he watched her cautiously put one arm in the air and then the other. Her body began to jerk to all angles. A crazed, wild-eyed look took her over.

Will whooped and laughed. "Thata girl! Now let loose with a yell."

"Yeah."

"Oh, come on. You can do better than that."

Laura caught his gaze in the rearview mirror. She threw her head back. "Wahoo! Yippee! Alright!"

This was exactly what Will had hoped to accomplish. He wanted her to feel carefree, lost in the moment, unselfconscious.

He braked, unbuckled his seatbelt, and scrambled up to stand in front of her. He stared across the roll bar at her. She stared back, smiling, her cheeks and nose red from the cold, her breath gushing out from exhilaration. Will grabbed the front of her jacket and brought their mouths forcefully together. They stood there, lips closed but pressed firm to the other. Then they opened their mouths and thrust their tongues, circling, angling their heads right, left, back to the right again.

As quickly as it had started, Will pulled back, kissed her once more hard on the mouth, and plopped back down into the driver's seat. "Ready for breakfast?"

Laura gave a jerky nod and fumbled with the security straps.

After she settled into the passenger seat, Will turned to her. "Wahoo? Yippee? Alright?"

She gave a quick nod. "Wahoo. Yippee. Alright."

They both laughed as he pulled out of the field.

* * *

Laura hummed the same tune she'd been plucking on her guitar, while cutting tomatoes for omelets. Outside, Will chopped wood. The sound of the ax coupled with the crackling fire inside the cabin made things homey. She heard him crunch across the frozen yard, then knock his boots against the side of the cabin. He opened the door, and she glanced over her shoulder. He looked like an adorable hoodlum in his dark toboggan and sweatshirt. Little black clumps of hair curled out from underneath his wool hat.

She went back to humming and preparing breakfast as he stacked the cut logs to the side of the fireplace. Then he came up behind her, braced his palms on the counter, and pressed his body against hers. Laura's hands stilled on the cutting board.

He moved her braided hair over her right shoulder and nuzzled the left side of her neck. She'd chosen not to wear a turtleneck this morning for this precise reason. Laura closed her eyes and tilted her head to the right to give his nibbling lips better access. "Your nose is cold."

"You think it's cold, wait until you feel this." He slid his hands under her sweatshirt and criss-crossed them over her bare stomach.

She gasped softly. He pulled her body tighter against his and rubbed his hands along her ribs and down across her stomach. "I love the feel of your body." He pressed a warm, open-mouthed kiss to the back of her neck.

"I'm making breakfast," she said on a mindless exhale, then realized it was probably a stupid thing to say.

Will let out a low, rumbly chuckle. "I can see that." He stepped away, leaned his hip against the counter beside her, reached for some sliced ham, and popped it into his mouth.

Slightly scatter-brained, Laura started chopping again.

He swallowed his ham bite. "So, tell me about that music."

She glanced at him inquiringly. "What music?"

"The guitar piece you were strumming when I arrived yesterday. The same one you were humming just now, identical to the one I heard you playing months ago on the road."

Laura shrugged. "It's nothing. Something I made up, that's all."

"Well, I think it's incredible, and I'm about to surprise you with something." He walked over to his suitcase, rummaged inside, then came back to the kitchen with his lyrics pad. "I've been messing around with this song for the better part of a year and haven't been able to put any notes to it. Then yesterday I walked in here, heard you playing, and knew they would go together perfectly."

Laura scooped the cut tomatoes and put them in a bowl. "Forget it, Will, I'm not a songwriter."

"Trust me, okay?"

She glanced at his pad and then up into his appealing eyes. This obviously meant a lot to him. She turned on the faucet and rinsed her hands. "Do you want me to get my guitar?"

Will shook his head. "You start humming, and I'll come in with the words when I feel it's right."

Laura dried her hands on the dishtowel. She closed her eyes and began to hum.

"Open up your heart and see what's inside.
Now that we're apart, can't you see love's blind?
I need you by my side to comfort me this night.
Cross the seas with me and join me in my flight."

She continued humming, soaking in the words as his smooth, baritone's voice enveloped them, filling the cabin with peace and love.

When Will finished, she opened her eyes and stared into his. "That's the most beautiful song I've ever heard. I felt it through my soul."

He leaned forward, pressed a lingering, tender kiss to her lips. "I'm glad you liked it," he whispered and kissed her again. "Where's the apple cider?"

Laura blinked at the swift change of topic. "Apple cider?"

He sucked her bottom lip into his mouth and held it between his teeth. "I can taste it on you."

Her stomach lurched to her feet. She pointed over his shoulder at the refrigerator. Will slowly released her lip, then grabbed a glass from the cabinet. She refocused on the cutting board. What had she been making? Omelets, right.

Will stared moodily into the flickering flames. Five days had gone by much quicker than he'd expected. Hard to believe he had to leave tomorrow. What wonderful days they'd been, though. He and Laura had walked the property, hand-in-hand, talking. They'd shared adventurous moments on his motorcycles and jogged the trails that cut through the woods. They'd played with Jake and tried without success to teach him tricks. They'd listened to music, sipped wine, cooked meals together. They'd kissed until Will felt he might explode.

He wanted to make love to her, more than life. He wanted to explore every inch of her beautiful body, stroke her curves, show her pleasure until it spiraled through her, and she felt it, too.

But something wasn't right. Each time he'd ventured further than kissing, she held back, had a look in her eyes that told him she wasn't ready. He was trying to understand and exercise patience, but he wanted more.

And now here they sat, on their last night together, side-by-side on the couch, his arm draped along the back cushions with her head resting against his shoulder. It'd been an hour since either of them had said anything. Will suspected Laura felt as down-and-out as he did.

"You okay?" she asked.

He dropped his arm from the back of the couch and circled her shoulders. "I'm fine."

"You're so quiet. I'm not use to that side of you."

Will hugged her to him. "Just thinking, that's all."

"About what?"

"You and me."

"Oh."

"Laura?"

"Yeah?"

"I want to make love to you."

Laura pushed up off the couch and went over to the fire. She grabbed the poker and picked at the logs. Will leaned forward, braced his elbows on his knees, and studied her. What was she thinking? Seconds ticked by as his heart banged harder and harder. Why wasn't she saying anything?

After the longest pause in history, she put the poker down and turned to him. "I've thought about that, too, and I want to experience that closeness with you. But I'm not ready now. Can you understand?"

Will sighed and dropped his head. "Is it me?" He lifted his eyes to hers. "Have I done something wrong?"

"No," she quickly responded. "You're fine. Perfect. I couldn't ask for a more wonderful man." Laura shifted her attention to the throw rug beneath her feet and idly fingered the corner. "I've never been intimate with anyone."

He'd suspected as much. "Are you scared?"

"Not really. Not anymore. Hesitant about the unknown. But more importantly I want to be whole, emotionally, before we take that step." She furrowed her brows. "I'll understand if you want to break things off."

Will's heart broke in half. He'd bet his life she felt inadequate right now. Sliding off the couch, he crawled over to her and took her hands in his. "I understand. You come to me when you're ready. I'll wait however long it takes. Last thing I want to do is pressure you into something you're not ready for."

He squeezed her hands. Laura lifted her eyes to his. "I have no intentions of breaking anything off. Okay?" She nodded. "I don't want you to be tense either. Relax and enjoy what we have." She smiled slightly. He leaned forward and touched his forehead to hers. "You don't mind if I kiss you silly, though, do you?"

Laura let out a weak laugh. Will pushed her back onto the rug and settled comfortably on top of her.

At the small, private airport the next morning, Will and Laura sat in the Jeep holding hands. They stared out the windshield, watching the workers prepare Will's rented twin-engine plane.

He sighed and turned to her. "I have something for you."

"Will, you shouldn't have–"

"Oh, hush, it's nothing really." He pulled a card from his pocket and handed it to her. "I wanted to get you a cell phone, but after talking to the salesperson I found out that you wouldn't get a signal at the cabin. Then I checked into getting a phone line installed, but they tell me it'll be weeks because it's so far out. So I got you a calling card instead. You've got my itinerary, so you know where to reach me. I'll make sure the hotel staff knows your name and to put you through to my suite anytime, day or night." He smiled. "You've also got my cell number. No excuses. Call me."

"I've already got a calling car–"

"Laura," he warned. "Take it and say thank you."

"Sorry. Thank you."

The pilot signaled it was time to leave. Will let go of her hand, cupped her face in his palms, and kissed her. "I'm going to miss you."

"Miss you, too."

He opened his door, grabbed his suitcase from the

backseat, and jogged toward the awaiting crew.

Laura watched him make his way across the tarmac, her heart feeling more empty with each step he took. What if months went by before they saw each other again? What if she never got her job back? What if...what if the plane crashed?

When the last horrible question reeled through her head, she gasped for air. She tried to memorize everything about him. The fit of his jeans, his well-worn Nikes, the dark blue suitcase in his left hand, his brown leather jacket, the sound of his laughter, his scent, his voice. Oh, God, what did he smell like? What about his voice? What did it sound like?

With a jittery hand, she reached for the door handle and stumbled out of the Jeep. "Will," she shouted, then clamped her hand over her mouth.

Every person on the field, including Will, turned toward her. He smiled, set his suitcase down, and opened his arms. She sprinted across the open field and landed hard against him. He squeezed her, rained kisses on her forehead, eyelids, cheeks, nose, mouth, and any other vacant spot on her face.

Then he pulled back and with twinkling eyes rubbed their noses together. "There. We've given these people a lot to talk about, haven't we?"

She nodded. "Be safe," she whispered and reluctantly released him.

Will boarded the plane, keeping his gaze glued to her tall, slender silhouette the entire time. As the plane taxied down the runway, he remembered the blue rabbit's foot. He'd forgotten to ask her about it.

Thirteen

Laura selected a can of corn beef hash, added it to her basket, and crossed over to the pet section. Jake was going through bones like candy. She picked his favorite off the shelf, turned toward the back of the store, and stopped cold.

Aunt Jane.

The older woman disappeared around the corner. Laura didn't even think. She dashed after her, rounded the aisle, and caught sight of her sidestepping a family.

"Stop," Laura yelled.

The family looked up at her. She sprinted toward them, waving for them to get out of her way, made it to the end, and saw Aunt Jane leaving the store. Laura dropped her basket and bolted past the cash registers and out the door.

She scanned the parking lot, the sidewalks, but saw no sign of her. A truck cranked its engine and pulled from its spot. Zeroing in, Laura studied the occupants. Two teenage boys.

Another car spurred to life. She whipped to the right and fixed her gaze on it, watched it slowly make its way toward her. It stopped in front of the store. An old gentleman climbed out and bought a newspaper from a stand.

"Miss, do you want these things you dropped?"

Laura turned toward the Piggly Wiggly worker. "Did you see that lady? Tall, skinny, shoulder length, straight brown hair."

The stock boy shook his head. "No, ma'am." He held up her basket. "Do you want these?"

She took it from him. "Yes. Sorry."

He held the door open for her, and she walked through.

As she stood in line at the register, she continued studying the parking lot through the bank of storefront windows.

Did she imagine her? Maybe. Seemed too real, though. But she hadn't cowered. She hadn't been afraid. For the first time in her life she reacted exactly how she always wanted–strong, fierce, determined, proud.

Laura paid for her groceries and exited the store, her chin up, back straight.

I've come a long way.

Then why did a sense of dread still loom over her shoulders?

Friday night came, and Jay had nothing better to do than hang out in an Irish pub and drown his misery in beer.

Around the curve of the bar sat two blondes. He'd told them he worked for *Tourist*, trying to impress them. It hadn't. They were flirting with another guy.

On the barstools to his left perched a couple. They'd met an hour ago and were already pawing and feeling everywhere publicly acceptable. Why couldn't Jay be lucky enough to pick up a chick and get some action?

Hunched beside him, an old man peered into the depths of his whiskey. He'd been that way for half an hour.

Jay looked up at the clock hanging above the bar. Midnight. The bartender swore it'd pick up around eleven, but only ten people occupied the pub. As busy as it would get, Jay suspected.

He reached for yet another cigarette. Did each one really take seven minutes off his life? Didn't matter, his life wasn't going anywhere anyway. All his careful maneuvering and planning had backfired.

Laura had been dismissed. Sure. But Ed stepped right back in, and Jay still held the same damn position–right hand flunky to the Head Sound Engineer.

Why had management skipped over him again? Didn't they think he could handle the job? Maybe Laura had recommended they call Ed back. The bitch. Jay had bent over backwards for her.

He downed his beer. "Bartender, another one here."

"Yo, Jay, you look about ready to keel over." Someone slapped him hard on the back.

Jay teetered forward from the impact and grabbed the bar for support. His head reeled. He had a pretty good buzz going. He glanced over and saw Kevin, one of the techies from the lighting crew, straddle the stool where the old man had been sitting. When had the old man left?

Kevin signaled for a beer, flashed a quick grin toward the blondes, and turned to Jay. "You sure you should be slopping back all that beer. We've got to be at set up in," he peeked at his watch, "seven hours."

Jay sent Kevin a scowl and gulped back more beer. "I'm calling in sick tomorrow."

Kevin's brows shot up. "The guys on the sound crew are gonna be pissed about that one. But, hey, I work lighting so what do I care?" He nudged Jay. "Don't worry, I won't rat on you."

"Whatever."

Kevin took a sip of his beer. "You okay, dude? You don't look like yourself."

"As a matter of fact, no, I'm not okay." Jay crushed his half-smoked cigarette in the metal ashtray. "Nothing ever goes my way. I've worked my ass off for Ed and *Tourist* for five years. Then when it's time for Ed to move on, he brings in some damn chick mixer to fill his slot."

Jay jammed his finger into his chest. "*I* was supposed to have that job! *I* deserved it! *I* was the next in line!"

"Jesus, I can hear you," Kevin hissed and glanced around the bar. "Lower your voice a few decibels."

Jay knocked back the rest of his beer, then wiped the back of his hand across his mouth. "I had it all figured out. I screwed around with the equipment, trying to get Laura fired so I'd be promoted. Ha! Wasn't I an idiot? Look what happened. They suspend Laura, bring Ed back, and I'm still exactly where I've always been. The next in line."

Jay threw some bills on the counter and stumbled off his stool. "Life sucks, Buddy. Don't let anybody tell you different."

Laura placed her right hand on her stomach and inhaled a nervous breath. She slid the airplane's window shade up and watched as they descended into Los Angeles. Will said he'd be there to greet her when she emerged from the terminal. How *would* they greet each other? A hug? A kiss? Maybe he'd simply shake her hand.

One week had gone by since his visit to the cabin. It felt more like ten. They'd talked a total of three times on the phone. Each conversation had been friendly and casual, laced with flirtatious remarks from Will. Laura longed for those remarks. They made her feel feminine and giddy.

Jay. Why did it have to be him? She'd trusted him more than anybody else on her sound crew, and he'd been sneaking around her back the whole time. Thank God he'd blabbed the whole thing to Kevin who'd told management the next day. Otherwise, who knew how long things would've gone on?

The plane touched down. Laura's stomach plummeted to her feet. She squeezed her eyes shut and forced herself to breathe slowly. But as soon as the captain told them they could unbuckle, Laura ripped the seat belt off, shot out of her seat, retrieved her bag from the overhead bin, then quickly made her way to the head of the line.

She emerged from the terminal, craning her neck, searching all the faces, but didn't see Will's dark head and quirky grin.

"Hey, green eyes, welcome to the city of angels."

Laura whirled around. "Ed? What are you doing here? I thought Wi–" She stopped in mid-sentence, realizing nobody knew about the two of them.

"Nice to see you, too." He reached for her duffel bag. "Ready?"

"Yeah." She scanned the crowd one last time.

"He said to tell you he'd meet you at the hotel. He couldn't chance coming here. The paparazzi have been hounding the group for days."

"He?" Laura inquired innocently.

Ed's mouth twitched. "Will."

"Oh."

"Good to you have back, Laura. And cut the crap with Will, I know you two have the hots for each other."

Laura felt her face grow warm. "I have no idea what you're talking about."

Ed snorted a laugh.

She cut a playful glare at him and pushed him in the shoulder. "Shut up, Ed."

Will darted toward his door when a knock sounded. He threw it open.

Ed grinned. "Hi. Wanted to let you know we're back."

Will swallowed. "Oh, well, then..." he ran his fingers through his hair. "I guess I should go down."

"Yeah," Ed nodded, clearly amused. "That's a good idea. I can tell she's excited to see you."

"Really?"

"Really. And the roses in her room were a nice touch. She couldn't take her eyes off of them."

"Really?"

"Really." Ed punched him on the arm. "See ya later."

Will dashed back inside his suite. He checked himself in the mirror, did the breath test, and then made his way to her room. Quietly, he tapped on her door, and when she opened it, he lost all coherent thought.

He'd recited his first words to her a hundred times over the last couple of days. But standing here looking at her, nothing came to his mind.

His gaze traveled from her excited, twinkling eyes down to her adorable, scattered freckles, over her perfectly formed, tiny nose, along the line of her heart shaped jaw, and stopped at her sweetly curved lips.

"Hi," he finally managed to get out.

"The roses are beautiful. No one's ever given me flowers."

"No one?"

"No one."

"Wow."

"Yeah."

Keeping his eyes locked with hers, Will stepped into her room, shut the door, and closed the small gap between them. He ran his fingers up the sides of Laura's face, into her hair, and followed the length of it all the way to her butt. He traced his hands down the backs of her legs to her knees.

"Grab on," he whispered and lifted her to straddle him.

Laura wrapped her legs around his waist, and Will melted with the mind-numbing feel of the new position. He clasped his hands under her hips. She released her grip from around his neck, ran her fingers through his hair, and feathered them across his brow and down his cheeks. She outlined his bottom lip with her thumb.

He grabbed that thumb between his lips and bit down. "Kiss me," he growled and walked toward the bed.

Laura wrapped her arms around his shoulders and lowered her mouth to meet his. She flicked the tip of her tongue under his top lip, sucked it into her mouth, then released it gradually with a scrape of her teeth. Will let out a low moan.

He watched her eyes take on a sultry, powerful look. She could do anything to him right now, and he'd let her. That alone was excitedly scary as hell.

Will landed hard with her on the bed and plundered her mouth with his tongue, angling his head one way, then the next, trying to get in deeper, desperate for more, craving satisfaction. He tore his lips from hers and moved to her neck, first the left side, then the right, half-conscious that he might be sucking too hard and leaving little love marks.

Frustrated with her restrictive clothing, Will tugged at the neckline of her fleece pullover, wanting access to her collarbone and further down. Laura squirmed and squeezed her inner thighs against his outer. Hungrily, he reacted and pressed his groin right where he knew she'd feel it.

Her swift intake of breath told him he'd hit the mark. Slipping his right arm beneath her back, he held her tight. Again, he pressed against her, but this time rotated his hips. She dug her fingers into his backside, pulled him closer, and circled her hips to the rhythm of his.

He groaned. Man, he needed her naked.

Will scooted her further onto the bed and pushed the hem of her shirt up for better access to her stomach. With his lips, he explored Laura's ribs, navel, the slightly concave lines of her stomach.

Running his fingers under the bunched fleece of her pullover, he traced the border of her bra. He circled his thumbs over her breasts and felt her nipples harden in response.

He glanced down her body. Laura's khaki pants rode an inch below her belly button. The gap in the waistband gave him a glimpse of yellow undies with tiny flowers. Will slid down and pressed a row of slow, sucking kisses along the waistline of her pants. He unsnapped and unzipped them and parted the material to reveal the cotton fabric underneath. With his index finger he traced the top of her panties, then slipped inside the elastic waistband.

Laura's accelerated pants for air caught his attention. Will looked up at her face, and what he saw there made him pause. She was watching him with wide, unblinking eyes. Her expression held a mixture of trust, yet uncertainty, passion, yet fright. He could go all the way with her; he knew that. But when they did make love, he wanted her face to show him fulfillment, abandonment, and yes, love.

With a deep breath, he affectionately rubbed his nose around her navel, then rested his cheek against her stomach. He waited patiently in that position until her breathing slowed and her nervousness subsided. Will reached for Laura's hand and linked his fingers with hers. Minutes went by as he studied the difference in their skin tone and listened to the activity of her stomach.

Laura squeezed her eyes shut. Something had gone wrong. Why had Will stopped? Part of her wanted to experience lovemaking with him, yet part of her remained hesitant as well. Why? Why couldn't she be normal? She knew he'd had a lot of women, none of them, surely, as complicated as she. Was he upset with her?

No.

Frustrated with her stupid, ridiculous thoughts, she sighed and rubbed her eyes. "I know you stopped because of me."

Will crossed his hands over her stomach and rested his chin on top. "You're right, I did stop because of you."

Miserable, Laura turned her head and looked the other way.

"But that's not a bad thing," he continued. "Don't you understand that making love to you is going to be so much more enjoyable when you're absolutely ready?"

"I wished I knew when that would be."

Will climbed up her body and kissed her cheek. He grabbed her chin and turned it so she would look at him. "I wish I knew that, too, but all this foreplay is a good thing." He wiggled against her. "Makes us all excited for the real event."

Laura smiled at his playfulness, loving the way he made an otherwise tense situation into an easier one. "Thanks for being so patient. I know you're used to a different kind of woman."

"You're right. I am. The women I've been intimate with have been different than you. But that's okay, because they were all just flings. You and me," he kissed her lips, "that's entirely different. There's something special between us, and I'm excited about it."

"How many–" she stopped, realizing she was about to ask a foolish question. "No, never mind, none of my business."

"Laura, if you want to know how many women I've been with, then ask."

"It's a stupid question. I'm sorry."

"It's not a stupid question, and I'll be honest and hope you won't think any less of me after I tell you the truth. When *Tourist* started getting recognition, the girls poured in from everywhere, and I sampled much more than I should have. But the novelty wore off after a while, and I became discreet and picky. I need you to understand that I was always careful about protection and never took chances."

Laura puckered her brows. "I don't think any less of you. Why would you think I would?"

He sighed and traced the outline of her jaw with his forefinger. "What you think matters a great deal to me."

"You're still the same old Will to me."

"Oh, so now I'm old am I?" He started tickling her sides.

She giggled and poked his ribs right where she knew he was especially sensitive. Will jumped, grabbed her hands, and pinned them above her head. They laughed and wrestled and rolled around on the bed.

"My clothes," Laura gasped a few minutes later. All their grappling had loosened her already undone pants and raised shirt.

Will gasped, too. "The last thing I'd want is for your clothes to come off."

She poked him in the ribs again. He chuckled and tugged her pants back into place, buttoned and zipped them, then pulled her shirt down to cover her belly. Will hugged her and rolled her over so she was stretched out on top of him. They lay that way for over an hour, listening to the outside traffic sounds and to each other's breathing.

The whole time Laura kept telling herself everything would be fine, her life was falling into place, and that the sick feeling in the pit of her stomach was only a false alarm.

Fourteen

Will strolled down the aisle of the convention center, making his way to the soundboard. Ed and Laura's matching blond heads were bent over a row of mikes as they fingered them, nodding to each other, discussing something technical.

Ed had agreed to stay with *Tourist* for an additional month in case someone else tampered with the equipment. Management didn't think that was likely, but had asked him anyway. With Laura having been gone from the job for weeks, Ed would be on hand during her transitional period.

Will hopped up on top a nearby speaker. "Hey, guys, how's it going?"

They both looked up at the same time through the exact vivid shade of green eyes. Why hadn't he noticed that before now?

Ed handed a mike to Laura and picked up another one. "Oh, fine. We're testing these new mikes to see if we want to buy them for the show."

Will nodded as he carefully studied the two of them. Ed stood about six inches taller than Laura. They had the same long, lean physiques.

Laura gave Will that delicious little smile he knew she reserved only for him. "You ready for tonight's show?"

He wanted to devour those tempting lips, but kept his butt planted on the speaker. "I'm always ready." Will sent her a smoldering look.

It worked because she blushed and quickly focused her attention on the mike in her hand. Will bit back a grin.

He and Laura had agreed anytime they were in public it would be best to act friendly to each other, but not overly affectionate. Neither of them wanted the press to find out about their relationship.

"I've always wondered what it's like to mix a show," Will said as he took in all the sound equipment scattered around their technical area.

Ed snapped excited eyes up to his. "It's the most incredible feeling to be in control of that stage. To know whatever you do, thousands of people will experience it. It's all right at your fingertips, and a slight move one way or the other could make or break a song. And when you get the EQ just right, when the acoustics in a place are perfect, it's like an orgasm or something."

"Orgasm, *hmmm*? That's sure descriptive." The two men chuckled, and Will glanced at Laura.

She ducked her head, mumbled something about going backstage, and brushed past him. As she hurried down the aisle, Will wondered if *she* was wondering what an orgasm felt like.

"Hey, guess who?"

"Will," Veronica squealed.

Will grinned at the sound of his little sister's excited voice and settled back into the hotel's desk chair. "So, what's going on, runt?"

"Oh, I'm as happy as ever," she sang through the phone. "Guesswhatguesswhatguesswhat?"

"You're pregnant?" He knew the question drove her crazy, but asked it anyway.

"*Nooo*," she groaned. "I'm certified to teach Tai Bo now, and I conduct my first class on Wednesday."

"Oh, well, that's great." Will had never understood her fascination with exercise. "What're you guys doing for the holidays?"

"Rico's mom's coming from Spain in February, and I'm

sure Dad already told you he's booked a singles cruise to Alaska. So we're here for Christmas. When ya coming?"

Will smiled at her question. He knew he wouldn't have to ask for an invitation. "We've got a holiday show with some other artists at Disney in Orlando on Christmas Eve. So I thought we'd drive up Christmas Day."

"We?"

"I'm bringing a friend. Her name's Laura."

"Laura?"

In all the years he'd been with *Tourist*, Will had never taken a woman home. Sure, in high school his dates had dropped in to say hi. But not since then had he deemed anyone important enough to meet the family. He knew his sister was biting her tongue on the other end, dying to ask a million questions.

Will decided to offer her a little bit of information. "Laura replaced Ed as Head Sound Engineer."

"Oh...well, okay, I'll have the guest room all ready for you two."

"Actually, sis, I'll sleep on the couch. Give Laura the guest room."

A long pause extended over the line. "Oookaaay. You know I'm dying over here. My curiosity's about to explode out of my head."

He laughed. "Wait 'til you meet her. She's something else."

"Oh, dear brother, you know I intend to snoop once you get here."

"I wouldn't expect any less, dear sister."

Veronica hooted. "I can't wait to tell Rico."

It was going to be an interesting holiday.

Laura tried not to fidget in the passenger side of the rental car. She'd be meeting Will's family in a few minutes. Maybe she'd made a mistake agreeing to this four-day trip. In the past she'd spent her holidays alone. They'd become like any other day. Either she'd worked or volunteered somewhere.

Would Will's sister have a turkey and a Christmas tree? Would they sit around the table to eat? Would there be lots of presents?

"This is the bridge to Amelia Island," Will informed her.

Laura sat up in her seat as they crossed the intercoastal waterway. Overgrown marsh bordered one side, a scattering of homes the other. Tiny canals zigzagged off the waterway with sailboats anchored in private coves.

Will pointed out his window. "Check out the marina. The boats have Christmas lights."

He'd been making little comments like that all the way from Orlando. Laura suspected he'd picked up on her anxiety and was trying to keep her mind occupied.

They drove a few more minutes until they reached the other side of the island. Will turned down a road that gave them a view of the Atlantic Ocean. "It looks like that every time I'm here."

Laura glanced out his window. The water alternated between shades of green, turquoise, and blue. The sun scattered dancing, sparkling prisms over the surface.

He took off his sunglasses. "It's beautiful, isn't it?"

"Yeah."

"Okay." He turned the car into a neighborhood. "We're here."

Laura put her hand on her stomach.

Will pulled the car over against a curb. He leaned over and gave her a kiss. "We're going to have a blast. Relax and enjoy yourself." He rubbed her stomach. "Don't be nervous."

Laura nodded. He drove the car another block and pulled up to a Spanish style house with a manicured lawn. They got out of the vehicle, made their way up a terracotta walkway, and right as they stepped onto the porch, the front door opened a few inches, and a tiny head peeked out.

Will had said his niece was adorable, but Laura hadn't imagined she'd be so beautiful. Her hair hung just past her shoulders with different shades of blond and brown streaming through it. Those features, along with her amber eyes and olive-toned skin, would make her gorgeous some day.

Will dropped his suitcase and swung his niece into his arms. She was small for an eight-year-old. He squeezed her until she squeaked and made loud chomping noises on her neck. She wiggled and giggled in his arms.

A man appeared next in the doorway. Laura assumed he must be Rico, Maria's father. They looked identical. He stood the same height as Will, but looked fuller through the shoulders and chest, like he lifted weights.

"I can't believe you're finally here, Uncle Will," his niece said, hugging his neck. Then she turned to Laura and extended her hand. "Hello, I'm Maria."

Surprised at her adult-like greeting, Laura shook the small hand. "Hello, I'm Laura."

Rico extended his hand as well. "Welcome to our home, Laura. I'm Rico. *Mi casa es su casa.*"

Will hadn't told her Rico had a Spanish accent. Laura shook his hand. "Thanks for inviting me."

Will put Maria down, and the two men embraced and exchanged greetings. Then like a whirlwind, a small woman burst through the door, her long, black hair flying behind her, and leapt into Will's arms.

"Will," she squealed.

"Veronica," he squealed back. They both laughed and hugged and kissed.

Veronica turned and gave Laura a huge hug, too, surprising her. "It's so nice to meet you, Laura. I'm Veronica."

Laura awkwardly received the embrace. "Thanks for

inviting me into your home."

Veronica pulled back and held Laura at an arm's length, studying her with twinkling, ebony eyes. Under other circumstances, Laura would've felt uneasy with the close scrutiny, but she found Veronica's smile warm and welcoming, much like Will's.

Veronica grabbed her hand and led her inside their home. "I'm so excited the two of you are here." She stopped and looked at her again. "You're so pretty." She glanced over her shoulder. "Will, she's very pretty."

"Um, thank you," Laura said.

"Veronica," Will warned.

She shrugged, turned back to Laura. "Let me show you around our place, then I'll let you get settled in."

Ten minutes later Veronica left Laura in the office, which doubled as a guestroom. A futon couch sat under the window, a desk and computer occupied the corner, a bookshelf loaded with novels, instructional manuals, and kid's books lined the wall. Someone had already placed her duffel bag on the futon.

"Hey, wha'd'ya think of the grand tour?" Will asked from the doorway.

Laura turned. "Their home is very nice, and your sister is beautiful. You two favor each other a lot."

"Well, thanks, but I prefer to be called handsome or sexy, not beautiful." He shot her a devilish, up-to-no-good grin and held out his hand. "Come on, there's eggnog to drink and Christmas presents to open."

She took his hand, and he led her into the living room where a sparkling tree decorated with white lights and shells filled one corner. Spanish holiday music played softly in the background. Maria was already kneeling beside the presents, bouncing with excitement. Rico and Veronica sat snuggled on the couch. Laura and Will settled on the floor.

Maria began handing out presents, and as the pile in front

of Laura grew bigger, she peeked at a few of the nametags to verify some mistake hadn't been made. They were all addressed to her. Giving into curiosity, she fingered the ribbons and wrapping and picked one up to feel the weight.

Will noticed Laura's child-like handling of the packages. Her inquisitive expression melted his heart. This was her first family Christmas, and he'd been able to give it to her.

"Usually we take turns opening gifts," Veronica said. "But how 'bout we all tear into them instead?"

With that, the place became a mad house. Will inconspicuously observed Laura as she gently pulled the ribbons and tape, but then she noticed everyone else ripping and clawing and got into the spirit. He had more fun watching her than he did opening his own gifts.

When she finished, she stared at the presents in front of her, a mixture of stunned delight and wonderment on her face. Maria had given her an Amelia Island T-shirt and a collection of shells in a blue bottle. Veronica had given her a lingerie catalogue with a gift certificate and a bath kit that smelled like vanilla. Rico had given her an inspirational book and a pen.

Will tried to get a closer look at the lingerie catalogue, but Laura had slipped it under the T-shirt out of his view.

"Thank you." Laura swept her gaze over all of them. "This is the most amazing Christmas I've ever had."

The emotion laced through her voice made everyone pause and look at her, at an obvious loss of words.

"You're welcome," Maria broke the silence. "Thank you for the play makeup set and fingernails."

"There's one more thing you haven't opened." Will pulled a small, flat, square package from under the couch and handed it to her.

Laura eyed it suspiciously. "What is it?"

"Open it and find out."

She untied the purple ribbon, then tipped the package

sideways. A CD slid into her hand. She glanced curiously at Will.

He smiled, hoping to the heavens she'd like it. "It's our song."

Laura blinked. "Are you serious?"

"Yep."

"When did you do this?"

"Ed mixed it for us when you were still at the cabin."

"Did the other guys like it?"

"They loved it. Now, are you going to ask me twenty questions or put it in the stereo?"

"Here, I'll do it." Veronica took the CD and placed it in the player.

The music started, and Will's voice filtered through the speakers. Laura slid a surprised look toward him. He knew she'd be shocked that he'd sung it himself instead of *Tourist's* lead singer.

Will scooted over behind her on the floor, stretched his legs along the sides of her body, and pulled her back to rest against his chest. He wrapped his arms around her, kissed her temple, and tenderly rocked her to the beat of their music.

The song they'd written together.

Will sat in an overstuffed leather chair, cradling Maria and reading her a bedtime story. Dressed in cloud-patterned pajamas, his niece lay curled in his arms with her head snuggled against his shoulder as she tried desperately to keep her eyes open. Laura watched them from across the room, warmed by the special moment they were sharing.

As if drawn by her stare, Will raised his eyes to hers. Her stomach did a slow roll as she held his gaze. The corners of his mouth curved up a little, then he went back to reading.

"Okay, sleepy head, time to put you to bed," Veronica called from the kitchen.

"*Nooo*," Maria whined. "I'm not tired."

"Way past your bedtime," Veronica said.

Will picked her up and sat her on her feet. He straightened her pajamas. "I'm gonna take a shower anyway, cutie."

Maria hugged him and kissed him on the cheek. "Night Uncle Will." With a yawn, she scooted into the kitchen while Will headed to the bathroom. "Night Mommy, night Papi."

"I'll be there in a few minutes to tuck you in," Rico told her.

Then Maria padded over to Laura and gave her a hug, too. "Sleep well, Laura."

Laura returned the small hug, loving the cuddle of it.

"Want some coffee, Laura?" Rico asked from the kitchen.

"Sure. Anything I can do to help?"

"Yes, come keep us company. Have a seat at the bar and tell us about your traveling."

Laura pulled out a stool and climbed up. "Well, let's see. I started with *Tourist* when they were in Canada, then–"

The bathroom door opened. Will emerged holding a towel around his waist. "Don't mind me. I forgot my razor." He walked over to his suitcase propped in the corner of the living room.

In all the months they'd known each other, Laura had never seen him without a shirt. She'd seen him in running shorts, jeans, T-shirts, long shirts, and a variety of other clothes, but never almost naked.

She told herself she shouldn't be staring, but couldn't tear her eyes away from him. Away from the tightly knit muscles in his stomach, the striated curves of his biceps and shoulders, the light dusting of dark hair across the top of his pecks, the line that started at his navel and disappeared down below.

Then he leaned over to grab his razor, and his towel opened, revealing his entire upper thigh.

Dragging her gaze away, Laura pondered the mug in front of her. Who'd set it there?

"Are you naked under that?" Veronica teased her brother.

Laura swallowed and skittered off the stool. "I-I-I'm going to step outside for a few moments."

Will followed her hasty retreat with his eyes down the hall and out the front door. He glanced inquiringly at Rico and Veronica.

"Brother, you scrambled that woman's brains."

Rico laughed. "That about sums it up."

Will looked down his body. He shouldn't have come out in a towel. He hadn't been thinking. "I hope she's not upset."

Veronica took a sip of her coffee. "I don't think she's upset. I think she's *very* aware of you, if you know what I mean."

He hadn't meant to make her uncomfortable. But maybe it wasn't such a bad thing that she'd seen him almost naked. It'd set off sparks. Make her feel alive inside.

Or in Laura's words–like a normal woman.

Fifteen

Laura smoothed her hand over her pregnant belly. She turned sideways and gazed lovingly at her round reflection in the mirror. She and Will would meet their daughter any day now. They couldn't wait to see her and hold her and hear her. Laura had suggested they name her after Will's grandmother. He loved the idea. So in a few days Emiline would be here, and they'd be a family.

Humming the song that he'd written for their baby, Laura moved about the nursery, tracing her fingers over everything, imagining Emiline there. A slight rustle in the doorway caught Laura's attention. She turned with a pleasant smile, expecting to see Will, and instead found Aunt Jane.

Laura blinked in confusion, assuming her aunt was a mirage. But then Jane moved from the doorway and glided across the room.

Laura backed up. "H-h-how did you get in here?"

Aunt Jane's face transitioned into an evil smirk as she approached her niece. Through eyes narrowed to skinny slits, Jane surveyed Laura from the top of her head down to her bare toes.

Laura placed her hands over her stomach and gathered her courage. She hiked her chin. "What do you want?"

"You always were a prissy one, thinking you were better than everyone else."

"Where's Will? Where's my husband?"

Aunt Jane let out a long, slow snicker. She tapped a red-tipped fingernail on Laura's stomach. "He can't come right now. He's busy."

"What have you done with him?" Laura demanded, hating

the frantic sound of her voice.

Jane placed her hand across her heart and fluttered her lashes. "Why, my dear niece, are you accusing me of something?"

Laura pushed past her and started for the door. Aunt Jane yanked her by the hair and slung her back against the wall. Pictures crashed to the floor. A sharp pain shot through Laura's side. She grimaced.

"Save your energy, you idiot, he's gone."

Laura grabbed her side. "Wh-what have you done with him?"

Hugging herself, Aunt Jane spun around with a sinister little laugh. "I love it when your voice gets shaky. It's food for my soul." She stopped and pinned her niece with an evil glare. "I killed him," she whispered.

Laura screamed and lunged at her aunt.

Jane dodged to the right, then used her foot to push her niece back against the wall. Laura stumbled and fell on the broken pictures. Her aunt charged forward.

Laura wrapped her arms around her stomach and curled up into a tight ball. "Get away from me! Don't hurt my baby!"

"I've always hated you!" Jane shouted and kicked Laura. "All you've done is ruin my life!"

"Stop. Please, stop," Laura cried. "Not my baby."

Jane aimed for her stomach with each kick. Laura crawled across the broken pictures, struggling to protect her daughter. She tried to fight back, but her cumbersome weight left her at a disadvantage. Every time she shifted her body, her aunt followed her, continuing the abuse.

Suddenly the assault halted, and Jane towered above her, heaving heavy breaths. Laura squeezed her eyes shut and prayed to God that it was all a nightmare, that the warmth seeping between her legs wasn't blood, that the pain in her stomach wasn't real. But when she opened her eyes again, her aunt knelt down, picked up a chunk of broken glass from the pictures, and squeezed it in her hand. Blood trickled down her fingers.

"I'm ending this once and for all," Jane hissed and raised the jagged glass high above her head.

"Noooo," Laura screamed as the glass plummeted toward her.

"Laura...Laura...Laura." Will shook her. "You've got to wake up."

Her arms flailed as she let out another guttural cry.

"Wake up."

Laura's legs kicked out. Her body thrashed from side-to-side. "Nooo," she moaned.

Will caught her shoulders and tried to pin them to the futon bed, but she was strong and quick and her knee connected with his side. His breath rushed out on a groan. He launched his body across hers, using his weight to keep her down.

"Wake up!"

Her eyes shot open. She stared unblinking into his face, her quick pants for air puffing against his cheeks.

"It's okay. You're alright. You were having a nightmare."

Laura swallowed, blinked a few times. He eased his weight off her body. She threw her arms around his neck. "Oh my God, you're alive. Oh, thank God you're alive."

Will held her as he turned and waved his sister's sleepy, concerned family back to bed. Laura's screams had awoken the whole house. He tightened his grip. "You're okay now. It was a horrible nightmare. That's all. I'm alive. You're alive. We're both okay."

How many of these had she gone through alone?

Laura pulled back in his arms. Her gaze touched the features of his face like she was trying to memorize every detail and reassure herself that he was definitely okay. Silent tears began to roll from her eyes. She reached up, wiped her hand across her cheek, and with furrowed brows, studied her wet fingers.

Will quietly watched her.

After a moment, she lifted her eyes to his. "I'm crying?"

Will smoothed his thumb over her damp cheek. "You deserve it after a dream like that."

Laura gave him a watery smile. "I didn't think I could do that anymore."

Puzzled, he asked, "Do what?"

She sniffed. "Cry. I don't remember crying before now. I thought I was too frigid. I thought Aunt Jane had taken that emotion from me." She inhaled a trembling breath and let more tears fall. "It feels really good."

Moisture welled in Will's eyes as he watched her experience the emotion. He leaned forward, kissed her wet lips, and gathered her into his arms. He held her until his T-shirt grew damp and her tears subsided.

He lay down with her on the futon bed and cuddled her in the spoon position. "You want to tell me about the dream?"

She slid her hand under her pillow and pulled out her blue rabbit's foot. "I was pregnant," she began in a hushed tone, "walking around the nursery, humming, touching the baby's things. Then Aunt Jane appeared in the doorway. I don't know where she came from. I thought I was imagining her. She said she'd killed you."

Will tightened his hold around Laura and pulled her tighter against him.

"She attacked me and kicked my stomach, my baby. There was some broken glass on the floor. She grabbed a chunk of it and came at me with it. She told me I'd ruined her life and deserved to die." Laura gripped Will's hand and pulled it under her chin. "There was blood between my legs," she whispered hoarsely.

Will leaned up and kissed her cheek. "It's okay. It's over now."

"Emiline. We we're going to name her Emiline after your grandmother."

He shut his eyes and placed his cheek against hers. "You were pregnant with my baby. Oh, Laura, I like the sound of that."

"Can you-can you stay in here with me?"

Will nodded and climbed beneath the covers. They lay curled together for a long time while she continued to slowly rub the rabbit's foot between her thumb and forefinger.

Finally, he asked, "Where did you get that?"

She shrugged a shoulder. "I'm not sure."

"How long have you had it?"

"As long as I can remember."

"Did Bizzy give it to you or Aunt Jane?"

"No."

Will reached for it, and she gave it to him. "Why do you carry it?"

"It settles me. It gives me peace." Laura's lips curved into a faint smile. "I know that sounds strange, but it's sort of like a kid's blanky."

"I don't think it's strange," he murmured, studying the blue rabbit's foot in the dim moonlight filtering through the window. A silver clasp held the fur together. Along the outer edge of the clasp danced a row of tiny, engraved, stick-figured boys and girls. "Do you ever give it to anybody for good luck?"

"No. Never."

"*Hmmm.*" He gave the charm back to her and pulled her into his arms. He kissed her temple and told her goodnight, and after she closed her eyes, Will lay there wondering what Ed's rabbit's foot looked like.

The digital clock beside the futon bed clicked to seven

a.m. Laura stared wide-eyed at it. She'd been that way for over an hour. She glanced over her shoulder. Will still lay dead to the world, curled on his side with his back to her. Careful not to wake him, Laura pushed the covers back, swung her legs over the side, then tiptoed from the guest room.

Five minutes later she emerged from the bathroom. No one was up yet. The entire house was dark except for a pale yellow beam escaping the crack in Maria's door. Laura padded over and peeked inside, expecting to see the child snuggled in bed, but instead she lay stretched out on the floor, coloring.

"Hey," Laura whispered. "What are you doing up so early?"

Maria turned and looked over her shoulder. "I couldn't sleep." She waved her inside.

Laura stepped into the aquatic-themed room and clicked the door closed behind her. She stretched out on the throw rug beside Maria and picked up a colored pencil. "Mind if I color this mermaid purple?"

The little girl shook her head and went back to highlighting a silver dolphin. "I used to get bad dreams a lot, but I don't anymore. Do you get them a lot?"

With anybody else, other than Will, Laura would've changed the subject. But something felt natural about lying beside this little girl, coloring and sharing. "I've had them my whole life."

Maria paused in her strokes and leveled concerned, adult-like eyes on Laura. "That's a long time."

"Yes it is, but last night was the first nightmare I'd had in a very long time."

"I'm glad. Bad dreams are no fun." Maria scooted over and hugged Laura's neck. "I'm happy you're Uncle Will's friend."

Laura smiled and hugged her back. Maria gave her a quick peck on the cheek, then went back to her dolphin. Laura picked up a pink pencil and started adding scales to the mermaid's body.

Will passed by Maria's door on the way to find Laura and paused when he heard their voices from within. He stood there for a few minutes, eavesdropping, smiling at their silly conversation. Quietly, he opened the door.

They lay stretched out on their stomachs, side-by-side, Maria's little body coming only to Laura's knees. They had their chins propped on the bends of their arms. Laura colored with her right hand while Maria used her left. Their pajamas pulled snug under them, outlining the shape of their butts and legs. Will enjoyed a savory moment of Laura's rear view before inching forward.

Carefully, he crawled on top and wrapped an arm around each of them. "Morning, girls." He kissed their cheeks. "Can I play, too?"

They giggled and scooted apart, making a place for him between them. Maria handed him a white crayon. "Here, Uncle Will, color the clouds."

Thirty minutes later Rico and Veronica found the three of them and did exactly what Will had done, crawled on top to make a body pyramid. They all laughed while Rico and Maria got into a tickling match.

"Anybody interested in pecan pancakes?" Veronica inquired somewhat airily. Everyone knew Maria loved pecan pancakes.

"Yeah, Mommy!" Maria wiggled out from under her Papi and started dancing. "*Comeoncomeoncomeon.*"

Rico laughed, snagged his daughter around the waist, and carried her out to the kitchen. Veronica elbowed her brother in the ribs one last time and followed her husband out. Will turned over on his side, propped his cheek in the palm of his hand, and wrapped his leg over Laura's.

She brushed her hair over her shoulder. "I like your family. Thank you so much for inviting me."

"You're welcome." Will moved in and nuzzled a nibbly line from her ear down the side of her neck.

Laura glanced toward the door.

"Don't worry, they won't come back. And if they do?" He pushed her over and stretched out on top of her. "Oh, well."

Cradling the sides of her face, Will brushed his lips back and forth across hers. Laura's tongue came out, and he responded by touching the tip of it with his own.

A little girl's giggle filled the air. He glanced over his shoulder to see Maria standing in the doorway, both hands planted over her mouth. She giggled again and pointed. "You're kissing." Will growled and lunged for her. She leapt out of his reach and sprinted toward the kitchen. "They're kissing, they're kissing, they're kissing, they're kissing."

He laughed and looked at Laura who buried her face in her hands. "I'm so embarrassed. I can't believe your niece caught us."

Prying her hands from her face, Will pulled her to her feet. "Don't worry about it. She sees plenty of kissy-kissy stuff between her parents."

Laura closed her eyes with a groan.

Settling into the couch, Will let out a muted whimper. His sister had worn them out with a four-hour bike ride on the trails of Fort Clinch, a local state park. She'd lied and said they were mildly challenging.

To her maybe.

With low-lying branches, rocks and stumps to jump, loose sand, steep inclines, and narrow, treacherous curves, the wooded trails were *definitely* more than mildly challenging. The only thing that had kept Will going was watching Laura's cute little rear as she pumped her bicycle through the paths.

"So, bro, I like your girlfriend." Veronica plopped down beside him on the couch.

He glared at her. "Go away. I hate you."

She gave him a pathetic little pat on the knee. "You're not worn out, are you?"

Will closed his eyes and dropped his head back with a moan.

"Here, I brought you a beer. Do you still love me?"

He inched open an eye and studied the icy bottle. Veronica waved it in front of him. He snagged it from her hand and took a gulp. "*Ahhh*, that's better. Where's Laura?"

"In Maria's room." Veronica leaned toward him. "Sooo, tell me about her."

"Strange. You called her my girlfriend a minute ago. I've never referred to her as my girlfriend. The last time I called somebody that was in high school."

"Well that's what she is, isn't she?"

Will took another swig. "I don't know. The term 'girlfriend' doesn't seem to apply to her in my mind. She's more special than that to me."

"I can see why. She's an amazing woman."

He looked down the hall toward Maria's room. "I've never felt this way about anybody. I'm excited, but scared, too. I don't know what the future holds. I don't know if this is called love. Hell, I've never been in love before. Half the time I'm with her I go with the flow and trust it all to pan out."

Tears gathered in Veronica's eyes. "I've been watching the two of you together. There's something wonderful there."

Will smiled at his sister's watery eyes. "Why are you crying?"

She sniffed. "I don't know. I'm so happy for you." She laughed and hugged her brother.

"Hey, you two, what's going on? What's up with the tears?" Rico asked.

Veronica grabbed her husband's hand. "Will's in love."

Will groaned and slung his arm over his eyes. "I can't believe you just told him that."

She patted his thigh. "Well, if I hadn't told him now, I would've told him later. What difference does a little timing make?"

Rico chuckled. "Come on, Will, let's check out that new construction down the street?"

Will jumped from the couch. "Gladly. Anything to get away from her." He glowered at his sister.

Veronica brightened. "Perfect. That'll give me time to invite Laura for a walk."

He shot her a warning look to which she fluttered her lashes. "Don't worry, I won't say anything I'm not supposed to."

Will gave Rico a "control your wife" look and made his way to Maria's room. Laura sat perched on a tiny stool, the left side of her hair hung in a dozen braids, curlers bobbed in the top, a clip held the back, and the right side was getting brushed by his niece. The smell of cheap hairspray permeated the room, and an assortment of combs, holders, and pins littered the bed. What an adorable picture they made.

He propped his shoulder in the door. "Looks like this place is an official hair salon."

Laura glanced up from some ribbons she was untangling. "Maria's making me beautiful."

"I can see that." Will walked over and placed a kiss on the tip of Laura's nose. "Rico and I are going down the street to check out a new construction site." He tweaked his niece's chin. "How 'bout you fix me up when I get back."

"Sure, Uncle Will."

Laura pondered his back as he left the room. Would he never cease to amaze her? He was going to play beauty parlor with Maria? Who would've guessed Will Burns, international rock star, would be such a fun-loving, easy-going, family man? What would *Tourist's* fans think?

They'd adore him even more. Good fortune seemed to follow some people. Laura had never been one of those people. Until recently. Until Will. He'd turned her life around.

Between horseback riding, a picnic on the beach, biking the trails, four wheeling on the dunes, building sandcastles, touring the island, and sailing, Laura felt like she'd packed two weeks worth of activities into the last four days.

She bent and retrieved a shell from the beach, smiling as she recalled Tai Bo last night. Veronica had been so enthusiastic about teaching the class. She'd begged for the family to join her. They'd piled in the car and headed to the local gym. Most of the people attending the class recognized Will, and it'd turned into an autograph session. He hadn't minded and even stayed an hour past time so some of the fans could run home and get their cameras.

"What are you thinking?" Veronica asked, interrupting Laura's thoughts.

She tossed the shell into the ocean. "What a wonderful time I've had here. I'll be sorry to leave tomorrow."

Veronica tucked her hands in her windbreaker. "I'm so glad you came."

They continued strolling, enjoying the crisp breeze. Will and Rico walked further up the beach, swinging Maria between them. Soon the sun would set, and they'd head home for grilled burgers.

"You've got a beautiful family."

Veronica grinned. "Thank you. We do make a nice looking unit even if I say so myself."

Laura laughed.

"I'll let you in on a little secret if you promise not to tell

Will." Veronica leaned in closer. "I'm trying to get pregnant."

"That's wonderful, but why don't you want your brother to know?"

"Because he wants to be an uncle again so badly he can't stand it. Every time I talk to him he asks me if I'm pregnant. I want to surprise him with the news when it happens."

"Well, I'm an expert at keeping secrets. So he won't hear a peep from my mouth."

"I haven't told anybody at all. You're the first person to know." Veronica skipped forward and spun a few circles. "It feels great to finally share that secret with somebody. I almost exploded trying to keep it in."

Laura jogged the few feet to catch up with her. Maria danced down the beach toward them, carrying something in her hand. When she reached them, she handed Laura a sand dollar, twirled and sprinted back to her father. Laura stared at the fragile shell in her hand.

I always wished for a family like this...fun, loving, kind-hearted.

Sixteen

Laura ran her finger over the crayon picture that she and Maria had completed. A purple mermaid with pink scales smiled up from the page. A silver dolphin danced on the water. Big billowy clouds floated in the sky.

Laura had found it tucked inside her duffel bag inscribed with, "I hope all your dreams are good ones. Love, Maria."

It'd been two weeks since the Christmas holiday. Laura had looked at that happy picture everyday.

Carefully, she folded the starched paper and slid it back inside her backpack. She grabbed an apple from the side pocket, polished it on her sweatshirt, hopped onto her stool, then kicked her legs up on the edge of the mixing board. Taking a crisp bite, Laura surveyed the stage. In twenty-minutes they'd do sound check. *Tourist* planned to perform Will and Laura's song tonight.

"Hello, Laura," a whisper floated across the air.

Laura paused in her crunching. Seconds ticked by.

"Hello, Laura," came the whisper again.

She forced the unchewed chunk of apple down her throat. She knew that eerie whisper. It'd been seven years since she'd heard it last. Moving only her eyes, she swept her gaze over the auditorium.

"Turn around and look at me," the voice hissed.

With a tense neck and locked muscles, Laura inched her head to the right and glanced over her shoulder.

Aunt Jane stood behind her.

Laura's legs fell from the edge of the soundboard. "Ar-are you real?"

* * *

Will strolled down the back hallway, whistling. He pushed through the door leading to the auditorium and hopped over a box of equipment. He hadn't seen Laura since yesterday afternoon. Between promotional work, concerts, early morning stage set-up, late night breakdown, and non-stop traveling, they were lucky if they stole ten minutes alone.

He'd picked up a Minneapolis patch for her duffel bag and wanted her to have it before sound check.

Peering across the concert hall toward her technical area, he saw a woman standing in front of Laura, looking very haughty and dominating. He watched as Laura slumped from her stool and grabbed the corner of it to steady herself. She looked shocked and horror-struck and clearly not happy to see the woman.

Will took off toward her.

Jane smirked. "Oh, yes, my darling niece. I'm real."

"H-how did you find me?"

"What? No, hello, Aunt Jane, I've missed you terribly. Didn't I teach you any manners?"

Laura inhaled a shaky breath and straightened her spine. "I said how did you find me?"

Jane pursed her lips. "Well, well, well. Look at how brave you've become, standing up to me like a big girl." She reached into her shoulder bag, pulled out a magazine, flipped through it, then held it up in front of Laura.

Laura looked from her aunt's face to the magazine. Colored pictures spread across two pages portraying her and Will at their most intimate moments. Hiding from the rain under the gazebo in Central Park, holding hands on a dimly lit street outside a pool hall in Texas, hugging on the escalator in the airport the day Bizzy left, kissing on the tarmac in Tennessee, jogging at his sister's house over Christmas.

Laura shut her eyes. It was the kind of publicity they'd

been trying to avoid. Who'd taken all those pictures?

Aunt Jane snapped the magazine back around. "'Will Burns, lead guitarist for *Tourist*, finds love with a roadie'," she read.

Laura opened her eyes. "What do you want?"

"So, you've found love have you?" Jane took a step forward. "What do I want?" She lifted the magazine and tapped Laura on the cheek. "I want you."

Refusing to cower down, Laura released her death grip on the stool and hiked her chin. Taller than her aunt, Laura purposefully looked down her nose at her. She knew what she wanted to say. She'd recited it hundreds of times over the years.

"You can't hurt me anymore," she began in a slow, even toned voice. "I'm through being intimidated and abused by you. I'm a grown woman with a new life, one that you are not a part of. I want you to leave now, and if you don't, I'll call security and have you removed from the premises."

Jane's eyes narrowed. "Why you inconsiderate brat. After all I did for you and this is how you treat me."

Will jogged up beside them. "What's going on here?"

Jane slid beady eyes to Will. "Who's this? Lover boy?"

Laura cleared her throat. "Will, this is my Aunt Jane."

Jane glared at her niece. "Apparently, you've forgotten everything I taught you. You're going to go to hell for this premarital fling you've got going on. Whoever thought you'd turn out to be such a whore."

"Hey," Will stepped forward.

Laura placed her hand on his arm and leveled a deadly stare on her aunt. "If anyone is going to hell, it's you. God, I'm sure, doesn't approve of the things you did to me."

"I gave you everything, and all you ever did was cause me problems," Jane hissed. "And don't you dare say I'm going to hell. I'm a God fearing woman."

Laura took a step forward and put her face right in Jane's. "You no longer have any control over me. You make me sick. I never want to see you again. Now leave, or I'll throw you out of this place myself."

Fury gathered in her aunt's eyes. Laura recognized the insane, twitchy look a second before Jane reared back and slapped her across the face. The unexpected impact sent her stumbling backward.

Will gripped her aunt's arm. "Security!"

Jane ripped her arm out of Will's grasp. She jabbed a finger in Laura's direction. "You will pay for this," she vowed and threw the magazine at her.

"There's nothing you can do to hurt me anymore," Laura yelled as her aunt flew from the auditorium.

Will didn't care if security got Jane or not. He spun to Laura who was following Jane's hasty retreat with her eyes. A red and white finger pattern marred her cheek.

He reached for her. "You okay?"

"I need to be alone," she answered and walked away.

He studied her back, wanting desperately to go to her, but knowing her well enough that she'd want time to think things through. With a sigh, Will scrubbed his fingers through his hair and looked down at the magazine. Every private moment that he cherished lay sprawled out in full color for the whole world to see.

"What's going on?" Ed asked, coming up beside him.

Will shook his head, at a loss for words.

"I saw what happened. I was up on stage. Is Laura okay?"

"She'll be alright." Will retrieved the magazine from the floor.

"Who was that woman? She looked familiar."

Will lifted his attention from the magazine. "What do you mean she looked familiar?"

Ed shrugged. "I don't know. I think I've seen her somewhere before."

"Where?"

"I don't know. Probably nowhere. I'm sure she's got one of those familiar faces." Someone yelled for Ed from the stage. He signaled them, then turned back to Will. "Listen, I've got a ton of work to do. You sure Laura's going to be okay?"

"Yep, I'll talk to her later."

"Okay then, but if I can help, let me know." Ed jogged down the aisle back to the stage.

Ed knew Laura's aunt, whether he realized it or not. Will was sure of it.

"How are you?" Will ventured guardedly when Laura opened her hotel door.

"Fine." She stepped aside to let him in.

He walked across her room and settled in the desk chair, relieved she hadn't turned him away. "Good show tonight," he said conversationally.

Laura closed the door and situated herself, cross-legged, in the center of the bed. "Yeah. You all did a good job with the new song."

In the pit of his stomach he'd been afraid she'd erect that icy barrier he hadn't seen in months.

"What are you smiling at?" she asked.

He didn't realize he *had* been smiling. "I was thinking how far you've come. If this had happened months ago, you'd be on the first plane out of here. And you certainly wouldn't have let me in your room."

Laura's lips curved into a peaceful smile. "Yeah, I have come a long way, haven't I?"

Will pulled the magazine from his back pocket and held it up. "I'm sorry about this. I had no idea these pictures had been taken. I suspected this one," he pointed to the picture of them hugging on the escalator. "I remember seeing a camera flashing, but the others–" he shook his head. "I guess my disguise doesn't work so well."

He'd never cared about pictures in magazines. He lived in the public eye and expected them. But the exploitation of his and Laura's relationship...it was too personal.

"It's okay. I was upset at first, but I'm fine now. Somewhere in the back of my mind I knew this would eventually happen."

Will blew out a long breath. "Thanks for taking it so good." He tossed the magazine into the garbage. "I was proud of you today, the way you handled your aunt."

"Thanks. At first I didn't think she was real, but when I realized she was, I felt like a little girl again, scared and unsure. But then an overwhelming flow of confidence filled my mind, and I recognized that I'm a grown woman, that she can't hurt me anymore. For the first time in my life I felt superior to her." She looked at him through wonder-filled eyes. "I'm taller than she is. I never realized that until today. I got satisfaction out of looking down my nose at her. Isn't that weird?"

Will smiled, his heart swelling with warmth and admiration. "No, it's not weird at all."

She sighed contentedly as her gaze drifted to the window. "Jane said I'd pay. I wonder what that means? She told me once that she'd kill me if I ever tried to run. I used to be so scared of that, consumed by it. But what can she do to me now?"

Kill her? Laura had never shared that with him before now.

He felt his teeth clamping together and told himself to stay calm. Pushing up out of the desk chair, Will crawled across the bed and stretched out on his back. He pulled Laura down beside him. "Idle threats. Don't worry about it."

She burrowed her cheek into his shoulder. "I'm not."

He lifted a handful of her hair, brought it to his face, and inhaled the freshly washed scent. Toying with the strands, Will stared at the ceiling, hoping to the heavens it really was an idle threat.

"Ed, can I have a minute with you?" Will asked, approaching him backstage the next day.

"Sure." He wiped his hands on a rag and tucked it in his back pocket. "What's up?"

"I'm sorry to bring this up, but do you remember telling me about your sister that day on the plane?"

Ed's expression flattened. He gave a brusque nod.

Clearly an uncomfortable subject, but Will forged ahead. "I saw you looking at a blue rabbit's foot. Can you tell me about it."

"Why?"

"Well, it looked very distinct and I was curious about it. I think I've seen it somewhere before."

Ed huffed an unamused chuckle. "I don't think so."

"What do you mean?"

"Because there's only two in the whole world, and my little sister had the other."

Will's pulse jumped to triple time. "You're right. I guess I made a mistake. Sorry." He wanted to ask why only two existed in the world, but knew he'd be pressing his luck.

Ed pulled the rag from his back pocket and went back to cleaning the generator, obviously ready to drop the discussion.

Knowing he was being pushy and rude, but not sure how to tactfully progress, Will asked, "Can I see it?"

Ed rolled an irritated glare toward him. "I don't have it on me."

"Can you tell me what it looks like?"

"Why?" Ed snapped.

"Because I'm curious."

Ed threw the rag down and got right in Will's face. "It's blue and has a silver clasp, and there's little stick figures engraved around the top of it. Does that satisfy your morbid curiosity?"

"Yes, thank you," Will muttered humbly.

Ed pushed him out of the way and charged off. Will wanted to explain the questioning. It was best to keep things to himself, though, until he could prove his hunch.

Ed had told Will that twenty years ago his family couldn't pay for a proper investigation into his sister's abduction and suspected murder. One thing Will possessed was plenty of money and the means to pay for a proper investigation.

An hour after his unpleasant query of Ed, Will dialed a private investigator recommended by a friend in the entertainment industry. A long time had transpired since Ed's little sister, Sandra, turned up missing. Will wasn't even sure a case that old *could* be investigated.

Armed with the bits and pieces of knowledge he'd accumulated, Will shared with the investigator everything he knew: five-year-old Sandra missing one day from her mom's garden, a description of the blue rabbit's foot, Laura's back ground including her name change from Franks to Genny, Aunt Jane's information and physical description, and Ed's comment that he'd seen Jane somewhere before.

After Will ended his conversation with the private investigator, he sat for a long time in his hotel room, mulling over everything, convinced a connection existed between Ed and Laura. Will hoped his suspicions came true. Because if they did, this was exactly what Laura needed to complete herself.

As Laura lit the vanilla scented candles in her hotel room, she remembered Jane's sudden and disturbing reappearance a few days ago. Her last words had been delivered in an idle threat. That's what Will had said, and Laura agreed. Aunt Jane was out of her life for good.

Will would be knocking on her door any minute now. Laura thought she'd be nervous about tonight, and she was, a little. But jitters from excitement, not fear, danced in her stomach. She'd worried about her lack of experience. Will would take things where they needed to go once she got them started. She'd wanted to wait until Valentine's Day to surprise him. But that still stretched weeks away, and now that she'd made the decision, she didn't want to wait.

Retrieving the grocery sack from the end table, Laura arranged the strawberries in a bowl, placed an assortment of chocolates on a plate, and positioned the wine and glasses next to them.

After almost twenty-six years of feeling alone in the world, wondering what she'd done to deserve her childhood, and experiencing bad luck around every corner, Laura finally felt her life swinging upward.

She'd landed the job of her dreams, and even though Jay had messed with things, that issue had resolved itself. With the help of Dr. Masters, Laura had worked through her upbringing and dealt with the painful memories. She would always wonder about her real mother and father, but knew not to dwell on such melancholy thoughts.

Masters had taught her to live in the present, plan for the future, and place the past where it belonged. Yet Laura had known she'd have to deal with her aunt in order to obtain inner peace, and that had happened a few days ago, finally putting closure on that part of her life.

Wandering into the bathroom, Laura checked her face in the mirror. She'd bought mascara and lip-gloss for the occasion. Would Will notice? Lifting her arm to her nose, she inhaled the peach scented lotion that she'd applied after her bubble bath. She'd never smelled so feminine and wonderful.

Will...

He'd turned her life around. With his never-ending patience, friendship, and witty humor, he brought an enticement to her existence that she never realized she needed. Her perpetual sense of loneliness had dissipated the moment she met him. After tonight, Laura would feel complete, emotionally and physically, like a normal woman.

A knock sounded on her door. Laura's stomach swooped to her feet. She took one last quick glance in the bathroom mirror, flicked out the light, hurried into the bedroom, swept her gaze around the room, assuring perfection, then inhaled a slow, fortifying breath.

She opened the door. Flickering candles caught Will's attention first, then the scent of vanilla wafted into the hall. Laura appeared from around the backside of the door dressed in a knee-length, white silk robe. She stood with one hand on the knob and one hand hidden behind her back. She'd left her hair loose and brushed it smooth and shiny. Her lips glistened like she'd just licked them.

She peered over his shoulder. "You better come in before someone wanders by and sees all this."

Will did as she requested. She closed the door behind him. He turned and continued to stare, more than aware of his erratic pulse.

Laura pulled a flower from behind her back and presented it to him. "It's a Bird of Paradise. The florist said it's a masculine flower."

He took the flower and held it poised in the air, too stunned to do much of anything else. Seconds later, Will remembered he should smell it and lifted it to his nose.

She indicated the room with a leisurely sweep of her hand. "Are you surprised?"

Will ran unsteady fingers through his hair. "Yep, you

could say that."

Laura walked over and poured them each a glass of wine. He followed her movement with his eyes, in awe of her relaxed confidence. He searched his mind for something to say and came up blank, like an awkward teenager on his first date.

She brought a glass to him. "To tonight," she toasted and clinked hers against his. They both took a sip, eyeing each other over the rims.

He swallowed the chardonnay and wandered over to the bank of windows overlooking the Chicago night skyline. Will took another sip of wine and refocused his vision on Laura's reflection behind him. She still stood in the same spot, holding her glass and watching his back. No wonder she'd turned him down when he'd asked her to spend their day off sightseeing. She'd been getting ready for tonight.

Will had fantasized about this night hundreds of times since they first met. He wanted everything to be perfect for her. He'd never expected her to initiate their lovemaking, and his heart melted into a warm puddle as he thought of her emotional journey to this pivotal point. Never in his life had he respected a woman more than Laura.

He turned to face her. "Candles, my flower, strawberries, wine. You've been busy."

Laura nodded in response and put her glass down on the end table. She reached for the belt of her robe and untied it. The silk slid down her body to her feet. "Make love to me, Will."

Seventeen

Rendered speechless and motionless, Will's throat convulsed in a nervous swallow.

Stunning.

Beautiful.

Lovely.

Goddess.

She'd chosen a peach colored, silk negligee that rode high on her thighs. Thin straps clung to her shoulders. The front dipped provocatively between her breasts.

"Touch me," she invited in a shaky voice, "before I lose my nerve."

Will quickly put his glass down and crossed the room. He reached for her hand and linked their fingers. "You look incredible," he whispered and placed a kiss to her bare shoulder. Wrapping his arms around her, he buried his face in her hair and inhaled her intoxicating scent. After a few deep breaths, he pulled away. "Laura, I need to say what's in my heart before we go any further."

Her lips curved into a sweet smile.

He lifted her hand and pressed his lips to her knuckles, gathering his thoughts, and when he felt ready, he lowered her fingers and lifted his eyes to hers. "Every since the first day I met you, I knew something was different. You had this barrier that intrigued me. I wanted to break through it and know you, really know you."

Will touched his fingers to her chest. "I wanted to know your heart," he glided his thumb across her forehead, "and your mind. The stronger our friendship became, the deeper I fell in love with you."

She glanced down to his chest. He put a finger under her chin and lifted until she looked him in the eyes again. "I love you, Laura. I've never said that to any other woman. You're the first."

He gazed at her with all the tenderness in his heart. "Sometimes I feel I can't go another minute until I see you, or hear you, or touch you. I never thought I'd get such joy out of a simple thing like your smile. You bring out every emotion in me. Happiness, sadness, anger, frustration. No other person has ever done that."

He took both her hands in his. "I admire and honor you. I watched you struggle to overcome your horrible past with such strength and bravery. You humble me. Inside and out, you're the most enchanting person I've ever known."

Will pressed a kiss to each eye. "The way you're looking at me right now makes my heart race."

He released her hands and skimmed his fingertips up her arms, over her shoulders, and down her back where the negligee's straps criss-crossed low. "Your skin amazes me. It makes me think of peaches and cream."

Laura's lips parted. Her chest began to rise and fall with heavy, slow breaths.

Will ran both hands up into her hair and then out, watching the candlelight flicker behind the cascading strands. "I've had so many fantasies about your hair falling like a curtain around me when we make love."

She blushed and looked away.

"That right there." He cradled her warm face in his hands and waited for her eyes to meet his. "The way your face goes flush makes me lustful." He stroked his thumbs across her cheeks. "Thank you for sharing your heart with me, for giving me tonight. I'll treasure it always."

"Will, I-I-lo-lo–"

He silenced her with his lips. "Don't feel pressured to tell me you love me. Tell me when you're ready, when you feel it in every particle of your being."

Laura closed her eyes and absorbed everything he'd said. Perfect, eloquent words. Everything she'd ever hoped to hear him say.

He moved away from her, and she opened her eyes to see him taking off his shirt, then he tossed it on the bed and came back to stand in front of her.

Hesitantly, she lifted her fingers and stroked them across his chest, mesmerized by the fine, black hairs moving under her touch. She lowered her hands to his abdomen and traced the ridges of his muscles. They twitched under her caress.

"You're so different from me," she marveled.

Will grabbed her hands to still them. "Are you absolutely sure about this? It's going to kill me to turn back, but if you have the least bit of doubt, I will."

And he would. Laura knew he would. "I'm sure." She smiled. "I'm absolutely sure. This night, you, me, making love, I need it. I want it. I'm ready for it."

He pulled her into his arms and kissed her deep and long, circling her tongue. While he held her in his embrace, he slid the straps of her negligee over her shoulders, down her arms, and across her hips to float to her feet.

Will released her and stepped back. His eyes traveled down the length of her body and back up again. "I knew you'd be extraordinary, but I had no idea how perfect you'd been created."

Lifting his hand, he traced the shape of her breast with his index finger, then rubbed his thumb back and forth across her nipple.

Laura caught her breath at the tingle that slowly spread across her chest and down through her stomach. She stared at his face, unable to look away. He seemed hypnotized by her breasts as he made love to them with his eyes and fingers. The longer he touched them, the more sensitized they became. He lowered his mouth to the left one and a wave of desire crashed over her body. Her head fell back in utter surrender.

He moved his lips up her chest and nibbled a path from her shoulder to her ear. "I can feel your pulse hammering in your neck," he murmured and circled around to the back of her. Reaching from behind, he brushed his hands over her sides, around her stomach, and pressed her against him.

She looked down at his hands resting on her lower abdomen and watched as he inched his fingers lower and caressed her more intimately. Laura inhaled a sharp breath and hunched forward. The throbbing sensation that she'd felt increased with his strokes.

"You feel so good." He nipped her shoulder, and sliding his finger away, came back to stand in front of her.

"Take your pants off," she commanded quietly.

"No. You do it," he challenged with a devilish gleam in his eyes.

Laura reached down and unsnapped his khaki pants, lowered the zipper. She looped her thumbs in the waistband and pushed them down his hips. Daffy Duck boxers stared back at her. "Cute."

Will kicked his shoes off. "I thought you'd like them."

She knelt down and pulled his pants and socks the rest of the way off. Then she reached for his boxers and paused, staring at the protruding portion, losing some of the bold sensuality that had driven her previous movements.

"I'd never hurt you," he said softly.

Laura looked up at him. "I know. I want to see you, all of you. I just lost my nerve for a second, though."

"It's okay." He held out his hand. "Come back up."

She slipped her hand into his, and when she was on her feet again, he wrapped his arms around her and cupped her hips. Lifting her a few inches off the ground, he carried her to the bed and threw back the covers. "Red satin sheets? You thought of everything, didn't you?"

She nodded, pleased with his surprised tone, and nuzzled her cheek against his. "I like it when your face hasn't been shaved."

"You do?" Will laid her on the bed. "Well, I'll have to remember that." He rubbed his whiskered chin across her stomach and up between her breasts, then stretched out on top of her and nestled his mouth into the curve of her neck.

Laura closed her eyes and moaned a sigh.

"I don't know why you made that sound, but I like it."

"It feels good."

"What does?"

"Our naked bodies together."

"I'm not naked yet."

"Well, what are you waiting for?"

Will chuckled and rolled off of her. "That's all you had to say." He removed his boxers and stretched back out on top of her.

Curious, Laura ventured, "Can I see?"

He buried his face in her hair, took a deep breath, then moved to his back. She propped herself up on her elbow and stared down at his erection. "Is it okay for me to touch you?"

Will stroked his hand lovingly over her hair and nodded.

She reached out and barely touched the tip, then trailed her fingers over the lines and contours, amazed at his texture and feel. Lightly, she grasped it in her hand, unsure of the amount of pressure.

He pushed her over onto her back. "Sorry," he breathed, "but that's it for now."

"Did I hurt you? I wasn't sure-I didn't know–"

"You didn't hurt me. I'm very sensitive right now. I want you so badly I just can't take much touching."

Will slid down her body and sucked her right nipple into

his mouth, scraping it on its release. With his hand, he smoothed a line from her neck, down between her breasts, over her stomach, and along the outer length of her leg. He brought his fingers up the inside and caressed her intimately again.

Laura moaned and closed her eyes. He removed his hand and settled his leg between hers, leaving her pulsing, desiring more. He pushed against her with his thigh and took her left nipple into his mouth. She dug her fingers into the back of his arms and arched her hips, searching for release.

He moved down her body, leaving a trail of warm, moist kisses over her stomach and thighs, and worked his way back up, parting her legs with his own. He lifted the back of her knees to cradle his hips and gazed into her eyes.

"I love you," he whispered and pushed slowly inside of her.

She gasped.

He stopped moving. "You okay?"

Laura gave him a reassuring smile. "It's not painful. It feels full. Complete."

He covered her mouth and shared a long, tender kiss. While their lips were sealed, he pulled out of her and carefully pushed back in. They stayed that way for a few seconds, then she moved her hips, wanting more.

Will slipped his hand between their bodies and stroked her. She lifted up and blindly latched on to his neck with her mouth. He slid out, back in, continuing to caress her with his fingers. She clamped down on his neck muscles with her teeth and heard her own breath rushing in and out, then she moved her hips again, making the pulsing sensation migrate up inside of her. She moved them again, then again, until her hips gyrated to their own rhythm.

He pulled his hand from between their bodies, gripped her hips, buried his face in her neck, and thrust to meet each of her upward arches.

She dug her nails into his backside and held him in place while she pumped, desperate to satisfy the throbbing, knowing it lay right within her reach. Then it hit her, pushing her deep into the mattress. She sucked in a breath, and another, while every nerve in her body spasmed.

Will pressed into her a few more times and with a groan, dropped lifelessly on top of her. She wrapped limp arms around his back, and they lay in that position until their breathing had slowed back to normal.

Laura moved first, lifting a lazy finger to trail down the middle of his back. He jolted when she ran over a sensitive spot. She curbed a smile and skimmed that spot again. He jerked, and she laughed.

"You're doing that on purpose," he mumbled.

She nipped his shoulder. "Yes."

Lifting his head, Will propped himself on his elbows and kissed her nose. "That was amazing."

Laura smiled and traced the outline of his dark brows with her index finger, recalling the details of the last hour. She'd responded to his love making without thinking, driven by some inner force to feel satisfaction. She hadn't any idea what to do. Her body had directed her. Had she done everything right?

Will brushed her hair across the pillow. "What are you thinking?"

She fixed her attention to a freckle on his shoulder. "Was that the way it's supposed to work?" She swallowed, feeling foolish about her question. "Did I do everything right?"

He moved his head into her line of vision, forcing her to look at him. "I can't describe to you how perfect it was. I've had sex before, but I've never made love. Loving you elevates the intimacy to a place I didn't think existed. And you," he rubbed his nose against hers, "responded more freely than I ever expected. You have such passion hiding under that quiet demeanor of yours. And you know what the best part is?"

Laura shook her head, looking so earnest it melted Will's heart.

"It's going to get better and better each and every time we make love."

She nuzzled her face into his neck. "Thank you for saying all that."

Will bent his head and cuddled her nuzzling face. "You're welcome." He lifted up and looked down the length of their bodies where they remained joined. The evidence of her virginity had smeared on both of them. "What do you say we get a shower?"

She nodded, and he pushed up off of her, grabbing her hand as he went. They walked across the hotel room to the bathroom.

"I can't believe I'm walking naked, holding hands with you."

He glanced over his shoulder. "Does it make you uncomfortable?"

"No. I feel desirable, womanly, special. I'm being silly I guess."

Tugging her into the bathroom, Will closed the door and backed her up against it. "You are very desirable." He pressed his body against hers. "And womanly."

He dropped a quick kiss on her lips and turned toward the shower. While he adjusted the temperature, she piled her hair on top of her head in a haphazard knot. When the water felt right, he moved behind her and watched in the mirror as she tucked a few last strands out of the way. He moved his lips along the back of her exposed neck and slid his hands around to cup her breasts. Perfect breasts. Medium size. Enough to fill his hands and nothing more.

"I can't keep my hands off you," he muttered against her neck. "It doesn't matter where I touch you. I love the feel of your skin."

"I like the feel of yours, too."

Will smiled at her sweet comment. He linked fingers with her and stepped into the shower. She hovered in the back, looking awkward and unsure of what to do. He wanted to hug her and rock her and kiss her and ravish her, all at the same time.

She reached for the bar of soap. He grabbed it from her. "That's my job." He worked it between his fingers until it foamed.

He put the bar down, then smoothed his hands between her legs, keeping his eyes glued to her adorable, wide-eyed, shocked expression. A look that would forever be implanted in his brain.

After he washed away the remnants of their lovemaking, he handed the soap to her. "Your turn."

She took the soap and lathered it, then gently touched him, clearly unsure of the amount of pressure to use. Will covered her hand with his and moved it over him, showing her she didn't have to be so careful. Quickly, he grew aroused. Laura snapped a surprised look from his erection to his eyes.

Will backed her up against the shower and grasped her hips. "I think we better get out of here before I ravish you again."

"That wouldn't be so bad," she replied in a sensual, husky voice.

He studied her face for a long moment, deciding. "There's nothing I want more, believe me. But I don't want to make you sore. Let's go drink some wine and have some strawberries."

Ten minutes later, they sat cross-legged on the bed, facing each other. Laura had slipped back into her white, silk robe. Will wore his boxers again. A bowl of strawberries and a plate of chocolates rested between them. He took a strawberry and held it up to her lips. She bit into it, and he popped the rest in to his mouth.

Laura swallowed her bite. "Your neck is bruised. I think I did that, didn't I?"

Will chuckled. "Yep, you did. And I loved every minute of it."

She laughed at that and plucked another strawberry from the bowl. They sat there for a few more minutes, munching on strawberries, sipping wine, silently watching each other. All he could think about was how much he loved her and wanted to share his life with her.

Right when he started to imagine their future together, it hit him. "We didn't use protection. Oh, shit. I can't believe I didn't even think of it. I'm sorry. I should've been more responsible. There's no excu–"

"I'm on the pill."

He cocked a brow. "When did you do that?"

"After the cabin. After you asked me to make love."

"So you went to a doctor and everything?"

She nodded.

"Well how did it go?" What a huge step for her.

Laura glanced away in obvious discomfort with the question.

He grabbed the back of her neck, pulled her forward, and planted a kiss on her lips. "We're lovers now. We're gonna talk about stuff like this. Don't be embarrassed."

Laura gave a shy little shrug. "I'm sorry. It's a lot to get used to, that's all."

"So, how was the doctor's visit?"

"It went okay. Better than expected, actually. I chose a woman doctor. She was real good about everything."

"Good. I'm happy." He picked a chocolate off the plate and bit into it. "*Mmmm*, my favorite."

Will dipped his finger into the hollow part and scooped out some caramel. He shot her a devilish grin and parted the lower half of her robe. He smeared the caramel along her inner thigh, then leaned forward and licked it off.

"Your inner thighs are shaking." He nipped where he'd licked and sat back.

Laura blinked a few times. "What?"

"I said you're shaking." He squeezed her inner thigh. "One of the after effects of good loving."

Laura regarded him through narrowed eyes. "You enjoy setting me off balance, don't you?"

Will chuckled and pressed her back into the pillows. "There's nothing I enjoy more."

She poked him in the ribs. He laughed and rolled across the bed with her, sending the strawberries and chocolates to the floor.

"Daffy Duck's coming to get you."

"What?"

He peered down at his boxers. She followed his eyes. A Daffy Duck head poked out with his erection.

Laura giggled. "Oh my God, that's so funny looking."

"Hey, don't give Daffy a complex."

A siren screamed past the hotel. Will awoke to the sound with his face lost in blond hair, Laura's naked bottom snuggled into his stomach, and his hand nestled warmly between her breasts. His lips curved into a content, sleepy smile. He could *definitely* wake up like this every morning for the rest of his life and never tire of it.

Will lifted his head and squinted at the shaft of light beaming through the slit in the curtains. What time was it? Seven in the morning, he noticed, locating the digital read-out on top of the television. Laura had to report to work at nine. He had a meeting with his agent at ten. Plenty of time for a leisurely breakfast.

He peered over her shoulder at her face. Still sleeping. Moving her hair aside, he pressed a kiss to her neck. "Good morning, sleepyhead."

Laura stirred and muttered something and turned her face toward the pillow. He wrapped his leg over hers and rolled her onto her back. With a low moan, she slit open one eye.

Will chuckled and stretched out on top of her, nuzzling her neck.

She rubbed her eyes. "Morning."

"Breakfast?"

She nodded.

He slid down her body, leaving a trail of quick kisses in his wake, and rolled off the bed. He padded over to the phone on the dresser and hit the room service button. While he waited for someone to pick up, Will turned and studied a very sleepy Laura. She'd moved back over onto her side and pulled the sheet up around her, leaving exposed a long leg and narrow back. His thoughts drifted to last night…

"Hello, is anybody there?" a man questioned from the other end of the line.

Will snapped back to reality. "Sorry, I'd like to order a plate of fruit, croissants, and strong coffee." He put his hand over the receiver. "Laura, does that sound good?" She groggily waved a hand in the air. He bit back a smile and finished, "I guess that's it."

After hanging up the phone, he crawled across the bed and rolled her onto her back again. "You're very distracting." He playfully sucked a nipple into his mouth.

Laura smiled and stretched her arms above her head. Will smoothed his hands over the entire length of her body.

She stretched again with a satisfied sigh. "I want to wake up like this every morning."

He nipped the inside of her elbow. "Now *that* I can do."

Thirteen days later on February 13, the day before Valentine's Day, Will entered his Miami hotel suite and headed straight to the bathroom. Laura would be arriving soon. She'd called thirty-minutes ago to tell him she was running late. He'd sensed the irritation in her tired voice and knew she was having a bad day.

He opened the bag he'd just bought from the hotel's salon and took out a bottle of massage oil. Smiling to himself, he conjured up an image of a naked Laura stretched across his bed while he worked the knots out of her sore muscles. Of course then one thing would lead to the next…

Will chuckled as he threw the bag away and turned to get the tub ready for her bubble bath. The last two weeks had gone by in a blur. They'd made love almost every day, even though their busy schedules hadn't afforded them much free time. Laura had surprised him with her healthy sexual appetite. Last week he'd put her on top, and since then she'd managed to get them in that position frequently.

She still hadn't told him she loved him, and that bothered him more and more each day. He felt it, though, every time she looked into his eyes, or smiled at him, or touched him, or made love to him. She didn't understand the emotion. He suspected she didn't really believe in it either. Why would she? Aunt Jane had certainly never showed her love.

Will flicked out the bathroom light and made his way into the living room. *Patience.* Laura would say the words when she felt ready.

Plopping onto the couch, he reached for the remote and spotted a maid's cart in the corner of the room. Strange. The cleaning staff didn't usually leave their stuff sitting around like that. He walked over to the cart and pulled it across his suite toward the door. *Heavy.* He hadn't realized these carts weighed so–

"Surprise!" A woman popped out of the laundry bag.

"What the–" Will stumbled backward and watched as she stepped from the cart onto the carpeted floor.

He stared at her, too shocked to do much of anything else. She was dressed in a French maid's uniform, complete with black garters, hose, and heels. She gave him a seductive smile and sauntered toward him.

Will backed away from her approach. "Ho-how did you get in here?"

She shrugged skinny shoulders, tossed her red hair, and stepped closer. "Doesn't matter."

Gaining back his coherence, he stopped his retreat. "You need to leave."

She ran a red-tipped nail down his chest and stomach and pressed her body against his. "No, I don't. I'm here for you." She fluttered her lashes coyly. "What ever will you do with me now?"

Gingerly, he grabbed her shoulders and tried to push her off of him. "Listen, stop this now. You have to leave."

She stood on tiptoes and brought her wet, red lips to his neck. "Come on, baby. I won't tell if you won't."

Laura stepped into the hotel's elevator.

Irritable.

No, that didn't describe her mood.

Mad.

A little better.

Fired up.

Getting closer.

Downright pissed off.

Yeah, that would do it.

It had all started that morning when the rain forced her and Will to cancel their run. Then, she'd showed up at the performance hall thirty-minutes early only to discover she was actually an hour late to a production meeting, which ticked her off because she'd double-checked her calendar the night before.

By mid-morning things had worsened. One of the semis

had gotten lost. Unfortunately, it happened to be the one carrying all the sound equipment. It finally arrived after lunch, but the delay had put Laura's crew hours behind all the other stage workers.

The venue's manager had been under her skin. Apparently, he wasn't comfortable with a woman sound engineer. He'd spent the whole day looking over her shoulder, questioning her work. The man had no concept of tone. Every word out of his mouth had been delivered in a scream. It'd split her head every time he spoke.

Maybe that was why she had a headache.

The elevator dinged and Laura limped out, cursing the stupid idiot who hadn't taped down the cables. She'd been walking, looking at her clipboard and not the floor, and caught her toe under the untaped cable. Her clipboard had gone one way, she the other, causing her to sprain her ankle *and* bruise her wrist.

Laura came to a stop in front of Will's door. She balanced on her good foot while she rummaged in her backpack for his key. All she wanted was a hug from Will and a Jack and Coke. She found the key and took a deep breath, ready for the end of her day.

But when she opened his door, what she saw put the cherry on top of her already horrible day.

Will glanced over at her. A frantic look crawled across his face. "Laura, this isn't what it looks like."

The redheaded, French maid looked over her shoulder. "Uh, oh. I've caused a lover's quarrel." She giggled and stepped away from Will. "Oopsy."

Laura clinched her teeth together and leveled a lethal glare on the tramp. She limped across the room, grabbed the redhead around the arm, and marched her to the door.

"Hey, ease up," the woman whined. "You don't have to be so rough."

Laura thrust her into the hall. "Don," she snapped and watched as the bodyguard jogged toward her.

"Come on lady." He took her from Laura's grip. "Let's go. You've had your fun."

Laura hobbled back into Will's suite, yanked the maid's cart across the floor, shoved it out into the hall, slammed the door behind it, then limped into the kitchenette. She jerked open the refrigerator, grabbed some ice cubes and threw them in a glass, popped a can of Coke, added some Jack Daniels, pushed herself up onto the counter top, closed her eyes, and took a long sip.

"Laura, you've got to believe me. I had no idea that woman was in here."

How is it possible to have so many terrible things happen in one day? Isn't there some law of physics that applies?

"I swear. I came out of the bathroom and there she was. She must have snuck past security in that cart."

Laura rubbed her fingers between her eyes. *One little thing goes wrong and that leads to another, then another, and another. God help me, the rest of my night better be good.*

Will touched her arm. "Laura? I'm dying here. Say something."

She opened her eyes and stared into his desperate, pleading ones. Confused by his expression, she recalled the things he'd just said. "Don't worry about it. It's already forgotten."

"Oh…you're not mad?"

"At you? No. At everything else? Yes."

"Want to tell me about it?"

Laura took another sip and then unloaded every miserable detail of her day.

When she finished, he blew out a quick breath. "Jeez, your day *has* sucked."

She felt the first smile of the day curve her lips, content

and happy to have Will. Someone to talk to, someone who listened. She took another sip and studied him over the rim, thinking of the scene she'd walked in on. "Does that kind of thing happen to you often?"

"That woman? It's happened once before. Lots try, but security usually catches them."

Laura grabbed a napkin from the counter top. "Come here."

Will stepped between her legs and cradled his arms around her backside. She rubbed the right side of his neck. "You've got her lipstick smeared on you."

He leaned his head sideways to give her better access. "Ya know, you looked sexy manhandling that floozy. I got all weak in the knees watching you take control."

She tossed the napkin into the sink and wrapped her arms around his neck. "I've been thinking about this all day."

Will kissed her lips. "What?"

"Jack Daniels and Will Burns."

He nuzzled the underside of her chin. "In that order?"

"*Hmmm*...maybe I thought of you first."

Will pinched her butt. "You'd better have been thinking of me first."

Laura jerked and laughed.

He unzipped her jacket. "I've got a tub full of hot bubbles waiting for you and me."

Her stomach did a slow roll. "Oh?"

Will slid the windbreaker over her shoulders. "And massage oil for afterwards."

"For you or me?"

He scooted her off the counter to straddle him and walked toward the bathroom. "You first. We'll see about me later."

She tightened her grip around his neck and pressed her body closer. "That doesn't sound fair."

"Oh, believe me," Will growled into her neck. "It's more

than fair."

Laura awoke next to Will. Her first Valentine's Day with a sweetheart. She glanced over at him. He lay spread out in what she'd learned was his favorite sleeping position–on his back with his left hand flung above his head, his right one straight down next to his body, and his legs separated by three feet of space. She smiled and fought back the urge to touch him. She couldn't wake him, not until she returned.

Quietly she slid from the bed, grabbed her clothes, and tiptoed into the bathroom. A few minutes later, she emerged and made her way out the door and down to the hotel's lobby. She'd prearranged with the gift shop to have a basket stuffed with all his favorite things. Chocolate covered caramels, Garfield boxers, macadamia nut coffee, Heineken beer, the latest Sports Illustrated, a Laker's ball cap, and a pack of cotton candy flavored bubble gum.

Laura loved him. And she planned to tell him as soon as she returned to his suite. She'd purposefully waited until Valentine's Day to share those three special words with him. She suspected he'd be more thrilled with them than the basket.

He'd been so patient with her over the last couple of weeks, never pressuring her to say the words. But she'd seen the hopeful expectancy in his eyes, even though he'd tried to disguise it.

Smiling, she opened the door to the gift shop. The lady with whom Laura had placed the order looked up from the register. "Oh, hi. You're right on time. I've got it in the back."

Laura watched her rush down the aisle and disappear through the rear door. She wandered over to the magazine rack and idly perused, waiting…

What she saw on display, right in front, drained every ounce of life-pumping blood from her body.

Eighteen

After one good whole-body stretch, Will slid his hand across the bed, intending to coerce Laura into some Valentine morning lovemaking. His fingers found nothing but empty sheets.

He opened his eyes and sat up. "Laura?"

No answer.

"Laura," he called a little louder.

Silence.

Will rolled from the mattress and shuffled to the bathroom. Dark. Nothing. He walked back into the living room, his gaze sweeping the area, looking for her clothes.

Gone.

Sitting on the edge of the bed, he picked up the phone and dialed her room extension. But after a half dozen rings, he clicked off and connected with the front desk. They told him they'd seen Laura walk into the gift shop an hour earlier. He thanked them and punched in that number.

"Yes, Mr. Burns, the young woman was in here an hour ago, but she disappeared. She didn't even take her basket with her."

Basket? What basket? He hung up the phone and pulled on jog pants and a T-shirt. He poured himself a glass of juice and stood in the kitchen sipping, staring at the door to his suite. She'd walk in any moment. She probably ran down the street to get something from a convenience store.

But when ten more minutes crawled by, he set his glass down and stuck his head out the door. "Roger," he called to the bodyguard on post. "Have you seen Laura?"

Roger looked up from down the hall. "Yes, sir. She went

into her room about an hour ago."

Will furrowed his brows. "Oh, is she still in there?"

"Yes, sir."

"Thanks," he mumbled and closed the door.

He picked up the phone and dialed her extension again. After a dozen rings, he hung up, snatched her key off his dresser, and made his way down the hall to her room.

Will knocked, which made him feel odd, he hadn't knocked on her door in weeks. But when she didn't answer, he slipped her key into the slot and let himself in.

She was sitting on the corner of the bed with her back to the door, staring out the windows. "Laura?" he ventured, stepping inside.

"Go away," she croaked.

His heart leapt into his throat. He'd never heard her voice sound like that. He closed the door and took a couple steps toward her. "What is it?"

"I said go away."

Something was wrong. Something was *really* wrong. He moved around the bed to stand in front of her. In a white-knuckled clench, she gripped a rolled up magazine. No emotion registered on her stony face. She didn't even raise her eyes to meet his.

He knelt down in front of her and touched her knee. "What is it? Talk to me."

She said nothing.

Will studied her blank eyes, then lowered his attention to the magazine. Whatever was bothering her had something to do with the tabloid. He reached for it, but she tightened her grip.

"It's okay," he reassured her softly. "Let me see."

He put his hand over her fist and pried her stiff fingers away. She stood, and in one swift abrupt motion, dropped the magazine in his lap and walked to the other side of the room.

Perplexed, Will followed her movement with his eyes. She folded her arms and stared at the wall, putting her back to him. He spread the crumpled pages out on the bed.

A knobby-kneed young girl, probably six-years-old, stood in full color on the front page. She stared back at him through huge, sad, green eyes. Her long, blond hair had been parted down the middle and brushed straight to hang behind her shoulders and down her back. She wore a short, yellow, frilly dress and white ankle socks. Her face held a stoic expression as if she'd never seen happiness in her life. The headline read, 'Born in a gutter. Twenty-five years later the truth is revealed. Does Will Burns know?'

His heart banged against his chest wall as he turned the page. Pictures of Laura at various ages littered the four-page spread. All of them looked much like the cover depicting her in ridiculously ruffled dresses, her face void, her eyes hazed in a brainwashed gloss.

The tabloid wove Laura's life story. Her mother had been a schizophrenic, drug-addicted prostitute who got pregnant from one of her tricks. After unsuccessfully trying to abort with a coat hanger, she had the baby in a filthy alley behind a dumpster. She wrapped it in some paper she found in the trash and carried it to her sister's house, Laura's Aunt Jane. Jane had taken the two in with a loving heart, and two weeks later, Laura's mother committed suicide, leaving Jane to raise the little girl.

The story described Laura as an emotionally unstable child who would lock herself in her room and refuse to eat or bathe or go to school. Sometimes she would even refuse to dress and walked around naked all day. She was a social outcast. The kids in the neighborhood were scared of her. As Laura grew into a teenager, she turned into a deceitful, wild child. She skipped classes, hooked up with a different boy every week, started using drugs, became addicted to pornographic magazines, and eventually ran away from home.

Fury gathered in Will as he read on. The reporter had interviewed Aunt Jane and quoted her as saying, "I haven't seen my dear niece since she was seventeen. I heard she's working for some rock 'n roll band now. I fear she's turned into her mother with the drugs and sex. I even heard she was a lesbian for a while. Schizophrenia is genetic. I always thought she showed signs of that disorder. I raised her in a loving, Christian home. I provided the best clothes and music lessons and church. I even refused to marry a man because he didn't want any children. My Laura was more important to me. My arms are open if she wants to come home."

Will balled up the pages and hurled it across the room. "This is bullshit," he hissed. "Laura, I don't want you to worry about this. It's a bunch of lies. Anybody can see that. We're going to sue." He marched over to the phone. "I'm calling my lawyer right now."

"Stop," she ordered quietly.

He glanced up from punching in the numbers. "What?"

Laura turned around to face him. Her eyes had taken on an odd, eerie gleam. "I said stop." Her jaw hardened into a square line. "Put the phone down."

Will did as she requested, eyeing her warily.

She turned and walked to the other end of the room, her arms still folded as she studied the floor beneath her feet. "I always wondered about my mother and father. Jane never told me the details, just that they didn't want me anymore."

"Laura, it's lies. You've got to realize that."

She stopped pacing and leveled an icy stare on him. "How do you know that?"

"Because…because…" he couldn't tell her that he'd hired a private investigator and she might be Ed's sister. What if it weren't true? It would crush her. Until Will saw the factual report he had to keep his mouth shut. No matter what stood at stake. "Because everyone knows that magazine makes money off false stories and fabrications."

"True. You and I both know that most of that crap is a twisted lie. I believe the stuff about my parents, though."

He reached out his hand, even though the space of a room separated them. "No. Don't say that."

"Why? Don't you want to be humping the daughter of a schizophrenic prostitute?"

Will flinched. Her voice had taken on a bitter quality that unsettled him. He crossed the room to her, but didn't touch her. "You're upset right now."

Laura let out a low, sardonic chuckle. "You don't get it do you?"

He didn't recognize this Laura. She almost seemed evil. "Get what?"

"You, me, us. What was I thinking?"

Blood rushed to his extremities, making him both hot and cold at the same time.

She bent and retrieved the magazine that he'd thrown. "I want to know who I pissed off in heaven."

He wet his lips. "What are you talking about?"

Laura snapped the magazine in his face. "This. My whole sad, pathetic life. Aunt Jane." She narrowed her eyes at him. "Who?" she demanded, her voice raising an octave. "Who did I piss off in heaven to have dealt me this life? What did I ever do to anybody to deserve the crap that happens to me?" She snapped the magazine again. "Who?" she shouted.

Will grabbed her upper arms. "You didn't do anything. You're the kindest, most wonderful woman I've known. I lo–"

She threw his hands off of her. "Shut up. You don't know what you're talking about."

"Yes I do." He took a step toward her. "I love you, Laura. I want to spend my whole life with you. And I think you love me, too."

Laura covered her ears with her hands and turned away. "No I don't. I don't believe in love."

He took her arm and spun her to face him. "Yes you do. You feel it with me every time we're together and even when we're apart."

She tore her hands from her ears and shoved him in the chest, sending him sprawling across the bed. "You can't have a life with me," she spat. "I have mental illness running in my blood, not just my mother, but look at Jane." Laura jabbed a finger in his direction. "You're famous. The public loves you. Bad luck follows me everywhere." She threw the magazine at him. "Take a good look at that, because you're going to have to answer to the media about all of that crap."

Will rolled from the bed and went to her again. "None of that matters. Please. We can be happy together. Build a life. Have a family."

"Who are you kidding?" she snapped. "My past will forever haunt us. It won't blow over. It'll keep coming up right when we least expect it. And a family? I can't have a family with you. What kind of mother do you think I'll be? I'll pass my mental problems on to our kids. I'll abuse them. I don't know how to be a mother. And our kids would have to live with that," she pointed at the magazine. "They'll be teased by other kids, and they'll wonder about me and question my past."

Laura pressed her fingers into her eyes. "God, I wish she would have just made good on her threat to kill me."

He fought back a wave of nausea. "Don't ever say that."

"You," she poked his chest with her finger. "My whole life was fine until I met you. Now everything I've tried to forget and put behind me is splashed across the media. I'm humiliated and embarrassed." She pointed toward the door. "Get out."

A sob lodged in his throat. He reached for her. "What are you doing?"

She turned away from him and covered her face with her hands. "Get out," she moaned.

With tears falling down his cheeks, he backed toward the door. He took one last look at her and slipped out. As he made his way back to his suite, a deliveryman approached him.

"Mr. Burns, this was left in the gift shop hours ago. It has your name on it."

Will mumbled his thanks and took the basket inside. He opened the envelope and read the card. "Happy Valentine's Day! Here are all your favorite goodies. Enjoy! Love, Laura."

Love, Laura.

Gripping the card in his fist, he dropped to his knees and fell onto his side. He lay there curled up, staring at the carpet for what felt like hours until a maid let herself in and found him.

By that afternoon, Laura had arranged for Ed to take over her position. She turned in a letter of resignation to *Tourist*, packed everything, and left. Will didn't find out about it until late the next morning.

"You look like hell," Eric said, stepping into Will's suite.

"What do you want?"

His best friend closed the door and made himself at home on the couch. "When was the last time you showered or shaved or slept, for that matter?"

Will walked into the kitchen and poured himself another cup of coffee. "Are you here for a reason or to bug the piss out of me?"

"We have a show tonight. You've got to get your act together."

Will took a sip. "The show must go on."

"I take it you heard about Laura's resignation."

"Yep."

"And that she took off and nobody knows where she

went."

"Yep." Will downed a gulp, wincing at the scalding in his throat. "Is there a reason for this conversation?"

Eric pushed off the couch and made his way over to the kitchen. He propped his elbows on the divider island and stared at Will for a good minute. "Everybody around here knows that story's a bunch of filth. But I'm telling you, the media is swarming outside this hotel. The next week is going to be hell for you. The press will hound you until you feel you're at the end of your rope."

"I know. I've got one thing to say to them. No comment."

"You know that's not good enough."

"Well it's going to have to be." Will tossed his coffee into the sink.

He charged out of the kitchen and into the bathroom where he stripped and stepped into the shower. Through the glass enclosure he saw Eric plop down on the toilet.

"Are you going after her?"

"No."

"Why the hell not?"

"Because she doesn't want to see me."

"You believe that? Will, she's hurt. She needs time to lick her wounds."

"I realize she's hurt, but she's supposed to lean on me, team up with me, fight this with me, not push me away."

"You love each other. Everyone can see that."

Will let out a humorless chuckle. "Try telling her that."

"Give her a few days to calm down, then go after her."

"No." Will squeezed some shampoo into his palm and lathered his head.

"I bet Bizzy knows where she is."

Will paused. Bizzy *would* know where Laura had gone. He could call her, ask, but Laura had probably sworn her friend to secrecy. He ducked his head under the spray. Bizzy would tell him. He'd convince her. Will shut off the shower, grabbed a towel, and stepped out.

Eric gave him a knowing smile. "I knew that'd get you to thinking."

Will quickly dried off and wrapped the towel around his waist. "Alright. You've got a point. Doesn't matter. I'm not going after her. Ever since I met her last summer, I've done nothing but pursue her. She's got to come to me this time."

"What are you talking about?"

Squirting some shaving cream onto his fingers, Will lathered his face. "She hurt me. I gave her my heart. She threw it back in my face. I pleaded with her, talked about life together, family. I'm humiliated. I've never begged a woman for anything in my life."

He picked up his razor and scraped it under his chin. "As a matter of fact, the more I think about it, the angrier I become. *Ow*!" He grabbed a tissue and held it to his bleeding neck. "Mother fu–"

"Listen," Eric shifted on the toilet seat, "I know you're angry. Take it from a married man, love isn't roses and rainbows. It's hard work, but it's worth it. You're going to say things to hurt each other. You're going to take each other for granted, and you're going to regret doing both. But in the end what it all comes back to is you and her and your love."

Will rinsed his face and toweled it off. "Thanks for your married man's advice, but I don't need it."

Eric grabbed his arm and jerked him around. "You ask yourself this question. Do you want to live the rest of your life without ever seeing her, touching her, smelling her, tasting her, making love to her, or holding the children you'll create together? If you're answer is yes, then you never really loved her."

Will watched his best friend storm off. When he heard the door to his suite slam shut, he buried his face in his hands and groaned.

The next three days were hell. Will weathered the media storm, answering the questions truthfully. He trudged through each day, eating when Eric shoved it down his throat and managing a few hours of sleep a night. A moment didn't tick by that Laura wasn't in his thoughts. Where was she? What was she doing? Was she okay?

On the evening of the fourth day, the private investigator called to tell Will he'd completed the report and would send it via overnight postal to his hotel. The next twenty-four hours ticked by at an interminable rate, and when the delivery man arrived, Will snatched it from his fingers, ripped it open, scanned the documents, and nearly fell over from what he read.

"Bizzy? It's Will Burns."

"I knew you'd call."

He tightened his grip on the phone. "Do you know where she is?"

Bizzy sighed. "Yes."

"Please tell me." Even he heard the desperation in his voice.

"Do you love her?"

"Man, yes."

"Jane leaked that story and pictures to the press. None of it's true."

"I know."

Bizzy sighed again. "She made me promise not to tell anybody where she went. But I don't care. She can hate me for the rest of my life."

"She won't hate you. I promise. Not after what she's about to learn."

"What are you talking about?"

"You'll know soon enough."

"She's at the Grand Canyon."

"What?"

"She's hiking. She's staying at a campground there."

He dropped his forehead into his palm. "What campground?"

"Just a minute. I have it written down." He heard her rifling through some papers. "Here it is. Mather, on the south rim."

"Thanks, Bizzy. You're a good friend."

He started to hang up, but heard Bizzy say, "Will?"

He put the phone back to his ear. "Yeah?"

"You're really good for her. Don't give up. She loves you. Don't ever question that."

"Thanks," he murmured. "I need to hear those words from her, though." He clicked off and dialed Ed.

Nineteen

Ed and Will's relationship had been strained ever since he'd asked Ed about his blue rabbit's foot. So when Will had suggested that Ed come to his suite to discuss something important, it was like pulling teeth getting him to agree.

Sitting down in the chair opposite Ed's, Will tried not to notice how defensive he looked. "I know you haven't been pleased with me since I asked you details about the rabbit's foot you carry all the time. But I had a reason, and I'd like to explain."

Ed shot up out of his seat and headed for the door. "I can't believe you. Aren't you ever going to let this die?"

Will stood. "Please. Give me fifteen minutes. It's about your sister."

Ed wrenched open the door.

"She's alive, and I can prove it."

Ed stopped and turned. "What are you talking about?"

"Have a seat. You won't be sorry."

He stared at Will for a long moment, then closed the door and walked back across the suite. He sat on the edge of his chair, making it obvious Will better have something concrete to say.

Will eased back down into his chair. He opened the file he'd placed on the coffee table and held up a picture. "Do you recognize this woman?"

"Looks like that woman who was bothering Laura."

"You're right. It is. Her real name is Mary Wood." Will held up another picture, watching Ed for signs of recognition. "This is the same woman twenty-five years ago. Do you recognize her?"

Realization donned on Ed's face. "Holy jeez," he breathed. "That's Mad Mary."

Will nodded. "Tell me what you know about her."

Ed slid all the way back in his chair. "She was this crazy lady who lived in my home town. All the kids were scared of her because she used to stand in the shadows and watch us play. She never spoke to any of us, except for my sister, Sandra. Mad Mary used to give her hair ribbons and tell her she was pretty. I remember how freaked out my mom got, but after awhile she thought she was just a sad lady who had taken a liking to Sandra."

"What happened to Mad Mary?" Will asked, already knowing the answer.

Ed shrugged. "I have no idea."

Will pulled a slip of paper from the file. "This is Mary Wood's background information. She had a horrible childhood. Her mother used to lock her in her room, make her go days without eating, beat her, tell her she wasn't pretty or good enough, yet she'd dress her up like a doll and take her out and show her around."

Ed grimaced.

"When Mary was fifteen she ran away from home and met an older man who claimed he loved her. Having had no love from her mother, Mary latched onto him immediately. She got pregnant, and when he found out, he abandoned her. She had the baby anyway and named her Laura." Will held up a picture. "This was Mary's daughter, Laura, at five-years-old. She had blond hair and green eyes."

Ed glanced at the picture, then back at Will.

"Worn down from her hideous childhood and having her heart broken by a man she loved, Mary took her daughter and moved in with another older man. In exchange for sex, she had a roof over her head and food in her belly. She vowed to raise her daughter better than the way she'd been raised, but unfortunately the cycle repeated itself. It started with her dressing Laura like a doll, trying to make her perfect. But unlike Mary had been as a child, Laura rebelled against her mother, and her disobedience led to horrid punishments. Beatings, locking in closets, and so forth."

Ed swallowed. "But what about the man they lived with. Didn't he do anything to stop it?"

"He never wanted kids to begin with. So he pretended not to see or hear what went on."

"Bastard."

"Yep. Well, when Laura, still quite the little rebel, turned fifteen, she seduced the man they still lived with. She got pregnant from him, Mary found out, she snapped, and killed Laura when she was two months pregnant."

Ed's mouth dropped open.

"The man called the police, and after evaluations with psychiatrists, they admitted Mary to a mental hospital where she stayed for the next fifteen years. At forty-five years of age, she moved to your home town." Will cocked a brow. "Now comes the part about your sister."

Ed squeezed his eyes shut.

"When Mary saw Sandra, she saw a pretty little girl with blond hair and green eyes that reminded her of her own daughter. I'm sure she must have thought if she could do it all over again, she'd do it right, be a better mom. She'd have a second chance. So one afternoon, while your sister played in your mom's garden, Mary took her and moved across the country to Mississippi."

Ed dropped his head back against the chair.

"She changed their names to Jane and Laura Franks and raised Laura as her niece, not her daughter."

Clutching his stomach, Ed bent forward with a groan.

Will got out of his chair and went to him. "Your sister's alive." He laid a hand on Ed's shoulder. "My Laura, our

Laura, she's your little sister."

"*Ohgodohgodohgod*, I think I'm going to throw up."

"No you're not. You're going to be fine." Will dashed into the kitchen and poured him a glass of water. When he returned to the living room, Ed had righted himself and was taking deep, gulping breaths. "Here, drink this." Will thrust the glass into Ed's hands.

He drank the contents in one huge gulp. "Does she know?"

"No. I wanted you to be the one to tell her."

"I don't understand. How did you put it all toge–" Ed's eyes widened in awareness. "Wait. The rabbit's foot."

Will grinned.

"She has it doesn't she?"

"Yep." Will sat on the edge of the coffee table. "I hired a private investigator. He did all the work."

Ed put the glass down and pushed out of his seat. He paced the living room, his gaze focused on nothing particular. Will stayed seated, following Ed's movement, knowing he had a lot to think about.

Finally, he stopped and turned to Will, his face looking perturbed and serious. "Mary could've snapped and killed her at any time."

Will nodded. He'd been trying not to think about that.

"Di-did Mary raise Sandra okay?"

He knew Ed would ask him that question. "I'm sorry. If you want to know Laura's past, you'll have to ask her yourself."

Ed frowned, clearly unsatisfied with his answer. "Alright. I'll respect that." He began to pace again. "We have to notify the authorities. Mary needs to be put away."

"It's already taken care of. Mary's in police custody right now."

"I didn't believe any of that stuff the magazine printed."

"Nobody did."

"Is Laura, Sandra, my sister going to sue?"

"In light of this new information, I think the media's going to be doing back flips for all of us."

Ed continued pacing, thinking. "Why did Mary assume the identity of her aunt instead of her mom? Why didn't she make Sandra believe they were mother-daughter?"

"I puzzled about that, too. A preliminary psychological profile said that Mary wanted to raise another little girl, but being her mother would somehow jinx it, make the cycle repeat itself."

"She's crazy."

"You can say that again."

Pivoting on his heel, Ed paced back toward Will. "Where's my sister?"

"The Grand Canyon."

"What?"

"That's what I said."

Ed headed for the door. "I've got to pack a bag." Then he stopped and walked back to Will. "Thank you. That seems so inadequate for what you've done, but that's all I can think to say."

Will stood and the two men hugged, then Ed pulled away. He gave Will a watery smile and darted from the room. Staring at the door, Will smiled, despite the fact he wished he were the one leaving for the Grand Canyon to see Laura. Her brother needed to be the one to tell her the news, though. She needed to know she had family, always had, and that her past had been out of her control, built on lies, some weird twist of fate. She wasn't alone anymore.

Lying on a blanket next to her tent, Laura stared at the stars illuminating the sky above the Grand Canyon. How naïve she'd been to believe her life was in an upswing. She should have known better. Her life had never been in an upswing.

How stupid of her to get her hopes up like that. She'd learned long ago not to have hopes, because inevitably, they'd be shot out from under her.

Laura sighed and watched her breath crystallize in the chilly air. She'd have to return to reality someday. But what would she do when she did?

Should she start over? Pick a new city, try again at life?

Should she return to Mississippi and confront Aunt Jane? What good would that do? Jane wouldn't suddenly realize that she'd wronged Laura and offer her an apology.

Should she go to the press with her own side of the story and obtain retribution? That wouldn't get her anywhere. Jane would issue a rebuttal and start a media war. More muck for the world to see.

Laura didn't care what people thought about her. She'd hardened her heart a long time ago to others' ignorance. They could believe what they wanted.

But all this had affected Will. He didn't deserve it, and now he had to deal with the after shocks. Although she'd been avoiding television and any print media, she knew the press had to be hounding him. Laura squeezed her eyes shut. Will was better off without her.

"Hi," came a voice from behind her.

She snapped open her eyes and rolled her head back. "Ed? What are–" She took an annoyed breath. "I take it Bizzy opened her big mouth."

"Bizzy cares about you. We all do."

Laura rolled to her feet. "Well you can tell everybody you saw me and I'm fine. You want a beer to take with you on your way home?"

Ed threw his duffel bag on the ground. "I'm staying."

She picked up his bag and handed it to him. "I don't want company."

He stepped around her, opened her cooler, and grabbed a

beer. "Drop the 'I don't care' act, Laura. You're rotten at it."

"Fine. Now goodbye."

Ed sat down on her blanket and crossed his legs. He pulled a file from the inside of his coat, placed it in front of him, then took a swig of beer. "Give me fifteen minutes. I promise if you still want me to leave, I will."

Laura eyed the file. "What's that?"

"A report."

"What kind of report?"

"About you. About your background."

She stiffened. "Who did that?"

"Will hired an investigator."

Laura closed her eyes. "Damn him. And damn you for coming here with that thing."

"He loves you."

Nausea bittered her mouth. She swallowed and turned away. Will *believed* he loved her. He'd figure out real quick that he should be with somebody else.

"Have a seat and give me fifteen minutes. That's all I'm asking for. You won't be sorry. I promise."

Laura sighed and made her way over to the blanket. She sat down across from Ed and stared at the file lying between them. He opened it and pulled out two pictures of Aunt Jane. One as Laura knew her, and one depicting her much younger. He told her about Mary Wood and her horrible childhood and how she'd had a little girl named Laura with blond hair and green eyes. He described how Mary had raised that little girl, repeating the cycle of her own childhood, then eventually went insane and murdered her pregnant daughter.

Laura listened to the details, her stomach clenched, feeling sorrow for the first time in her life for Aunt Jane. What a horrible upbringing she'd had.

Then Ed went on to say how Mary had spent time in a mental institution, and after being released, she moved to his hometown. He then turned the story to his family and talked about his mother and father and little sister, Sandra. He told Laura about his sister's abduction, the follow-up investigation, and the conclusion that she'd been murdered.

The nighttime sounds surrounding them became mute as Laura slowly realized where the story was heading. She heard only Ed's words and her own deep, rapid breathing. He backtracked in his story and told her about Mad Mary, how all the kids were scared of her, and how Mary talked to one of them, and that had been Sandra. And one day Mary stole Sandra from his mom's garden and never returned.

Laura watched Ed through her blurred, teary vision as he reached inside his coat pocket with a shaky hand, pulled out a blue rabbit's foot, and put it between them. "There are only two like it in the whole world," he whispered in a quivering voice. "And my little sister has the other."

Laura covered her face with her hands and let out a loud gut cramping, "*Nooo*!"

She gasped for air as her stomach caved in on a sobbing breath. Ed wrapped his arms around her and rocked. She clutched his coat, moaning, and slumped into his chest. Her breath hitched as tears pressed the backs of her eyes and gushed down her cheeks. Her nearly inaudible, high-pitched wails filled the air around them.

Her whole childhood reeled through her mind. Sitting for hours trying to learn the flute. Being locked in a closet for crying. Having to wear baby doll clothes. Enduring the whippings. Feeling inadequate and being told she wasn't pretty enough or good at anything. Taking the beating for that man walking out on Aunt Jane. Sprawled on the examining table while the doctor verified her virginity. The lies and contorted views of religion and discipline. The years Jane had robbed her from a real family.

Jane had been repeating her own twisted, horrible

childhood. She'd gone insane early on, and none of it had been Laura's fault. All the years of wondering *why me?* There were no answers. She'd been kidnapped for one reason and one reason only. She had blond hair and green eyes, like Mary Wood's daughter.

Laura sniffed, her crying having subsided. Ed stroked her head, still rocking her. She pulled back and stared into his eyes. *Her brother's eyes.*

He let out a choppy breath, his cheeks wet from tears, and touched her face. "You grew into such a beautiful woman."

She rubbed the backs of her hands across her eyes, then started to cry again.

Ed grabbed her face and brushed the tears away. "Why are you crying again," he asked, even though he'd started to also.

"Because I'm so happy." She threw her arms around his neck. They squeezed each other hard, and Laura started to laugh. "Do I have any other brothers or sisters? What about a mom and dad?" She pulled away, delight bubbling in her stomach, and looked him in the eyes. "Grandparents? Do I have grandparents?"

Ed pulled a wad of tissues out of his pocket and gave her half. "Here. I figured we'd need these." He blew his nose while Laura did hers. "No more brothers or sisters. It's you and me kid. Both Mom and Dad are alive. We have a grandmother from each side of the family. One of our grandfathers died before you were born. The other died about ten years ago."

Laura's heart did a happy little pitter-patter. "Do they know about me?"

"Not yet. I wanted to see you first."

"Wait." She grabbed his arm. "Your last name's Barslow."

He nodded.

"Sandra Barslow," she said slowly, trying the name out. She glanced past his shoulder into the night and said it again, "Sandra Barslow." She refocused on him and smiled. "Hi, my name's Sandra Barslow and this is my brother, Ed."

He laughed and gave her a quick hug.

She slipped her rabbit's foot out of her front pocket. "Tell me about this."

"Our father's an artist. He made those in his workshop when you turned two years old." Ed took the foot from her fingers and held it up. "Ya know the engraved stick-figured boys and girls circling the top?"

Sandra nodded.

"They're holding hands. Dad made them for us because when you learned to walk you were holding my hand, and every time after that, you'd ask for me. You always wanted my hand, not Mom or Dad's."

"Oh, Ed," she sighed. They sat there, staring at each other, their lips curved into pleasant, peaceful smiles. "I have so many questions."

He grinned. "I figured you would. We've got all night, lil' sis."

Early the next morning, Sandra flopped down into her tiny, two-man tent, exhausted, but more happy and content than she'd been in her entire life. She and Ed had stayed up the whole night talking. There'd always been a small void, a missing chunk, something she knew had to be sated before feeling complete and whole.

She'd been right. She had a family now. *A real family.* Sandra smiled, for what felt like the millionth time since Ed had told her the news, and rolled over onto her side.

She didn't have any mental illness running in her blood. She wasn't the daughter of a schizophrenic prostitute. She hadn't been born in an alley behind a dumpster. Her mother didn't try to abort her with a coat hanger. Her father hadn't been a whore's trick. She wasn't even related to Aunt Jane.

Sandra closed her eyes on a groan. How could she have believed those ugly things?

Flopping onto her back again, she threw her arm over her eyes and thought of Will. She'd been so mean to him. She'd said things she wished she wouldn't have. She'd acted out of hurt and anger and feeling lost. She'd yelled at him. She'd never yelled at anybody in her whole life. She'd made him cry. And all along he'd had the investigation going on. It must have killed him to keep it a secret, especially when she'd pushed him away.

Why had she pushed him away? Weren't people supposed to rely on those they loved? Maybe that meant she didn't love him, which didn't feel right, but what else could it mean?

Sandra inhaled a frustrated breath. If only she had somebody to talk to, somebody older and wiser. She'd never had that before, hadn't needed it until now.

A snore filled the air. Ed. He'd pitched a tent right beside hers. She smiled. Her brother snored.

Snuggling deeper into her sleeping bag, she recalled Ed's inquiry about her past. He'd wanted to know the details of her life with Aunt Jane. Sandra would never tell her family the whole story. They'd had enough pain and sorrow over the last twenty years. It was time for all of them to build a future together. And tomorrow she'd finally meet them.

Twenty

"Sandra, you okay, dear?"

She looked up at her mom, approaching from across the yard, still not used to her new name. "Yes, Mom, I'm fine."

Mom. Sandra had said that word every chance she could over the last five days.

Mom squatted down on the other side of the garden. "Do you realize that's where you were the last time I saw you twenty years ago."

Sandra turned and surveyed the dense woods behind her. Had that been Aunt Jane's, Mary Wood's, hiding place? "No, I didn't know that."

"I made some hot chocolate. Feel like visiting with me on the porch?"

Tucking her hands in her coat pockets, Sandra got to her feet. "Sure. Sounds good." It sounded more than good. Her whole life she'd fantasized about sitting on a porch with her mom, talking, sipping hot chocolate. "Where's Dad?"

"Gone to get some steaks for tonight."

"Oh." Just the sort of thing a normal, real dad would do.

A few minutes later they settled on the back porch, each with a warm mug, side-by-side on the swing. Sandra gazed out over the yard, the garden, the woods, and the creek beyond. She visualized her and Ed playing as kids. Her parents had thought they were completely safe in this secluded location.

No child was ever safe.

Mom shifted and placed her hand on Sandra's thigh. "Ed called last night."

Sandra slipped her arm under her mom's and lowered her head to her shoulder. A comfortable, easy affection had developed between them over the last five days. "What did he say?"

"Oh, the usual. *Tourist's* latest city, a little bit of gossip, asked how you were doing. Wanted to know if we had any problems with reporters."

Nothing about Will? "Did you tell him what I've decided?"

"Yes. He thinks it's a great idea."

She'd decided to sue the magazine that printed the original story. Not for money, but she did want them to admit their wrongdoing in not investigating the facts. She'd also put together a press release detailing the true story of the kidnapping and how her family had come to be reunited twenty years later. It was an amazing saga that deserved to be told and maybe give other families, who were going through the same thing, hope.

Mom took a sip of hot chocolate. "Tell me about Will."

Tears pressed the back of Sandra's eyes. She'd wanted to talk to her mother about him, but hadn't known how to bring it up. "I've made a muck of things," she mumbled, lifting her head from her mom's shoulder.

"Oh, now, I doubt that. It's never as bad as it seems."

"I hurt him. I said things I wished I wouldn't have. I pushed him away when he reached out to me." Sandra watched the steam from her hot chocolate lazily stream upward. "I made him cry," she whispered achingly.

Mom reached over and smoothed a lock of hair behind Sandra's ear. "Your dad and I have been married a lot of years. Do you know how many times we've hurt each other and regretted it? A lot. Saying things you wished you wouldn't have is human. You acted out of your emotions. Tell me, do you love Will?"

"Yes," Sandra answered without hesitation, more sure of her feelings than ever before. Everything about her life had clarity now. All the pieces of the puzzle had fallen into place.

"Have you told him?"

Sandra shook her head. "No."

"Little words like 'I'm sorry' and 'I love you' go a long way, especially when they come straight from your heart."

"You don't think it's too late?"

Mom chuckled. "Oh, honey, where love's concerned it's never too late. I'll bet you that young man can't think of anything else."

Sandra inhaled a contented breath. Her mom had spoken the exact words she'd needed to hear.

"By the way, I met Will Burns a few years ago when your dad and I visited Ed on the road."

Sandra's stomach did a slow roll. She looked at her mom expectantly, waiting to hear what she thought of him.

"He's very funny and...well, heck. He's extremely appealing."

Sandra laughed and gave her mom a hug. "Thanks, Mom. I love you."

"I love you, too, dear."

Will stared moodily out his hotel window down at Nashville. Laura had worked here last year before coming to *Tourist*, at the same arena, in fact, that they'd perform in tomorrow tonight. It'd been thirteen days since he saw her last, five she'd been at the Grand Canyon and eight at her parents in Oregon. The only reason he knew she was at her parents was because Ed had told him. Laura certainly hadn't contacted him.

Will had read her press release in the papers. It was excellent, done with an angle of awareness for missing children. She'd touched briefly on Mary Wood's past, but only to explain why the kidnapping occurred. Laura hadn't gone into the details of her own childhood, and he understood why. Those were private, personal details that she'd worked through.

There was no reason to splash it all over the media.

With a sigh, he dropped his forehead to the glass. He missed her so much. Every single day that ticked by, Will wanted to go to her. But every day he told himself to wait. She needed time to reunite with her family, work through all that had happened, gather her thoughts, formulate a plan for her future, and realize that she wanted him in it...*hopefully*.

He'd give her one more day, and then go for her. Who was he kidding? He'd wait until the end of time for Laura–his life, his love, his heart, his soul.

A knock sounded at his door. "Go away, Eric, I'm fine." His best friend had been checking on him regularly. Eric's good intentions were beginning to annoy him.

A knock sounded again, this time a little more persistent.

"I said I'm fine," Will shouted.

The knock came again.

Will pushed away from the window with a growl and stomped across his suite. He reached for the knob and wrenched open the door. "What do you wa–"

Laura stood in the threshold, looking more beautiful than he ever remembered, and he had a superb memory when it came to her. His aggravation slowly dissolved as he stared at her face curved into that delicious, sweet, shy smile he adored. He closed his mouth and swallowed.

"I love you, Will Burns."

He sucked in a gulp of air as his heart leapt into his throat. He reached out, grabbed her wrist, and pulled her into his arms. "Oh, Laura, I missed you so much."

"I'm sorry."

Will reached past her and shut the door. He kissed her cheek. "Don't apologize." He kissed her forehead. "I understood." He kissed her other cheek. "I knew you were upset." He kissed the tip of her nose. "Don't ever leave me again." He kissed her eyelids. "I was so miserable without you." He pressed his cheek against hers. "I love you. Tell me you love me again."

Laura took his face between her palms. She put her lips against his, held them there for long seconds, then pulled back and looked him in the eyes. "I love you with every fiber of my being. I give you my whole heart. Make love to me, Will."

His heart melted at her soft-spoken request. He linked fingers with her and led her to the bed. Slowly they undressed each other, exploring every inch of skin, cherishing every curve, every corner, elbow, knee, finger, toe. When he finally entered her it felt like home, like everything clicked into place as their souls merged to one.

Afterward, they lay in each other's arms, their eyes closed, listening to the other breathe. Will had no idea how much time went by. Minutes, hours.

"I changed my name. I'm going by Sandra Barslow now. Do you mind?"

He nuzzled the top of her head with his cheek. "I don't care if your name is Winky Dink. As long as you're in my arms, that's all that matters."

She laughed softly and snuggled deeper into his chest. "I get my green eyes from my mom."

Will's lips curved. "Yeah?" He ran his fingers through her hair. "What about your hair? Who do you get that from?"

"Both. Dad and Mom both have blond hair."

He opened his eyes and scooted down to look at her face. "Tell me more."

Sandra rolled onto her back. "They live in Oregon in a woodsy, secluded area. There's a creek and a garden and they have two dogs. Mom's a music teacher. That's where I get my musical ability, and Dad's a retired fireman and an artist. He made the blue rabbit's foot."

With his cheek propped in the palm of his hand, Will smiled down at her, falling in love with her all over again as she delightedly described her family.

"They've lived in the same house for thirty years. Can you imagine that? My dad's name is Chris and mom is Helen. I have two grandmothers. We call them Mams and Nana. Both my grandfathers are gone, but I've heard all about them. Oh," Sandra put her finger in the air, "my parents don't make any noise when they laugh. It's the strangest thing. Mom does this cute little giggle where she holds her breath and hunches her shoulders, but no sound comes out. And dad, he grins and slaps his thigh every time something's funny, but he doesn't make any noise either."

Will trailed a leisurely finger down between her breasts. "Who do you get your amazing body from?"

"My dad's side of the family gives me and Ed our height."

"Oh." He traced a line to her naval, twirled a few slow circles around her belly button.

She reached up and toyed with a lock of his hair. "Mom wants us to come visit on our next break. Is that okay?"

He turned his head and kissed the inside of her wrist. "That's more than okay."

"Oh, and I had an idea."

Will bit back a smile. She'd never been so bubbly chatty. "What?"

"Our song, the one we did together. I thought it'd be a good idea if we donated the profit to helping families find their missing children."

He cupped the side of her face with his palm, filled with pride and admiration for the woman he loved. "You're amazing. I think that's a fantastic idea."

"Yeah?"

"Yeah."

Sandra rolled onto her side and snuggled their bodies together. "I guess I can tell you the news now."

Will wrapped his arm around her back and pulled her

closer. "What news?"

"I talked to management a few days ago, and to make a long story short, I'm *Tourist's* sound engineer again. I'm mixing tomorrow's show."

He gave her a quick squeeze. "You little sneak. Nobody even let on they knew. I could've been out of my misery days ago."

She pushed him over onto his back and pouted her lower lip. "I'm sorry you were in so much misery. How will I ever make it up to you?"

Will pretended to give the question a lot of thought. "Well you can start by kissing the hurt away."

Sandra nuzzled her nose against his chest. "Where all does it hurt?"

He pointed to his cheek, and she slid up his body and pressed her lips there.

He pointed to his mouth, and she followed.

He pointed to his neck, and she followed.

He pointed to his chest, and she followed.

He pointed to his stomach, and she followed.

He pointed…

Twenty-One

Grammy night. *Tourist* had been nominated for album of the year, but as Will sat in his suite five minutes before leaving, only Sandra occupied his thoughts. He replayed their entire time together in his mind…

Meeting her that day in Canada and wondering what lay beneath her haunted eyes. Watching her pounce in muddy puddles in a rainy Central Park. Holding her hand for the first time after one of her nightmares. Giving her a state patch for her duffel bag and feeling as if he'd given her a diamond ring instead. Pulling her secrets from her little by little. Losing to her in a game of pool. Falling asleep on the couch with her in his arms. Wrestling on the floor of his suite. Spending four gut-wrenching weeks away from her when she'd gone to his cabin. Kissing her for the first time. Hearing her screech for joy on the back of his Jeep. Putting her guitar music together with his lyrics. Spending the holiday at his sister's house. Meeting Aunt Jane. Linking the blue rabbit's foot with Ed. Making love to Sandra. Showering together. Losing her on Valentine's Day when all those lies hit the tabloids. Sending Ed after her and wondering if she'd ever return.

Hearing her say, "I love you."

Will flipped open the small box he held. Inside, her engagement ring twinkled back at him. He'd chosen twenty tiny emeralds and had the jeweler set them in a zigzagging pattern over a platinum band. It matched Sandra's eyes.

Tonight would be their first public appearance together. *Ever*. Before Aunt Jane had returned, Will and Sandra rarely went out unless they'd worn a disguise. It'd been two months since the truth about Mary Wood hit the press. Since then,

Will and Sandra hadn't ventured beyond their hotel or whatever venue *Tourist* performed in. There'd been plenty of stories and photos in the tabloids about their relationship, but tonight Will would cement the rumors. He was proposing. They'd appear hand-in-hand, no more hiding. He was going to show her off.

Will clicked the box closed and slid it into his jacket pocket. Someone banged on his door. He blew out a breath, wiped his damp palms down his pants, then joined everyone in the hotel's corridor.

"Well it's about time. What were you doing in there? Fixing your makeup?"

Will ignored his blockheaded best friend and gave Eric's wife a quick peck on the cheek. "How do you put up with him?"

"Love blinds," she muttered through the side of her mouth.

Eric slapped him on the back. "You clean up real nice."

"Thanks. Black's easy and it matches." Will turned to greet the other guys' dates, all clinging proprietarily to their arms. He didn't recognize any of them. *Flavors of the month.*

The drummer let out a slow whistle. "Check it out. I knew she was hiding the goods under those jeans and caps."

Will watched as Sandra emerged from her doorway down the hall. Now he knew why she'd insisted on getting ready in her own room. They wouldn't have made it to the Grammy's if he'd seen her in that dress.

His fantasy of her long legs in high heels had come true. She wore a floor length, silver gown with a slit running all the way to her upper thigh. Tiny straps held it onto her shoulders and gave the appearance it'd been casually draped over her breasts. She'd left her hair down, just like he liked it.

She walked toward the group, and even though she held her head high and shoulders back, Will knew his Sandra. All eyes focused silently on her made her uncomfortable. But how could they not stare? She looked incredible.

He managed to tear his gaze away from her exposed thigh and looked her in the eyes. She gave him a small smile and made him feel like the luckiest man in the whole world.

"Well, I don't know about you all, but I think we've got the sexiest sound mixer in the whole industry," the band's manager said. The other guys showed their agreement with good-natured catcalls and whistling.

Sandra blushed, and Will's heart melted. He went to her. "You look amazing," he whispered against her ear, then inhaled her scent. "Your perfume is intoxicating. I've never seen you in a dress before."

"Thanks," she whispered back. "I haven't worn one since high school."

Will slipped his hand under her hair and trailed his fingers between her shoulder blades down to her lower back, discovering it bare. "I hope this thing doesn't come off of you."

"It won't." She grabbed his gaze and held it seductively. "That is unless you make it."

His heart triple timed. There was a time when he'd fantasized about her saying such bold, flirtatious statements. She'd gotten good at it. Real good. "Lady, you have no idea what you do to me."

Her lips curved knowingly.

"You're wearing makeup," he realized suddenly. Other than the night they'd first made love, she'd never worn makeup.

"Yes. Is it too much?"

"No. It's perfect. You're perfect. You're beautiful." He lowered his lips to within a few tempting inches of her coral colored ones. "I want to kiss you, but I'm afraid to mess up your lipstick."

"You won't. It's one of those non-smudge brands."

"Oh goodie." Will moved his mouth to hers.

A clearing throat interrupted them. He scowled and turned from Sandra to find the drummer standing behind them.

Will cocked his brow. "Yes?"

The drummer looked down at his black boots and shoved his hands in his pockets. "I wanted to say I'm happy for you two." He glanced up at Will. "And I'm sorry I've made things tense between us."

Will studied his sincere expression. "We've been together a long time."

The drummer nodded. "Yeah."

"Let bygones be bygones?"

"Thanks, man." The drummer gave him a relieved smile. "I appreciate it."

"Sure." Will socked him on the shoulder. "Better get back to your date. She's looking lost."

The drummer turned and shuffled away.

"That was nice of you."

Will linked fingers with Sandra. "He's a good guy, just annoying at times." He flicked his hand in the air. "But forget about that. I have news." He grinned. "Guess what?"

"What?"

"Veronica called a little while ago." He puffed his chest up proudly. "I'm gonna be an uncle."

Sandra laughed. "Well, congratulations, Uncle Will."

He steered her toward the elevators. "She's six weeks along. She and Rico are ecstatic. They're already picking out names. You should've heard Maria's little excited voice. She was..."

Sandra followed him into the elevator, listening to him jabber about becoming an uncle. Imagine what he'd be like when he became a father. He'd make a great daddy.

Five minutes later, they sat across from each other in their limo. Sandra held Will's stare as he thoughtfully considered her. What was he thinking?

A few seconds later his face softened into a loving smile.

She smiled back.

"I heard Nighttime Production wants to buy our song for a movie," he said. "I also heard a rumor that it may be up for a Grammy next year."

Sandra blinked. "Are you serious?"

"Yep."

"Wow."

They grew quiet again and continued to study each other. Then Sandra remembered. "My mom called me while I was getting ready. Mary Wood had a heart attack and died."

Will sat up. "What? And you waited this long to tell me? That's the last thing I expected to hear. How do you feel?"

She shrugged. "I don't feel the loss. I don't mean to sound callous, but the news didn't phase me. I'm not going to be mean and say she got what she deserved, but it's almost like I expected something like this to happen."

What a waste of life with the childhood Mary had been subjected to and the bitter, hateful woman it'd made her.

He slid back into his seat with a contemplative look. "You don't sound callous."

That was all they said about Mary Wood as they slipped back into silently staring at each other. Moments ticked by. Sandra shifted and crossed one knee over the other, giving him a view of her bare thigh.

He lowered his attention from her eyes to her leg, then reached forward and ran his hand inside the dress's slit and up to the curve of her hip. "You did that on purpose."

Sandra nodded slowly.

Will kissed her exposed thigh. "What are you wearing under that?"

"You'll find out later."

He groaned and dropped his head to her lap. She laughed and skimmed her fingers through his hair. He had a way of making her feel sensual, desirable, uninhibited.

Will moved to sit beside her in the limo. He lifted her left hand and stroked his thumb back and forth across the tops of her fingers, studying them intently, deep in thought, as if looking for something. She'd hardly ever seen him that way.

Finally he lowered her hand and leveled serious eyes on her. "Sandra, I'm so lost in love with you I don't know what to do with myself."

She let out a silent breath of relief. For a minute there she wasn't sure what was going to come out of his mouth. With a smile that she hoped showed how much she cherished him, she traced the outline of his face with her finger.

He slipped his hand inside his pocket and then placed a tiny, white box in her lap.

Sandra stared at it, afraid to open it, afraid it might be something other than an engagement ring. She'd wanted this for months, ever since their reconciliation. She'd hoped that he'd propose, but neither of them had brought up the subject of marriage. They both had said they wanted to spend their lives together, but they'd never talked in concrete terms.

Almost a year had gone by since they first met. If somebody had said to her twelve months ago she'd be living without flashbacks or nightmares, she'd experience every emotion from laughter to tears, she'd be reunited with her real family, Aunt Jane would die of a heart attack, and Will Burns would be in love with her, Sandra would've laughed and walked off. But all of it was true, and every day she counted her blessings for her amazing life story.

"Open it," he encouraged quietly.

She took it in her hands and lifted the lid. "*Ooohhh*," she breathed. "It's gorgeous."

Will pulled the ring from its satin case and slid it on her finger. "Marry me, Sandra. Please."

She searched his face with all the love in her heart. "I-I had hoped–I mean..." She closed her eyes. "Oh, Will. My life has been so incredible lately, and you've just completed it.

There isn't anything I want right now, but this."

"Is that a yes?"

Laughing, she threw her arms around his neck. "Of course it's a yes."

Will squeezed her. "You don't mind if I announce it to the world tonight, do you?"

She shook her head, too emotional to talk.

The limo stopped and somebody opened the door. Will grabbed Sandra's hand and tugged her out behind him. Flashing bulbs went off and reporters rushed toward them.

"Will, do you think *Tourist* will grab the Grammy tonight?"

"I certainly hope so." He pulled Sandra into his side.

"Who's your date tonight?" another person asked.

Will linked fingers with her. "Everyone, this is Sandra Barslow." He kissed her hand. "My fiancée."

People sucked in surprised breaths. Microphones were shoved in front of her face. Cameras seemed to come out of nowhere. Flashes erupted before her eyes. Then she felt Will's fingers squeeze hers reassuringly. She smiled and basked in the loving warmth that flowed through her body.

Meet the author:

Shannon Greenland is the award-winning author of two novels. She lives with her husband and adopted mutt off the coast of Florida. Shannon uses both sides of her brain by teaching math during the day and writing at every opportunity. Her novels have repeatedly hit the top seller list and been used for instruction in high schools and universities. When she's not teaching or writing, she's enjoying school holidays, sailing, and relaxing on the beach.

You can e-mail Shannon at

SGreenland@echelonpress.com

Or visit

www.shannongreenland.com

Coming May 2005 from Echelon Press

Maid to Order

By Rekha Ambardar

CHAPTER ONE

Mark Runyon sprinted up the steps of the modernized brownstone in Chicago's 'Jefferson Park and pulled open the grill-reinforced door. He stepped inside and grinned at Jack Delaney, the supervisor, through the long glass window of his office in Tivoli Terrace Apartments.

He glanced at the elevator briefly and shook his head. No, not the easy way up today. He'd been in meetings all day the last few days, and had had no time for his usual tennis game. Better take the stairs. He could handle four flights, no problem.

He loosened his tie and started climbing. In his briefcase, he carried the graphical representations of the new senior citizens' condominium he wanted to look over. David Roth, an associate, had commended Mark on the new advertising slant for REA Inc.–"You'll Know You're Home." The words sang in his mind like a jingle. It reminded him of the company's mission statement of putting the client first. This new project was his baby and he had had a special person in mind when he developed this idea.

Mark caught his breath as he remembered something. He hadn't been able to make the Children's Heart Foundation fundraiser the other evening, and now he'd never hear the end of it from Gran. Dear, lovable Gran. What was it she'd mentioned? That she had found a new housekeeper to replace dragon lady, Mrs. Babbitt. Good, he could stop ordering Chinese takeout from now on.

Footsteps slowing, Mark climbed on. He reached the fourth floor, unlocked the door, and walked into a large apartment bathed in the late afternoon sun. He stashed his briefcase on the side table in the hall and pulled off the tie that felt like a choke chain better used in dog obedience classes.

Suddenly, something appeared strangely wrong. Things were in place all right–the expensive oil paintings in their silver-bracketed frames in the hall, and the living room billowing out at the far end with its soft chamois leather upholstery furniture. The vases were filled with flowers, Mark's standing request to the cleaning temp.

Then why did he feel like the three bears walking in on Goldilocks? At the end of the hall, he spied two suitcases partly hidden by the wall, and a sneaker tumbled against it nearby. Alert to the last nerve, he followed the signs as a nature lover might follow markings in the woods.

On the sprawling living room sofa, a small, blonde, tousle-haired waif lay curled with an arm resting on a rounded cheek, her sneaker-clad foot dangling over the edge of the sofa. Her blue jeans were molded over eye-catching curves as she lay fast asleep, breathing evenly.

Mark stood there, his tie draped around his neck, a hand on one hip, and watched her for a few moments. A frown formed on his forehead and then slowly disappeared. Curled on the sofa in that childlike way, she looked pretty. Thick sooty lashes lay like veils over her eyes, and the white long-sleeved shirt with its sleeves rolled up gave her a tomboyish air that was curiously attractive.

Mark pulled himself together. He had no business standing here getting an eyeful of Sleeping Beauty. But who was she and how did she get in?

The girl stirred and opened her eyes. Green, he noticed, sea green. Mark cleared his throat. "Miss, I think you're in the wrong place."

"What? Oh...I..." She sat up, her hand going to her head. "Ouch! This is Tivoli Terrace Apartments, isn't it? Ellen Carstens sent me. I'm Nikki Slater, the new housekeeper."

Mark slowly pulled the dangling tie off his neck and crumpled it in his hand. Had Gran lost her mind? Was this another one of the charity cases she forever championed? Did she really think this elf-like girl could handle the work of Mrs. Babbitt? Mrs. Babbitt even scared dust away, and when she left, she had brought in a temp just like herself–frontline combat material, the original drill sergeant. He unbuttoned his collar. "How did you get in?" This ought to be good, he thought.

"The super let me in. I have a note from Ellen." She fumbled in her jeans pocket for a while, wriggling every which way.

Mark looked away, very conscious of the girl's allure, the hair around her face in curly wisps, the perfect mouth.

"Here it is," she said finally, fishing out a crumpled piece of paper. "It's addressed to you, so the super agreed to let me in."

Mark took the note from her. "Dear Mark," it said. "I'm sending Nikki as promised. She's a good worker and will be a help to you. She needs a place to stay. Perhaps she could use the spare apartment adjoining yours? Take care of yourself and try not to work too hard. Love, Gran."

Mark allowed himself a half-chuckle, recognizing his grandmother's concern for him. But how like her to spring a surprise like this on him! The girl looked as if she had packed her life's belongings into two suitcases. She probably needed the money badly and Ellen stepped in to help. Fine with him, he could go along with a gag to humor his grandmother.

The extent of the situation dawned on Mark like a neon light gaining power by the second. The girl sat groggily on the sofa and pushed the hair away from her eyes. It suddenly hit him that she was to stay in his spare apartment. Mark swallowed hard on that one. Too bad she couldn't leave at the end of the day as Mrs. Babbitt had done. Someone like her was too much to handle when the new construction project was just getting underway. He didn't want a distracting female hovering next door.

Mark raked his fingers through his hair. "If you can cook and keep the apartment clean, it's fine with me. The apartment you will use has a separate entrance. In fact," he said, going to a narrow closet and pulling out a key that hung on the inside of the door, "I'll show you around." He glanced at her suitcases. "You might want to bring those."

Nikki got up. Small built, she barely reached his shoulder. What was Gran thinking when she sent this puny little urchin his way? He hoped like heck she could do some work, though he doubted if she was much good. Mild irritation assaulted him as he led the way to the other apartment. He opened the door and stood aside to let her enter. "This door is left unlocked," he said.

They stood in the foyer flooded with the light of the setting sun. Mark watched with amusement as Nikki walked over to the window and stared at the scenery outside. He had to admit it looked nice this time of year when leaves were starting to come in the trees.

"It's beautiful," she said, coming away from the window. Her gaze fell on a glass and steel abstract structure on the black marble-topped table in the foyer.

"Like it?" he asked.

Nikki nodded. "But what is it?"

"It's a miniature skyscraper. It's in there somewhere, if you look hard enough." Mark laughed. "What's the matter?"

The dimpled smile that had looked promising turned into a puzzled expression. "What do you do?" Her eyes opened wide and a sharpness laced her tone.

"Construct buildings."

"You work for the Runyon Corporation?"

"My father and I own it. I'm Mark Runyon. We also have a battalion of relatives working for us. You sure you're okay? You look ill." Mark lurched forward suddenly and caught her by the arm to steady her. "Whoa."

What *was* the matter with her? This was an odd time to be groggy. Was she one of those party animals in a perpetual state of hangover? Or maybe she was just hungry, which was probably why Gran got involved. The girl was probably too poor to afford a square meal a day.

"Are you hungry? I was going to order Chinese food." He was, after all, a volunteer for Big Brothers, he could help one more down-and-out person, except he had to admit she didn't make him feel like any brother. Not with her curves and those come-hither bedroom eyes.

"No, no. I'm fine." She appeared to gain control of herself.

"Well, let me show you the apartment. Then you can settle in. Is this all the luggage you have?"

"For now. I sold my furniture since this place came furnished."

"Of course." Mark hoped he sounded convincing in accepting her words at face value.

He helped her carry the suitcases and crossed an archway leading to a suite of rooms: a living room, bedroom, and kitchen.

"This is it. Think you can manage here?" He hardly expected her to balk–it was furnished in a neat, elegant style. "When you're ready, you can come over to my apartment. I'd like to go over a few things with you."

He strode out leaving her standing in the hallway, suitcases standing on either side of her like two short, protective pillars. Did Gran have any idea what she'd gotten him into? Foisting on him a young woman with a propensity for taking naps in strange surroundings?

Printed in the United States
26607LVS00001B/55